THE SCRAPPER

Stepping between the men and the girl, Cuno spoke with a hard edge.

"The girl doesn't seem to want your business, so why don't you gentlemen look for one that does?"

The men looked at him, percolating anger coloring their cheeks beneath their ruddy tans. In a moment, they had surrounded Cuno and moved in. The boy went to work with his fists, swinging furiously, ducking, feinting this way and that, dodging right, then left, then right again, and flinging haymakers, jabs, roundhouses, jawbreakers, and even something he and his father had called a Silly Willy.

An experienced sport fighter at county fairs, he had all the men down at least once, lips and eyes swelling, before they coordinated their efforts against him. They pummeled him with their fists. But Cuno was thinking more about Anderson than about them, knowing with a keen frustration that the kill-crazy hider was only a few feet away.

PRAISE FOR THE NOVELS OF PETER BRANDVOLD

"An action-packed, entertaining read for fans of traditional Westerns."
—*Booklist*

"Brandvold writes a lot like L'Amour." —*Fargo Forum*

"Recommended to anyone who loves the West as I do. A very good read."
—Jack Ballas

"Takes off like a shot." —Douglas Hirt

Berkley titles by Peter Brandvold

.45-CALIBER REVENGE
THE DEVIL GETS HIS DUE
ONCE LATE WITH A .38
RIDING WITH THE DEVIL'S MISTRESS
ONCE UPON A DEAD MAN
DEALT THE DEVIL'S HAND
ONCE A RENEGADE
THE DEVIL AND LOU PROPHET
ONCE HELL FREEZES OVER
ONCE A LAWMAN
ONCE MORE WITH A .44
BLOOD MOUNTAIN
ONCE A MARSHAL

Other titles

DAKOTA KILL
THE ROMANTICS

.45-CALIBER REVENGE

Happy Trails!

PETER BRANDVOLD

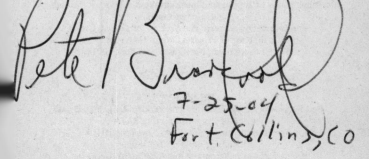

Pete Brandvold
7-25-04
Fort Collins, CO

BERKLEY BOOKS, NEW YORK

.45-CALIBER REVENGE

A Berkley Book / published by arrangement with
the author

PRINTING HISTORY
Berkley edition / June 2004

Cover illustration by Bruce Emmitt.
Cover design by Jill Boltin.

For information address: The Berkley Publishing Group,
a division of Penguin Group (USA) Inc.,
375 Hudson Street, New York, New York 10014.

ISBN: 0-425-19700-X

BERKLEY®
Berkley Books are published by The Berkley Publishing Group,
a division of Penguin Group (USA) Inc.,
375 Hudson Street, New York, New York 10014.
BERKLEY and the "B" design
are trademarks belonging to Penguin Group (USA) Inc.

PRINTED IN THE UNITED STATES OF AMERICA

10 9 8 7 6 5 4 3 2 1

For Mike and Brenda Cline
with much love
and many thanks
for all the great food and wine

1

LATE IN THE day, when the false-fronted buildings canted their bulky shadows across the dusty, rutted street and shopkeepers lazily swept their boardwalks or smoked on loafers' benches while basking in the weakening summer light, two strangers rode into the hamlet of Valoria, Nebraska Territory.

Looking up from his sweeping and spying the strangers, the barber tensed. One of the men was a tall, broad gent with a full red beard and small, deep-set eyes under sun-bleached brows. He wore a cream Stetson, a fringed buckskin shirt, and buckskin breeches stained with blood and camp smoke.

The other man was shorter and leaner than the first, with quick, darting eyes and a hawkish face bespeaking high emotion. Russet-complected, he obviously had some Indian blood. Black pigtails wrapped in greased rawhide fell from under his high-crowned black hat. He wore a black cotton vest over a ratty tunic, buckskin breeches, and moccasins.

Both men were well-armed with revolvers, Sharps

hunting rifles, and bowie knives. In addition, the red-bearded man carried a double-barreled shotgun in a heavy leather boot decorated with silver conchos.

The two were obviously killers of either buffalo or men, or both. They had that soulless look about them, too, that air of inbred evil, and they carried the right weapons for both jobs.

As Valoria was on one of the main western trails, many such men had ridden through town. That was all right with the shopkeepers and barmen, as long as after the hardcases had spent a few dollars, they mounted their horses again and fogged it down the trail.

On the street, the half-breed, Sammy Spoon, regarded his partner curiously. "What is it, Rolf?"

Rolf Anderson had halted his beefy buckskin in the middle of the street and was looking around, rubbing his bearded jaw. "I'm tryin' to remember which saloon Corsica Landreau works. She was the best-lookin' whore between Nebraska City and Denver, and that ain't no lie. She didn't come cheap, but she didn't come green, neither."

Sammy Spoon chuckled. "Well, which one was it? Come on, Rolf. We been on the trail for nigh two weeks now. I'm about burstin' at the seams."

"Let's try the Pasttime over yonder," Anderson said, gigging his horse to the two-story milled lumber building on the north side of the street.

He and Spoon tied their horses to the hitchrack and strolled through the batwings. The Pasttime was like a hundred other saloons in the West. A long bar stretched across the right side of the room, and about ten tables were arranged haphazardly on the left. Toward the back, near stairs leading to the second story where rooms were rented by the day or by the hour, a battered, upright piano clattered off-key under the hands of a girl clad in a skimpy, spangled dress, the powder-blue feathers in her hair swaying gently.

A desultory poker game was in progress at one of the tables, and several groups of men sat around the others, drinking and chatting or listening to the music. A couple men had girls on their knees. A lanky brunette playfully slapped a man's hand away from her cleavage and said, "No more till you pay, Sandy!"

"What can I get for you boys?" the beefy barman asked Anderson and Spoon, taking a wary measure of the pair.

"Corsica Landreau works here, don't she?" Anderson asked.

The barman shook his head. "Not any more she don't." He smiled thinly. "She got married. I got plenty of other girls, though." He turned his head to indicate the four girls working the room.

"Married, eh?" Anderson growled, his disappointment evident on his rawhide face, matted red beard bleached nearly blond by the harsh prairie sun. "Who'd she marry?"

"A freighter by the name of Lloyd Massey."

"Massey, eh? They live in town?"

The barman nodded. "That's right, but she's out of the business now, Corsica is."

Spoon chuckled. "There ain't no such thing, amigo," he said. "Once a whore, always a whore . . . for the right price. Ain't that right, Rolf?" His amusement was out of place on his savage, unkept countenance, making him seem insane, which he was. Dangerously so.

Ignoring his partner, Anderson faced the barman. "Where does she live?"

The barman frowned, flushing. "Why?"

In a calm voice but with a taut jaw and dark eyes, Anderson said, " 'Cause I'll blow a hole through your belly if you don't tell me."

The barman's face turned a deeper shade of crimson as he stepped away from the bar, turning slightly to his right and glancing down. Anderson whipped one of his matched Colts from its holster and clicked back the hammer, holding the gun close to the bartop, so it wouldn't be obvious to the other customers.

"Don't even think about going for your greener, or I'll splatter your brains all over that nice, clean mirror behind you."

The barman froze, his body rigid. "Hey, now, I don't want no trouble."

"And you won't have any if you tell me where Corsica lives."

The barman shifted his troubled gaze to the other tables, to see if any of the other customers had noticed the gun aimed at his belly. Seeing that none had, he returned his eyes to Anderson.

"All right, all right," he said, holding up his hands placatingly. "She lives north of here a couple blocks, on Wichita Street. A little blue house with a white picket fence, and a buggy shed out back."

Anderson grinned and turned to Spoon. "A little blue house with a white picket fence. Ain't that sweet?"

Spoon chuckled.

Anderson depressed the hammer of his Colt and reholstered the weapon. "Much obliged, friend," he told the barman. "Just curious, that's all. Now, why don't you set up me and my friend here with a bottle of rye and two glasses."

The barman studied Anderson with a cautious gaze, gray-flecked brows twitching. "You ain't gonna go over to Corsica's?"

"Nah," Anderson said. "I was just curious about her. If she's out of the business, she's out of the business. What can a man do?"

"Well, I'll tell you what this man's gonna do," Spoon said with an air of desperation, staring at the girl banging on the piano.

He grabbed the bottle the barman had set on the counter, bit off the cork, and sloshed whiskey into a shot glass. He threw the drink back, slammed the empty glass on the counter while smacking his lips, and stalked over to the piano.

"Come on, honey," he said, grabbing the girl's arm. "You and me got business upstairs."

The girl, fussing against his brusque grip, nevertheless allowed herself to be half-led, half-dragged up the stairs. Watching them, Anderson smiled and sipped his whiskey.

"How 'bout you, Mister?" the barman asked. "Don't you wanna girl? Rates are cheap on weekdays."

"Nah," Anderson said. "I had my mind set on Corsica. Since she ain't available no more, I think I'll just enjoy my bottle."

He tossed a few coins on the bar, then grabbed his bottle and his glass and headed for an empty table. Collapsing with a sigh, he tossed down his drink and poured another, then sat back in his chair to watch the light fade over the false fronts across the street.

"A little blue house with a white picket fence, eh?" he said softly to himself, a shrewd light in his eyes.

When Corsica Massey had finished hanging the wash on the line in her backyard, she brushed the stray wisps of auburn hair from her eyes and walked back into the blue frame house on the north end of Valoria.

It was a tight little house that her husband, Lloyd Massey, had built before they were married. He'd had it ready for them to move into on their wedding day a little over a year ago. Lloyd's son, Cuno, had moved in, as well, occupying one of the two small rooms upstairs.

As Corsica filled a percolator with coffee and with water from the kitchen pump, she reflected on how her life had changed in only a little over a year. Not long ago, she was turning tricks at the Pasttime Saloon on Valoria's main drag. She had been, to put it bluntly, a whore. Her mother had died in St. Joseph, Missouri, and after Corsica's father had taken his daughter west to homestead a farm in Nebraska, he'd died when a stud bull had run him through a barbed wire fence, leaving Corsica to fend for herself.

Oh, she might have hired out to another farm family for room and board, she supposed, or to one of the businessmen in Valoria. But when she'd learned what men were willing to pay to spend time in bed with her, she put her innate beauty and charm to practical use. She accepted the job Sherman Wood had offered her at the Pasttime. She'd have been the first to admit she was not the most ambitious of God's creatures, and she'd found that allowing men to lie between her legs was better than slaving for only room and board for some crotchety farm wife.

It was better than that, but only just barely. It was also humiliating and often dangerous. So when Lloyd Massey had come along, first as a customer after his wife had died, and then as a suitor, and had so obviously fallen in love with her, she readily accepted his offer for her hand in marriage.

He was nearly twenty years her senior, and he certainly had his faults, though fewer than most of the men she'd known. But he was almost always gentle—he'd never laid a hand on her and rarely raised his voice—and he was a hard worker and provider. His son, Cuno, had been a problem at first, not approving of Corsica's past, but finally he'd come to accept her as well as any young man can accept his mother's replacement. What's more, he was often even protective of her, quick to defend her against slights by those in town who had not forgiven her for her previous occupation.

Thinking of Lloyd turned Corsica's head to the kitchen clock. Nearly six o'clock. He and Cuno would be home soon, as they were returning mid-evening from a freight run between Valoria and St. Mary, on the other side of the Platte. They'd been gone for five nights, and Corsica was so eager to see them—she hated staying alone—that she'd bought three hefty steaks from Mrs. MacGregor down the street, whose husband raised the most succulent beef in town. Tonight, Corsica would surprise Lloyd with a festive homecoming meal.

Donning her apron and gloves, she went outside and harvested peas and potatoes from her garden patch. When she'd scrubbed the potatoes and had shelled the peas at the kitchen table, she heated water for a bath.

By seven o'clock she was bathed and dressed in her best green dress—the one Lloyd had bought her for her birthday. In hers and Lloyd's bedroom off the kitchen, she was adjusting her mother's ivory cameo pin on her collar when she heard a knock on the front door.

Her heart quickened. Could it be Lloyd and Cuno already? She hadn't been expecting them until around nine. Besides, they wouldn't bother knocking on their own door.

In spite of her doubts, she hurried to the door with a hopeful light in her eyes. Twisting the knob, she opened the door with a smile that faded slowly to a frown when she saw the big, red-bearded man standing on the porch.

He had to be at least six and a half feet tall. His clothes were dusty and sweat-stained, and they reeked of rotten flesh and whiskey. He wore a battered, dust-colored Stetson. Two cartridge belts were wrapped around his waist, with two holsters, matching pistols, and a savage-looking, horn-handled knife.

"Yes?" she said, her voice faltering, tentative.

"Hi there, Miss Corsica," the man said in a deep, rumbling voice, removing his hat and placing it over his chest. His eyes were rheumy and red-ringed from drink.

"Hello," she said, uncertainly. "Can . . . can I help you?"

The man smiled, showing big, yellow teeth. "Don't you remember me?"

All at once, she did. How could she not remember such a man?

"Oh," she said, "yes." Realizing what he must be here for, she hurried to say, "But I'm afraid I'm not in that line of work anymore."

Since leaving the Pasttime, she'd been afraid that one of her former customers would come calling at her house. None had, however. Virtually all the men she'd known when she was working had accepted the fact that she was now a married woman, and most she met on the street appeared happy for her and seemed in no way eager to cause trouble. Such treatment, she knew, was due in no small part to the fact that her husband, Lloyd, was so well-liked and respected.

But this man, not from around here, was another sort altogether.

She started to close the door, but the brute stuck a boot just over the jamb, stopping the door with a wooden shudder.

"Look," Corsica said, her heart beginning to thud with anger, "I told you—"

"Oh, come on now, Miss Corsica. Don't you remember all the good times we had together? Why, I used to come visit you twice a month when I was shootin' game for the railroad. I may have been gone a little over a year, but certainly you haven't forgotten ole Rolf Anderson. Why, ole Rolf sure hasn't forgotten you!"

"Yes, I remember you, Rolf," she said, apprehension making her heart flutter. "But, like I told you, I'm married now, and I don't do that kind of work anymore. I'm sure you can find what you're looking for at the Pasttime."

"No, Miss Corsica," Anderson said in a deep, guttural voice, slowly shaking his head. "I've found what I'm looking for right here." His hungry eyes dropped to the ample mounds of her breasts, well-covered by her gray-green, lace-edged dress, and smoldered there.

"I told you to get out of here," Corsica raged suddenly, widening the door and then slinging it back toward its frame. Again, his boot stopped it, and Corsica turned and ran for the Winchester Lloyd always kept in an antler rack over the fireplace.

She grabbed the gun, but before she could cock it and bring it to her shoulder, Anderson had followed her in, his boots pounding the floor, and grabbed it out of her hands. She hadn't had any chance of holding onto the gun at all, for Anderson's strength was monstrous. He tossed the gun across the room as if it were no more than a stick, and it clattered across a table, breaking several pictures and a lamp.

Grabbing her around the waist, Anderson said, "Where's your husband?"

Struggling against him, trying to kick him with her heels, Corsica wasn't sure how to reply, so she said nothing. It would only be to her advantage if he thought Lloyd and Cuno were here.

Anderson laughed as she fought ineffectually against him. Holding her around the waist with one arm, like a flopping doll, he called, "Mr. Massey—you home?" He laughed with infuriating mockery, his voice a bear's roar in the small sitting room. "No? Well, I guess not," he roared again. "Must be out mule-skinnin'!"

"Let me go!" Corsica screamed, hoping one of the neighbors would hear. "Please, let me go!"

Anderson asked her where the bedroom was, and when she replied with only screams of protest, he carried her into the kitchen and discovered the open bedroom door.

"Here we go," he laughed as Corsica raged and fought against him.

"No!" she shouted as he pulled her through the door, jerking her hands loose from the frame she'd grabbed. *"No!"*

"Oh, come on now, Miss Corsica," Anderson said as he threw her on the bed. "We're gonna have us a good ole time, just like before!"

With that, he turned and slammed the door. Turning

back, he began unbuckling his belt, breathing harshly through his nose, as though his lust had caused a constriction in his throat.

Lying dazed on the bed, for her head had hit the wall, Corsica stared at the big man fearfully, sobs rising in her throat, tears washing down her cheeks. Her worst fears had come true: her grim past had come calling.

She knew her only hope was Lloyd. If only he and Cuno would return soon . . .

2

AROUND NINE-THIRTY THAT evening, the two big Murphy wagons wheeled into Valoria behind eight sweat-lathered mules. Stay chains rattled and barked, and the great oak beds groaned under two tons of freight.

The wagons passed down Main Street where tin-panny music jangled behind the lantern-lit windows of the Pasttime Saloon and Dance Hall.

Cuno Massey followed his father's wagon around behind Donovan's Mercantile and leaned back on the reins, checking the mules down to a halt. Lloyd Massey pulled his team up to the loading dock before the slant-roofed storage shed. When he'd halted the tired team, he fished his tarnished Waltham timepiece from his pocket, flipped the lid, and tipped the face toward the weakening light.

"We made good time, for the late start we got," the elder Massey said, glancing over his shoulder at his son.

"It helped that they finally got that bridge up across Salt Creek." Cuno set the wagon brake. "Why don't you go on home and surprise Corsica with that new dress you bought her in Estherville, Pa? I'll unload the wagons."

Lloyd Massey glanced again at his son, and smiled. He hadn't realized that his eagerness to get back home to his wife had been that obvious. Lowering his gaze to the ton of dry goods piled behind him, his smile turned to a frown, and he shook his head. "This is too much for you to unload all by yourself, Cuno."

Cuno wagged his head as he crawled down from the wagon seat—a thick-bodied, stout-necked eighteen-year-old wearing a shabby bowler hat and linsey-woolsey jeans held up with rawhide galluses. Long red underwear, stained by sweat and wheel dope, strained against the work-defined muscles of his chest. The sleeves had been pulled up his tanned, corded forearms.

"Pa, I know your back's ailing. You go on home. I can off-load these wagons in no time. Tell Corsica to fix me a big plate of whatever she's got in the oven."

Lloyd thought it over, chewing his lip. His back was bad, that was for sure. He'd need to rest it if he was going to make tomorrow's run. "All right," he said. "You'll bed the horses down?"

"Don't I always?"

Lloyd Massey chuckled as he climbed stiffly down from his wagon, a wry grin on his darkly handsome face with its three-day growth of salt-and-pepper beard stubble. Nearing his forty-seventh birthday, he'd come West as a young man, doing everything from trapping beaver in the Wind River Range to driving stagecoach before turning to freight hauling when he'd married Cuno's mother Katherine, who had died three years ago of a milk fever. A little over a year ago, he'd married Corsica Landreau. She may have worked as a soiled dove, but she'd helped Lloyd through a bad time, and he was not ashamed to have fallen in love with the girl.

"Well, I can go and come back after supper, after I've given my back a rest," Lloyd said, reaching for the gift-wrapped package beneath the seat. "Remember, we need both wagons free for the run to Kearney tomorrow."

Cuno was removing the tarpaulin from the bed of his father's wagon. "Don't worry, Pa. I got it covered."

"I'll be back in an hour."

"If you say so, but you don't have to."

The gift-wrapped box under his arm, Lloyd slouched down the alley, favoring his back and the knee all those icy snowmelt waters in the Wind Rivers had grieved with rheumatism. As Cuno rolled the tarpaulin and tied it, he couldn't help smiling as he thought of his father and Corsica. They may have been twenty years apart, and Corsica may have come from a shady past, but Cuno knew his father would be dead now if it hadn't been for her. Lloyd Massey would have either drunk himself to death or gotten himself killed in one of his infamous saloon fights.

Cuno was glad his father was alive and happy once again, for, in spite of Lloyd's drinking and carousing, he and Cuno had become nearly as close as brothers in the lonely years after Cuno's mother had died.

Cuno's attention returned to the job at hand when, in the gathering darkness, he banged his knee on one of the Murphy's steel-rimmed wheels. He cursed aloud, then looked around to see if anyone had heard. He did not want to become known as a boy with a foul mouth, for his mother, God rest her soul, had taught him better than that.

He was lucky. The alley behind the mercantile was deserted. Mr. Donovan was probably still crouched over his book work in his office, for the second-story window was lit, but Cuno doubted the man could have heard the epithet from this distance.

Chastising himself for his tongue slip, he lifted the weather-stained bowler to run his big hands through his ash-blond hair, the longish waves of which brushed his ears and shirt collar. Snugging his hat back on his head, he opened the warehouse doors, lit the bull's-eye lantern on the center post, and set to work off-loading the freight. It took only a few minutes of back-and-bellying the crates, barrels, and sacks before Cuno had worked the sting out of his knee and the trail-weariness out of his bones. He and his father had been on the road five nights, sleeping under the stars. Now Cuno's body became a fluid, graceful, adrenalin-pumping machine. Sweat quickly soaked his shirt under his arms and down his back.

By the time he'd begun off-loading the second Murphy, he'd forgotten that his father had said he'd return to help. A cat appeared while Cuno muscled two feed sacks into the warehouse—the orange tabby that lived in the alleys of Valoria.

"Go away, Moose," Cuno said, setting the feed sacks on the neat pyramid he'd built against the warehouse's north wall. "I don't have any food for you now, but I'll fetch you some jerky from my war bag before I head home for the night."

The big tom stiffened its tail and gloved against Cuno's leg, nearly tripping the lad. "Darn it, cat!" he exclaimed. "You're gonna—"

He stopped when he heard hoofbeats, and turned to look down the alley. A horseback rider was approaching in the darkness. He was a paunchy man with something silver flashing on his tan vest.

"Hey, Massey, that you in there?" It was Ned McPheeters, the deputy town sheriff.

Cuno stiffened, tense. He knew he'd been a bur in the deputy's shorts since he'd beaten the man at arm-wrestling two weeks ago, during the town's Fourth of July celebration. He'd beaten McPheeters three out of three matches, winning twenty dollars. Cuno hadn't intended to shame the man, but as he'd collected his winnings before the cheering crowd, he'd seen the humiliation in the deputy's flushed, sweat-beaded face, and knew he'd made an enemy right then and there.

"It's me, Mr. McPheeters," Cuno said, ingratiating himself. One thing you wanted on your side in this rough little burg was the law.

The deputy reined his horse up beside the wagon and sat slouched in his saddle. He was a short, stocky man, sloppily dressed, and with a perpetual three-day growth of beard. "You got trouble to home, young Massey. The sheriff wanted me to find you and take you over to the jailhouse, to wait for your old man."

Cuno's jaw dropped. His heart thudded as he stared at the deputy. "Wait for my old man . . . at the jailhouse? Why?"

The hint of a smile pulled the corners of McPheeters's heavy lips. "Appears he went and killed your step-ma. Come on now, I don't have all night. I'll send someone else over to tend your teams and wagons."

Cuno just stared at the man dully. His mouth went dry, and he swallowed, feeling a lump rise in his throat. Slowly, the words worked their way through Cuno's suddenly sluggish brain as his ears began ringing softly.

"Killed my . . . step-ma," Cuno whispered, repeating the words, turning them over in his mind. Swallowing again, he said, "What are you talkin' about, McPheeters? There must be some mistake. Pa was just here . . . an hour ago."

"Yeah, well, he went home, I reckon, and found your step-ma with some other man." McPheeters had given special, mocking emphasis to "step-ma." He'd always been one of those around town who'd sneered at Lloyd and Corsica behind their backs, despite the fact that McPheeters was one of the Pasttime girls' most frequent customers.

Cuno stared at McPheeters, the ringing in his ears increasing in volume. Vaguely, he wondered if this were some cruel practical joke the deputy was pulling on him, to get him back for the arm-wrestling defeat. More than horror at the news, he felt an angry heat rise in his back and neck.

"There's a mistake, or you're lyin', McPheeters!" Cuno suddenly raged, balling his fists at his sides and giving the deputy a challenging glare. All impulse to ingratiate himself to this man had dissolved, and he now wanted to pummel him with his fists.

Half-grinning, thoroughly enjoying himself, the deputy wagged his head. "No, there ain't no mistake, and that's a fact. I been there; I seen it. Now climb down from there and follow me over to the jailhouse. Sheriff's orders. I guess he don't want you walkin' into the house and seein' the carnage."

"Pa's home?" Cuno asked the deputy, his voice quavering with barely restrained emotion. More than he wanted to beat the deputy now, he felt the urgent need to find his pa and get this mess sorted out. And when he did, when he knew for sure the deputy was hornswoggling him, Cuno would beat the fat-faced man to within an inch of his life.

"That's right, but he'll be headin' for the jail pretty soon, so—"

"I have to go home, then," Cuno said as he jumped off the loading dock and turned around the wagon, heading east down the alley.

Corsica was dead?

Pa had killed her?

It was obviously a cruel, sick joke. Lloyd Massey was no more likely to kill Corsica than he was to kill Cuno.

"Hey, where do you think you're goin', Massey?" McPheeters barked as he gigged his horse ahead of Cuno, cutting him off. "I told you we're headin' for the jailhouse."

"I ain't headin' for no jailhouse, McPheeters," Cuno raged, his broad, sun-browned face flushed with fury. "Now get your horse out of my way, or I'll move it."

This seemed to be just what the deputy was waiting for. Grinning, he reached for the revolver on his right hip. But before he could draw it, Cuno reached up, grabbed the deputy's left arm, and pulled him from his saddle with one powerful yank.

McPheeters yelled as he hit the ground in a heap, his gun falling out of its holster. The horse jerked and skittered as Cuno quickly grabbed the reins and saddle horn and climbed aboard, instantly heeling the mount into a ground-eating gallop down the alley.

Behind him, McPheeters shouted and cursed, but Cuno didn't hear. He was too intent on getting home to find out what all this was about, hoping against hope it was all just a cruel joke and he'd find his pa and Corsica sitting around the kitchen table, smiling and laughing like they always did, horsing around.

Or maybe Corsica would be trying on that new dress Pa had bought her . . .

Crossing Main Street, Cuno hunkered low in the saddle and wheeled the horse down Third Avenue past the new school and the Johnson barn. He hung a left across a vacant lot, past the Roddenberrys' woodpile, through a stand of pine trees, and into his own yard.

A saddle horse, a carriage, and the buckboard Cuno recognized as belonging to the undertaker sat under the tall oak tree, outside the picket fence. The horses were tied to the hitchrail. By now, several dogs were barking at the sound of Cuno's horse's hooffalls, but Cuno was only vaguely aware of them as he slid out of the saddle, dropped the reins, marched onto the porch, and pushed through the front door.

"Pa?" he called as he stepped into the small sitting room, the screen door slapping shut behind him.

He turned to the kitchen, where several lamps spread a buttery glow over the table and rough-hewn cupboards. Two men were sitting at the table, and Cuno recognized one as his father. Lloyd's shirt was covered with blood, and there were smears on his face, as well. A third man, Doc

Sutton, stood behind Lloyd Massey, wrapping a white bandage around his head.

"Cuno," the elder Massey said. It wasn't so much a call as a bewildered exclamation.

The other man sitting at the table turned suddenly to Cuno and stood, lifting his arms and spreading his hands. He had a five-pointed star on his chest, and Cuno recognized him as another of the sheriff's deputies, Lon Sykes. He was a big, dark-haired man in a frock coat and a string tie. A cheroot smoldered in an ashtray before his place at the table.

"Hold on there, Cuno. You can't come in here now. The sheriff sent Ned to take you to the jailhouse."

"I wanna see my pa. I wanna know what's going on," Cuno exclaimed, looking around the big deputy at his father. "Pa, what happened? Ned said Corsica's dead and you killed her!"

The young man shook his head, his face flushed with befuddlement. It was slowly becoming clear that something awful had happened, but Cuno was not yet ready to believe what McPheeters had told him. Pa would not have killed Corsica.

The bedroom door opened to Cuno's left, and a corpulent man with a ruddy complexion and thin, salt and pepper hair appeared. He was in his fifties, dressed in a cheap, brown suit with a sheriff's star pinned to his wool vest. A Colt Army .44 rode high in a black holster on his hip.

To the deputy, Sheriff Manget said, "It's all right, Lon. Let him talk to his father. I'll sit here, too. You can go in and help Isaac carry the body out to his wagon."

Nodding, the deputy retrieved his cheroot from the ashtray, stuck it between his lips, and walked into the bedroom. Cuno's heart jerked. There was a body, which meant someone really had been killed. Corsica . . . Cuno felt his knees trying to buckle. The ringing in his ears had risen to a witch's shrill, incessant scream.

"Pa," he mumbled, turning his eyes to his father, who stared at him wanly, reflecting the confusion and sorrow and horror in Cuno's own heart.

The front screen door squawked open and Ned McPheeters rushed in, looking flushed and harried, his eyes turning angry as they found Cuno in the kitchen. "Sorry, Sheriff, but the crazy, sumbitch kid caught me by surprise!"

Manget held up his hands placatingly. "It's all right, Ned. Go into the bedroom and help Lon and Isaac carry the body out."

"You're gonna pay for that, boy!" McPheeters warned, jerking a rancorous arm at Cuno.

"Let it go, Ned," the sheriff ordered with strained patience as he settled his ample girth in a chair.

Still eyeing Cuno angrily, the deputy turned and walked into the bedroom. Cuno didn't notice. He was fixating on the word "body" again and trying to keep his knees from buckling.

What horrible tragedy had befallen them?

Stiffly, as if in a dream, Cuno shuffled to the table and collapsed in a chair. He sat there rigidly, staring at his father, who was not looking at him now. Lloyd Massey gazed incomprehendingly at the closed bedroom door, his face drawn with shock.

"Tell your son what happened," Sheriff Manget told Lloyd as he fished a small notepad and pencil from a pocket of his coat. "And tell me again, too, so I can get it straight in my head."

Lloyd was silent for nearly a minute, dully blinking his eyes, and Cuno could see he was addlepated by whatever or whoever had hit him in the head. Finally, Lloyd swallowed and licked his lips, his gaze wandering unseeing around the kitchen.

"I-I just come home from the freight yards, and I didn't think anyone was here. The house was dark. I went into the bedroom, to see if Corsica was in there."

Lloyd winced as the doctor adjusted the bandage on his head.

"That hurt, Lloyd?" Doc Sutton asked. He was a slight man in a gray suit with a ball-tipped nose. His thin, gray hair was pomaded to his head.

Lloyd didn't answer, and the sheriff told him to continue.

Cuno sat there in stunned silence, feeling as though he were experiencing a bad dream. He watched as his father dropped his gaze to his hands and wagged his head slowly from side to side.

"I opened the door and stepped in." His voice caught in his throat, and he continued hoarsely, "I saw Corsica layin' on the bed . . . covered with blood." Anger darkened his eyes and carved deep lines in his forehead, raised a flush in his cheeks. "Then I heard something behind the door, an' I turned and, just for a second I saw a big, red-haired gent in a buckskin shirt just before he hit me in the head. That's all I remember until the sheriff here doused me with water."

Lloyd turned to Manget, his eyes wide and flashing exasperation. "It was the red-bearded man—he killed Corsica, Sam!"

"Lloyd," the sheriff said slowly, grimly, "your clothes were covered in blood, and there was a bloody ashtray in your hand."

Lloyd stared at him hard. "So what are you sayin'—I killed Corsica?" Lloyd's eyes filmed but the anger did not leave them. "Why would I kill my wife? I loved her. It was him . . . that man with the red beard. I seen him, Sheriff!"

The sheriff swallowed and sat back in his chair. "Lloyd, are you sure you didn't come home and find Corsica with another man?"

Lloyd wagged his head uncomprehendingly but said nothing.

"Are you sure the man didn't skin out that broken window in there, and then you, in a jealous rage, beat your wife with this here ashtray?" Manget slapped a brown paper sack apparently containing the ashtray on the table.

"No, Sheriff!" Cuno cried. "Pa wouldn't do that. He wouldn't kill Corsica!"

Manget stared at Lloyd. "Are you sure, Lloyd? Are you sure that isn't what happened? These pleasure women—sometimes it's kind of hard for them to give up their old ways. Sometimes they try to get married to nice, honest sorts like yourself, but after a while . . ."

His voice trailed off when he saw Lloyd stand, the freighter's eyes on fire, his fists bunched at his sides. "Don't you talk about her like that, Manget!" Lloyd shouted. "Don't you dare—!"

Lloyd moved toward the sheriff menacingly, but stopped when Manget lifted his Colt above the table.

The sheriff's voice had a hard, incriminating edge. "What about the blood on your shirt there, Lloyd? What about the fact you were lying on the bed, beside your wife, and not just inside the door like you would have been if you'd been hit when you first came into the room?"

The doctor turned to the sheriff. "If it happened like that, who hit him in the head?"

"Corsica," Manget said. "Maybe he was beating her with his fists, and she grabbed that off the bed table, and let him have it. He used the ashtray on her before he passed out himself. He's got quite a welt there, don't he, George?"

The doctor glanced at Lloyd regretfully and shrugged, nodding. "I reckon he does, and he's lost quite a bit of blood. That might've caused him to pass out after a few minutes . . . Sorry, Lloyd," he added.

Lloyd shook his head and sat back down, looking miserable and defeated. "Th-that just ain't how it happened." He took his head in his big, rope-burned hands and heaved a ragged sigh. "It was the man with the red beard who done it."

"Lloyd, I haven't seen no big man with a red beard in town," Manget said sympathetically. "Have you, Doc?"

Sutton shrugged reluctantly and shook his head.

"Pa wouldn't do that," Cuno said softly. He'd been sitting frozen in his chair, unable to move, taking in the conversation but only vaguely understanding. That Corsica was dead and that his father was sitting here being blamed for her murder was just too much to comprehend.

"Everyone knows your father has a temper, Cuno," the sheriff said. "He's shown that in the saloons often enough."

"That was back when I was drinking, after Katherine died," Lloyd said. "I'm a changed man. She—Corsica—changed me." His voice broke with a sob and he lowered his face to his hands again, his shoulders bobbing, his body racked with crying.

The bedroom door clicked open, and the sheriff, Lloyd, Doc Sutton, and Cuno watched the two deputies carry each end of a sagging, sheet-wrapped body out of the bedroom. The sheet was spotted with blood, and as the two men grunted the bundle through the kitchen, a flap opened, and Corsica's exposed face rolled toward the table, glassy eyes open and seemingly staring right at Cuno.

Cuno stiffened, and his stomach heaved. Lloyd Massey groaned and took his face in his hands. Without bothering to cover the dead woman's face, the men maneuvered their grim burden past the table, through the dark sitting room, and out the door.

The undertaker, a tall, gaunt man in a threadbare suit, followed them while keeping his eyes glued to the floor.

Watching, Cuno's throat constricted, and he fought back tears. The second, and probably the last, love of his father's life was dead. And Lloyd was being blamed for her murder.

It wasn't real. It was a bad dream.

It couldn't be real.

"Pa didn't kill Corsica," he said tightly, staring after the deputies. "If he said it was a red-bearded man in buckskins, then that's who it was."

Manget turned to Cuno and nodded slowly. "I'll look into it, boy. In the meantime, I'm afraid I'm going to have to take your pa down to the jail."

Cuno looked at his father. Lloyd looked at Cuno. The son had not seen the father so heartbroken since Katherine Massey had died.

Cuno grabbed his father's arm, sobbing. "No, Pa. *No!*"

3

AFTER THE SHERIFF had led Lloyd off to jail, Cuno returned to the mercantile and finished unloading the wagons. It was exhausting work now, and his head spun from emotional fatigue.

When he'd bedded the mules down in the livery barn, he returned home and slept fitfully, haunted by dreams and nightmares. He must have finally nodded off around dawn, because when he opened his eyes, full morning light angled through his upstairs bedroom window.

He dressed and went down to the kitchen, ignoring the door he'd closed last night after allowing himself only one look around the bedroom, one look at the blood-splattered bed and the broken window. Although he wasn't hungry, he grabbed a biscuit from one of Corsica's storage tins—he needed to keep his strength up—and munched it as he grabbed his hat and headed out the door.

He paused, remembering the broken window, and walked around the side of the house. The window had been broken from the inside, all right, and whoever had broken it had used the chair that now lay on its side a few feet away from the house.

Looking around, Cuno saw that the grass, which had gotten shaggy after the several inches of rain that had recently fallen, did not appear trampled anywhere around the window, as it would have if someone had jumped out, like the sheriff believed. Obviously, old Manget had not inspected the grass out here last night. He would today if Cuno had anything to say about it.

The lack of footprints in the grass meant that someone had only wanted it to appear he'd been surprised by Lloyd's arrival, wanted it only to appear that he'd jumped out the window to get away from an encounter with a jealous husband—a husband who, in his rage, had killed his unfaithful wife.

But, in reality, whoever had been in the room with Corsica had killed her before Lloyd had arrived. The lack of footprints in the dewy grass was proof. The real killer was the red-bearded man in buckskins.

Cuno left the yard and tramped to Main Street, which was bustling now at nine o'clock, farm and ranch wagons clattering this way and that, several matrons in long dresses strolling along the boardwalks. Cuno headed for the sheriff's peak-roofed, log office, and pushed through the door.

Manget was sitting at his desk, a mug of coffee before him, doing paperwork. His jacket was off, and his sleeves were rolled up his arms. He looked up as Cuno entered, but before he could say anything, Cuno started in with, "Sheriff, did you take a good look at the grass out that broken window last night? Well, I just did, and—"

"Hold on, hold on," the sheriff said, waving Cuno to silence.

The boy wouldn't have it. "No, Sheriff. Don't you see? If there's no tracks in the yard, that means—"

Cuno was cut off again as the door to the cell block

opened. His father appeared, flanked by the deputy, Lon Sykes. Lloyd looked wan and red-eyed and ten years older than Cuno remembered, but he wasn't wearing handcuffs as he stepped into the office and locked eyes with his son.

"Pa?" Cuno said, startled. He'd expected his father to be locked in his cell, waiting for a visit from his lawyer.

"Hello, son," Lloyd Massey said, his features grim.

"What's going on?" Cuno asked hopefully.

"Your pa is free to go," the sheriff told Cuno as he opened a drawer, producing a small burlap bag and tossing it on his desk. "There's your personals, Lloyd. Make sure everything's there, then put your John Henry on this form, here. It says neither me or my deputies stole anything."

Cuno blinked with amazement as Lloyd walked over to the desk and opened the bag. "What? Why?" Cuno stammered, unable to believe the sudden good turn of events.

The sheriff leaned back in his swivel chair and removed his reading glasses, twirling them in his right hand. "The undertaker said Corsica was beaten with what appeared to be a pistol butt, not the ashtray we found near your father. Also, she had blood and skin under her fingernails, as though she scratched someone deep. Well, your father don't have any scratches on him. I checked."

Cuno nodded, barely able to contain his relief. "I knew he didn't do it."

The sheriff mirrored the nod. "I figured he didn't, too, but I have to go by the evidence, you know. Sorry, Lloyd."

"I know you were just doing your job, Sam," Lloyd said as he stuffed his wallet, timepiece, and a small leather notebook in his pockets. "But I hope you'll start looking for the man I saw in our room last night. That's the son of a bitch that killed my wife." His voice was taut with anger.

"I know, I know," the sheriff said. "The red-bearded man. I'll have my deputies keep an eye out for him, but we can't just go arresting any man with a red beard and buckskins, you know, Lloyd. We have to have proof he killed her."

"Check him for scratches."

The sheriff flushed, his jaw hardening as he looked up at the sorrow-wracked freighter. "Now, don't start tellin' me how to do my job, Lloyd. Go on home and get some sleep."

Lloyd turned and headed for the door. "I'll sleep when the man who killed my wife has been found," he said. Opening the door, he added, "Not before. Come on, Cuno."

When Cuno had followed him onto the stoop, he said, "Where to, Pa?"

"The undertaker's," Lloyd said, turning and walking north.

When he'd walked half a block, Cuno following silently, pensively behind, he angled across the street to a low, shed-like building with a shingle that read ISAAC GRAYSON—UNDERTAKER.

"Wait here," Lloyd told Cuno. The older Massey turned the doorknob and stepped inside, shutting the door behind him.

Cuno waited on the stoop, staring at the traffic, his thoughts with his father. Lloyd had gone into the undertaker's to see Corsica. The thought of it broke the boy's heart, and he sniffed back tears as he stared sightlessly across the street, at the townsmen and cowboys and farmers going about their day.

How quickly everything had changed. Yesterday at this time, Lloyd and Cuno had been on the trail, heading their mules home. Lloyd had been full of boisterous cheer as he looked ahead to giving his lovely young wife the dress he'd bought her in Estherville. Now, only a few hours later, Corsica was dead, and Lloyd grieved over her inert body in the undertaker's parlor.

Nearly a half hour passed before the door opened behind Cuno, and Lloyd stepped out, his eyes red and his face swollen from crying.

"You okay, Pa?" Cuno asked. The only other time he'd seen his father this shaken was after Cuno's mother died.

"I'll be all right, son," Lloyd replied. He sighed deeply. "I tell you what, though, I sure could use a drink. How 'bout if I buy you a beer?"

Cuno hesitated. He hoped his father was not going to start frequenting saloons again, as he'd done after they'd buried Cuno's mother. The fights he'd instigated when drunk and hating the world were still discussed around the county.

"Why not?" Cuno said, knowing his father could probably use a drink right now, to calm his nerves. He'd make sure Lloyd didn't overindulge.

A few regulars stood at the Pasttime's bar, one foot on the brass rail. A few more hunkered over beers at the tables.

"Two beers," Lloyd told the morning barman, Clyde Proust.

"You got it, Lloyd," Proust said grimly. "Sorry to hear about your loss. It's just awful. I never knew Corsica—I came a few months after she and you got married—but I heard she was a real fine girl."

Ignoring the comment, Lloyd said pointedly, "You haven't seen a big, red-bearded man in buckskins around, have you?"

"Nope, can't say as I have, but then I just work mornings, you know," Proust said, shaking his head as he filled the second beer at the tap. "Why? Is that who you think killed your wife?"

"It sure enough is," Lloyd said, "and when I find the son of a bitch, I'm gonna chop him up in little square chunks of wolf bait."

"I don't blame you, Lloyd," said one of the regulars standing at the bar. "That Corsica was one fine lady."

"How 'bout you, Dan?" Lloyd said as he tossed several coins on the bar to pay for the beers. "You see a big, red-bearded man in buckskins around town lately?"

Dan wagged his head. "Nope, can't say as I have. I just got back to town this morning, though. I was off selling hay to a livery barn in Marnett."

Lloyd nodded. To Cuno, he said, "Come on, son. Let's get us a table and relax a little."

Warily, Cuno followed his father to a table back by the piano.

"I sure am sorry about this, Pa," Cuno said, when they'd each taken a seat.

Lloyd shook his head and took another long sip from his beer. "I don't want to talk about it," he said dully. "I don't want to talk about anything. I just want to sit here and drink my beer."

Cuno nodded and sucked the foam off his own beer. He considered reminding his father that they were supposed to haul a load of seed corn from the train station in Kearney today, but decided against it. He knew his father was in no condition for work. Later, Cuno would wire the freight manager in Kearney that the pickup would be delayed a few days.

Lloyd finished his beer and ordered another. Not having acquired a taste for alcohol, Cuno only sipped his. A half hour after they'd sat down, Ned McPheeters pushed through the batwings. He paused before the door when he saw Cuno and Lloyd, then poked the brim of his shabby hat onto the back of his head. Scratching his jaw, he swaggered over to Lloyd and Cuno's table, pulled a chair out, and sat down.

"Have a seat, Ned," Lloyd said, fashioning a diplomatic smile.

The deputy looked at Lloyd gravely and said, "I'm sorry about your loss, Lloyd. I truly am." Then, turning to Cuno, he added, "I just want your son to know that the only reason I ain't gonna arrest him for that crazy stunt he pulled last night—yankin' me off my horse, takin' me by surprise—is cause I'm sympathetic to the situation."

Lloyd glanced at Cuno. "And Cuno appreciates that—don't you, son?"

Cuno nodded sheepishly. "Yes, sir. I'm sorry about pulling you off your horse, Mr. McPheeters."

"You do anything like that again," McPheeters said, leaning over the table and looking at Cuno directly, "I'll make sure your horns get clipped but good. You understand?"

Before Cuno could say anything, Lloyd spoke. "Now, hold on, Ned. The boy apologized. You said yourself you understood the situation. Let's leave it at that, shall we?"

He reached out and grabbed Cuno's shoulder. "I don't blame you for bein' sore, but listen, this kid has licked bigger and better men than you or me. Look at his arms. Look at those shoulders. Those are a mule-skinner's, back-and-bellyin', freighter's shoulders. Why, he'll knock your ears down so's they'll do you for wings." Lloyd's voice had gradually hardened and lowered, like a painter's growl. "So you best swallow your pride and lay off the prod, Ned, or my boy here'll kick your ass from dusk to dawn, so's you'd think you'd just fracased with a grizzly in a one-hole privy."

McPheeters's face had turned the pink of a Nebraska sunset. His mouth opened to speak, but before he could say anything, boots and boisterous voices sounded on the stairs at the back of the room, and he turned that way.

Cuno and Lloyd turned, as well. Two men were coming down the stairs, chuckling. One was a wiry whip with black braids and who appeared to be at least half Indian. The other, Cuno noticed as the blood froze in his veins, was a big, red-bearded man in greasy, smoke-stained buckskins.

Two deep, recent scratches trailed from just below his right eye into his beard on his right cheek, and another shone on the left. There were several nicks on his neck.

"I told you not to say that," the big man affably cajoled the other as he beat the half-breed playfully with his hat. "My mother weren't no Viking. She was Scotch. Now those girls are gonna think I'm a damn savage!" He laughed boisterously at this, his deep, resonant voice booming around the room as he and the half-breed reached the bottom of the stairs and headed for the bar.

"Did you see the tattoo on the one calls herself Springtime?" the half-breed said through a face-wide grin. "I never seen such—" He stopped midsentence when he noticed, like the big man had, that everyone in the saloon had fallen silent and was now staring at them in awe.

"I'll be goddamned," Lloyd growled. Cuno turned to him. His father's face was a taut mask, his eyes frozen on the pair at the bar. "It's him."

The bearded man, standing beside his diminutive, hawk-faced buddy at the bar, looked around the room curiously. "What the hell ye all starin' at?"

Heart thudding, Cuno glanced at McPheeters. The deputy was staring at the pair, his expression befuddled and apprehensive, in stark contrast to Lloyd's building rage. Cuno was glad his father wasn't carrying a gun. If he were, he'd probably have tried to use it by now, and been dead. It was obvious the pair at the bar were good with the weapons they wore prominently displayed on their belts, their holsters secured to their thighs with leather thongs.

"I said, what ye all starin' at?" the big man repeated, his voice booming even more loudly as his anger grew.

Cuno glanced at his father again and felt bile fill his guts when he saw the little, taut smile pulling at the corners of Lloyd's mouth and drawing his lids slightly over his eyes.

McPheeters saw it, too; and said, "Now simmer down, Lloyd."

Cuno said to the deputy, "Maybe you better get the sheriff."

"What for?" the deputy said, his reluctant gaze returning to the renegades at the bar.

"Murder—that's what for," Lloyd growled.

Overhearing the conversation, the big man said, "Hey, what are you two talkin' about? If it's about me, I don't like bein' tongue-whipped behind my back. You got somethin' to say, say it."

"Okay," Lloyd said, shoving his chair back and rising to his feet.

"Pa!" Cuno urged.

Ignoring the boy, Lloyd said to the big man, in a wire-taut monotone through clamped jaws, "I think you killed my wife last night."

"Say what?" the big man laughed, glancing at his friend, who grinned.

"How'd you get those scratches on your face?"

"These?" the big man said jovially. "Why, those girls workin' upstairs get a might excited, they do. Of course, who can blame 'em? I'm sure none ever seen the likes of me before—most of 'em bein' new an' all. Now, there was a girl who used to work here. Let's see—what was her name? Oh, yeah, it was Corsica. Corsica Landreau. Now, she liked it when I—"

"Shut up!" Lloyd raged, balling his fists at his sides. "You killed her, you son of a bitch! And if I had a gun right now, I'd blow your goddamn heart out!"

"Pa, don't!" Cuno urged as he bolted to his feet and pushed his father back several steps. "Let the law take care of it."

"Yeah, let the law take care of it," the big man said, turning his eyes on McPheeters, who stood there stiffly, obviously wondering what to do. His face was pale.

"Clyde," he said to the bartender evenly, "go get the sheriff."

"You got it, Ned," Clyde said, tossing his bar rag on the counter, moving out from behind the counter and disappearing through the batwings.

The room was so silent that the outside clatter of buggies and buckboards and the vigorous hails of the working men resounded off the walls. Chickens squawked from cages in a passing wagon.

Still trying to hold his father at bay, Cuno glanced behind him and up, seeing several of the pleasure girls, clothed in light wrappers, their faces drawn from sleep, staring apprehensively down from the second-story balcony.

The wiry half-breed looked at Lloyd. "My friend here didn't do nothin' to your wife, man. He was with me and the girls up there all night long."

Lloyd's voice trembled with emotion, but Cuno kept him from lunging for the pair at the bar. "He as much as admitted it by bringin' up her name!" the elder Massey bellowed. "Cuno, let me go!"

"No, Pa! They'll kill you. Now settle down!"

"Yeah, settle down, Lloyd," McPheeters admonished, keeping his eyes on the pair by the bar. "Let me and the sheriff take care of it."

"Yeah, let the law take care of it," the big man said to the deputy, adding with a sneer, "If they think they can."

"Oh, we can," McPheeters said, mustering up his courage, knowing that all eyes in the room, including those of the girls, were on him. He couldn't keep a slight tremble from his voice, however.

"Then you better draw that hogleg on your hip," the big man said, "or get your hand off of it."

The deputy glanced down and appeared surprised to see his right hand on his pistol butt. When he looked up at the renegades again, his face turned a lighter shade of pale and his eyes were even more uncertain. He swallowed, considering. Cuno could tell he did not want to remove his hand from the gun. Doing so would brand him a coward. But if he didn't, he'd have to use it.

Cuno had loosened his grip on his father now. Lloyd's body had relaxed as he watched the activity between McPheeters and the renegades.

"Don't do it, Ned," Lloyd said, his old anger at the deputy having been deflected by the two cutthroats. "Wait for Manget."

"Listen to Lloyd, Ned," one of the girls in the balcony counseled.

The big man glanced at the girl, then turned to the deputy, grinning mockingly. McPheeters flushed and licked his lips.

"Get your hand off the pistol, mister," the half-breed advised through his customary grin, showing his teeth, his obsidian eyes flashing. It was more of a challenge than a warning, and McPheeters knew it.

He couldn't do it, Cuno saw. He couldn't remove his hand from his gun and still lift his chin around town, much less strut like the cock of the walk.

Cuno was about to yell when McPheeters's right arm jerked as his hand clawed his gun from its holster. He wasn't able to raise it, however, before both renegades had their own out. They both fired at once, smoke billowing and the reports echoing like thunder, jouncing the chandeliers. The bullets plunked through McPheeters's chest and out his back, splashing blood.

The deputy stumbled back, firing his own weapon into the floor. He rolled across the table, screaming, and fell to the puncheons in a heap.

Before Cuno knew it, his father had bolted to his right. Lloyd clawed a pistol from another customer's holster and pivoted toward the renegades, shouting, "You killed her, you bastards!"

He raised the gun and fired. The bullet sailed between the two renegades, shattering a gallon jar of pig's knuckles on the bar.

"No, Pa!" Cuno yelled.

As if in a dream, he watched the two renegades swing their pistols at his father, guns barking, smoke billowing. As the slugs punched through Lloyd, the elder Massey stood, stiffening, throwing his head back, his mouth open and raging. Blood stained his shirt and back and face as he stumbled backward, twisting, tumbling over a chair and falling face forward into the piano.

The renegades continued firing through the smoke haze, riddling Lloyd's back with bullets, until the freighter slid down the piano to the floor, leaving the old, bullet-pocked upright a smeared mess of red.

Suddenly, the shooting stopped. The silence returned, almost palpable, the air fetid with the rotten-egg odor of black powder.

His eyes stinging from the smoke, Cuno stood rigidly staring at his father on the floor, unable to comprehend what had just transpired. His ears rang and his heart shuddered, his knees turning to putty. Cold steel had been shoved up his spine.

He stared at his bullet-riddled father until "Pa!" erupted from his throat. He ran to Lloyd and dropped to his knees. "Oh, Pa!" Cuno sobbed.

"Hold it there!" he heard at the periphery of his consciousness.

Lifting his head feebly, he saw the sheriff and Lon Sykes run through the batwings, both men wielding shotguns. Looking right, Cuno saw the big man slapping the loading gate of his pistol closed as he turned to the lawmen.

Simultaneously, the half-breed jumped up from behind the bar, wielding the house greener. His sudden appearance surprised the lawmen. As they jerked their heads toward him, the half-breed tripped the two-bore's first trigger, nearly vaporizing the sheriff's head.

As the sheriff flew back through the batwings, the big man triggered his revolver at the deputy, who was still staring in shock at the half-breed. The slugs punched through the deputy's gut and shoulder, throwing him back against the wall, where he stood yelling and trying to raise the shotgun. His effort was terminated when the half-breed tripped the two-bore's second chamber, nearly cutting the man in half.

Cuno watched, horrified, barely able to see anything through the thick smoke webbing under the rafters. By now, everyone else in the saloon had hit the floor, and the girls were no longer staring down from the balcony.

Through his shock, Cuno realized all the lawmen were dead, as his father was dead. No one else in the saloon was moving to do anything. His exasperation reaching up through his shock to spur him on, Cuno bolted off his haunches and dove for the pistol his father had dropped on the floor.

He'd just raised the barrel when several more shots rang out, flames geysering through the smoke haze, stabbing at Cuno, who felt something cold sear his head.

When he hit the floor, everything went black.

4

IN DREAMS, CUNO Massey watched his father die, over and over again, the bullets punching through Lloyd till he flew to the floor with a crash. Cuno tossed and turned and ground his teeth. He cried out, "Pa! Please don't die!"

Then he drifted for a while in a thick, black soup until the images came to him again, like flotsam shunting in a deep-water current.

Corsica was there, too, the deputies carrying her nude, bloody body out of her room and through the kitchen. Her arms and hair dangled, and when her head flopped toward Cuno, her sightless blue eyes bore into him.

Somehow, everyone in town had gathered in the kitchen to watch. Cuno was yelling for the deputies to cover her body with a sheet, but the men didn't seem to hear him, and for some reason, Cuno could not retrieve a sheet himself.

Outraged at the townspeople for standing there gawking, Cuno yelled, "Get the hell out of our house!"

That woke him up. He opened his eyes, blinking groggily, looking around. The room seemed strange—a bedroom with a mirrored dresser, bureau, clothes rack, and a small table and hide-bottomed chair. There was a water basin and cracked pitcher on the table, with several rags and a roll of bandages piled around it. A thick, green book lay open on the table, as well.

Two windows lay across from him, the lace curtains drawn. But the afternoon sunlight still seeped through—a springy saffron color. Cuno could hear the birds and the distant clucking of chickens.

Cuno looked at the bed and the quilt covering him. This was definitely not his room, his bed. Then he realized his head ached like the blazes, and he reached up, felt the thick bandage wrapped around his forehead.

Then he allowed in the memory of what had happened to his father and Corsica and to himself in the saloon, in the aftermath of his father's death. The memory had been inside his sleeping self, wallowing around, rising up to attack him in dreams. And now it attacked his waking self, as well. His insides heaved; his heart clenched and twisted.

Pa was dead. Corsica was dead.

And that meant Cuno was now alone . . .

He remembered the red-bearded face of the man who had shot his father, and his fists tightened on the quilt.

The doorknob rattled. Cuno turned his head as the door opened and a slight old man with a bulbous nose appeared. Doc Sutton wore a tattered suit with a tarnished watch chain flapping at his vest. His hair was thin atop his head but long and gray and of the texture of corn silk on the sides.

The man's clear blue eyes scrutinized Cuno from the open door. "Awake?"

Cuno nodded.

"I figured you'd wake today. Your fever broke yesterday around noon." The doctor ambled over to Cuno. Bending down, the old man set his hand on Cuno's forehead, over the bandage. The hand was smooth and gunmetal cold.

"Yep, I think it's done settled. You should be on your feet soon. Hungry?"

Cuno shook his head. "How long have I been out?"

"Four days."

"Four days." Cuno tried working his mind around it. "What . . . what about . . .?"

"Your father's dead, Cuno," the doctor said, his voice barely above a whisper. He gazed at Cuno directly, and the corners of his wide mouth were slightly turned down. "I'm very sorry. Corsica is dead, too. So's the sheriff and . . . well, I guess you remember all that, don't you?"

Cuno was speechless as it all flashed in his head, a waking nightmare. It was so vivid he could hear the gunfire and smell the rotten-egg odor of the smoke. He could hear the red-bearded man's sneering voice, see his flat eyes as he fired his gun. He could hear his father's dying cry, hear Lloyd's body smacking the floor.

"What about the man who killed my father?" Cuno asked, turning to the doctor, who had swung the hide-bottomed chair around and sat down only a few inches from the bed. "The red-bearded man."

"Him and his compatriot done rode out after they left the saloon." Doc Sutton shook his head and rubbed his big nose thoughtfully. "Just climbed onto their horses like nothing had happened, and jogged north out of town. Word has it they're headin' for the gold camps Montana-way."

Cuno thought about that, squeezing out the nightmare images with the image of the red-bearded man and his friend—the short, slimmer, younger man with the greased braids. He wanted to remember their faces and the clothes they wore. He didn't know why he wanted to remember them; his lust for vengeance was not yet fully conscious. He knew only that he wanted—needed—to remember.

In his mind, he saw the two men ride out of town after killing Corsica and Cuno's father, as though they'd done nothing more than kill a couple of buffalo.

That's what they were, Cuno knew—buffalo hunters. He knew the breed. They rode through town often. He knew how they dressed and the guns they carried and the smell they wore—the smell you could detect from a block away. The smell of camp smoke and death.

Word has it they're headin' for the gold camps Montana-way.

"Am I gonna be okay, Doc?"

The doctor nodded. "Should be. That bullet creased you good, rattled your brains around. But you should be on your feet again in a couple days."

"A couple days?" Cuno wanted to get up right now.

Doc Sutton shook his head. "Give it time, Cuno. You get up now, you won't make it to the door. You're weak; you need to rest. I'm gonna get Carmen to heat you up some soup."

The old medico patted the young man's shoulder placatingly as he climbed to his feet and turned to the door.

"Doc?" Cuno called. "What about Pa and Corsica?"

The stoop-shouldered Sutton turned around. "We buried them, Cuno. Sorry. We couldn't wait for you." He jerked his head to indicate south. "We buried 'em in the Lutheran cemetery, side-by-side. Wally Knutson carved 'em up a real nice stone. Reverend Johannson said a nice sermon."

Cuno choked back a wave of emotion, squeezed his eyes closed. "I wish I could have been there."

Later, when Carmen Polly, the middle-aged woman who cooked and cleaned for the doctor, had brought Cuno a tray with soup and bread on it, Cuno dug in. He'd eaten only half the soup and bread when the doctor came in again, scrutinizing the tray from the door.

"That all you can get down?"

"I'm not very hungry, Doc."

Sutton nodded. "No, I suppose you wouldn't be. You'll be hungrier tomorrow."

"I reckon," Cuno said dully, staring off. A thought occurred to him. "Doc, what about the sheriff and the deputy? What about the law . . .? I mean, who's goin' after them?" He knew Sutton knew who he meant.

"We don't have a new sheriff yet, but a couple of men went out, Cuno," the doctor said halfheartedly, shrugging a shoulder. "They didn't find anything. They didn't ride very far, though. I reckon no one really wanted to tangle with Rolf Anderson and Sammy Spoon."

"You know who they were?" Cuno said eagerly. He hadn't heard of them, but it was good to know their names.

The doctor nodded. "They used to come to town whenever they were in the area, hunting game for the railroad. They'd do some awful hoorawing in the saloons. Nothing real bad, but it was obvious they were violent men. It's been said they've hired out to kill more than just buffalo, if you get my drift."

"Doc?" Cuno said after a long silence.

"Yes, boy?"

"I'm going to hunt them down and kill them—that Rolf Anderson and Sammy Spoon."

The doctor stared at Cuno for a long time, expressionless. His nostrils flared a little. "I figured you might, boy. It isn't a good idea, but to tell you the truth, if I was young like you and in your shoes, I'd try to do the same thing."

"I'm not just going to try, Doc," Cuno said, cocking an eyebrow for emphasis. "I'm going to do it."

The doctor nodded and pursed his lips with mute skepticism.

Cuno turned away and stared through the window. He could hear Carmen out there, scolding a dog.

"Well," Sutton said, "I'll tell Carmen to get your dishes. Maybe you'll eat some more for supper."

"Yeah, maybe," Cuno said. His heart wasn't in the reply.

He was still staring out the window, a slow fire kindling in his eyes.

A week and a half later, Cuno Massey shook hands with Ray Bennett, the man who'd bought Massey's Freighting, and climbed atop the horse—a skewbald paint—he'd bought from the livery owner. Renegade was the horse's name. The gelding was sixteen hands high with a deep chest, stout legs, and a restless light in its eyes. If what the liveryman said about him was true, Renegade was really more horse than Cuno could handle, for he'd rarely ridden horseback, having grown up in the driver's box of a stout Murphy wagon. But he knew he'd need a good horse to get where he was going.

He'd rigged Renegade out with an old saddle he'd bought for ten dollars, a bedroll, saddlebags, and a canvas war bag he'd looped around the horn. In his saddle boot rode the old Spencer rifle he and his father had always packed on their freight runs. It was a bit rusty and tarnished, and its walnut stock was gray as a weather-beaten barn, but it was the only gun he had, and it would have to do for now. He'd made twenty-five hundred dollars when he'd sold the freight business and the house, but he didn't know how far the money would have to stretch. He didn't know how long it would take him to hunt down Rolf Anderson and Sammy Spoon.

He knew only that he was heading for the gold camps in Montana, because that's where Anderson and Spoon were heading.

Reining the horse around uncertainly and glancing around self-consciously—he had lots to learn about horseback riding—he gigged the skewbald paint onto a trail that curved south of town. He rode in the warm summer sunlight, curving around a bend in the trail shaded by two large cottonwood trees. Ahead, on a low, grassy rise, lay the cemetery. He rode to the gate in the rod-iron fence and tethered Renegade to the hitching rail.

The afternoon sun was warm on his neck and shoulders, and his weathered bowler did little to shade his face. He'd need a new hat, with a broader brim. Grasshoppers arced through the air. Meadowlarks and blackbirds sang in the cattails in the slough just north of the burial ground.

He removed the hat as he strode through the gate. This was the first time he'd visited the cemetery since leaving the doctor's house, and he was hesitant, afraid of his own emotion, of losing control.

Looking around, he saw two black mounds of fresh earth lying under a cottonwood tree, in the northwest corner of the cemetery.

He hesitated, choking down the dry knot in his throat, feeling the muscles in his face contract. Taking a deep breath, he walked around the gravestones and stopped under a stout branch of the cottonwood. He looked down at the two mounds. One stone marker marked both graves.

Massey, it read in arcing letters across the top. Below, side-by-side, were the names Lloyd (1820–1867) and Corsica (1837–1867).

On the other side of Lloyd's grave lay Cuno's mother, with her own marker and the words BELOVED WIFE AND MOTHER etched beneath her name and the date she'd died.

"Well, you're together again, I reckon," Cuno told his father and mother. "I hope you don't mind Corsica bein' here with Pa, Ma." His voice broke; he sniffed back tears. "She sure was a good woman and she really got pa's wolf back in its cage after you left us."

A sob racked Cuno's body, and he dropped his head. Tears rolled down his cheeks.

"I'm so sorry, Pa. Those men had no right to kill you. You were a good man . . . a kind, gentle man, and you taught me a lot." He cried openly now, dropped to his knees and stared through a haze of tears at his father's freshly chiseled tombstone. "I don't know . . . I don't know how I'm ever gonna get on without you, Pa. But if I do one thing in my life . . . I'm gonna see to it I settle the score. For both of us, Pa. For both of us, and for Corsica, too."

Cuno knelt there and cried until the midday sun angled around, drawing shadows from the tombstones. He occasionally lifted his head to glance around and see if anyone had come and had seen him, kneeling here and bawling like a baby. No one came, however, and he let the tears flow of their own accord, letting out the anguish that had gotten a stranglehold on his heart.

Finally, feeling somewhat lighter but wrung out from the explosion of emotion, he climbed back to his feet. He bid his parents and Corsica good-bye and promised he'd be back again someday.

"Sorry I didn't bring flowers," he said as he donned his hat. "I'll bring some next time."

He turned away and strode through the gate—a big, broad-shouldered lad dressed in rough mule-skinner's duck pants and faded shirt and suspenders, a tattered bowler on his down-canted head, blond hair curling over his ears and down his collar. Awkwardly, he mounted the skewbald paint. Still afraid of its reluctant and hesitant new owner, Renegade skitter-stepped away from Cuno, nearly throwing the boy, before he finally got settled in the saddle.

"Sorry. I know you don't like me, boy," Cuno told the horse. "You give me a chance and I'll give you a chance, all right?"

With that, he rode down the hill to the road and followed the trail west through the buttes, toward a dark line of rimrocks rising like bad teeth on the far horizon.

Word has it they're headin' for the gold camps Montana-way . . .

5

"SO WHAT ARE you gonna do with yours?" Sammy Spoon said as he and Anderson rode single-file down a thin, powdery trail in western Nebraska.

"My what?"

"The gold we been talkin' about?" Spoon chuckled. "The gold we're gonna take out o' Montany."

"Didn't know we were still on that subject," Anderson said, characteristically laconic. "Thought we'd moved on."

"Moved on to what?" Spoon asked. "We weren't sayin' anything."

"Yeah," Anderson said grimly. "Wasn't it sweet?"

Spoon spat chaw on a white, saucer-shaped stone along the trail. "Don't see no harm in talkin'. Like I said, when I'm rich on Montany gold, I'm gonna go on a whorin' rampage across the West, find out who all the best whores are and bed 'em all." Spoon cackled. "I'll bed two, three, maybe even four at a time. Then I'm gonna get me a big house—one of those big Mex ranch houses, made of adobe—and just live there with a hundred whores to serve my every need."

"Haciendas."

Spoon chortled a laugh, his small, dark eyes flashing merrily. "What's that?"

"They're called haciendas, and you're gonna have to make one hell of a killing to afford one, I shit you not."

"That's all right," Spoon said. "My old man always said I'd go far one day." Spoon cackled his boyishly evil cackle, tossing his greased braids as he wagged his head. "Of course, he also said I'd burn in hell."

Anderson hipped around in his saddle to give his younger, half-breed sidekick an angry glower. His bushy red beard was coated with alkali dust and seeds from the cottonwoods along the creek they'd crossed a half hour ago. "Shut up for a while, will you?"

Accustomed to his partner's owly moods, Spoon fell silent. He forgot himself a few minutes later and snickered, dropping his chin and shaking his head reflectively. "Did you see what I done to that ole sheriff's head back in Valoria? Boom, and it was gone. I mean, *gone!*"

They were crossing a low sandstone scarp, following an old settler's trail. Anderson lifted a silencing hand and jerked on his reins, checking the buckskin down to a stop. He glanced around, his eyebrows furrowing like bushy red caterpillars, hiding his blue eyes deep within their doughy sockets. The knobs of his cheeks were pink and sun-blistered.

"What is it?" Spoon asked, reining his mouse-brown dun to a halt just off the tail of Anderson's buckskin.

"Shut up, goddamn ye. I heard somethin'."

Both men canted their heads around, listening. Anderson gigged his horse higher on the scarp and cast his gaze southeast. "Sure enough," he said, pointing. "Stage."

Spoon's voice was eager. "Yeah?"

"Yeah."

"Well, I'll be jiggered. You wanna try for it?"

Anderson turned his glowering features on the half-breed, spat on a yucca, then reined his horse off the scarp and into a small gully hidden from the stage trail. Spoon watched him, chuckling, both reluctant and amused. He never knew what was going to set Anderson off. It could be a simple look or a careless word. Sometimes you didn't have to say or do anything at all.

No, you just never knew. And if the burly hide-hunter and seasoned regulator hadn't been so kill-crazy and money-hungry, Spoon would have lit out on his own a long time ago. As it was, Sammy Spoon just chuckled and followed his partner into the draw to wait for the stage.

One week later, Cuno Massey reined his paint to a halt on the stage road east of Kendle, Nebraska Territory. He'd been on the trail for five days, and he was tired and hungry. His clothes were still damp from the rain he'd endured the last three nights. He wasn't used to camping out on his own, and he was hungry for table food and coffee he hadn't scorched on a cookfire.

That's why the long, gray cabin lying in the valley before him looked so good. Most likely there'd be a woman there who might cook him a meal if he asked politely and offered payment.

His mouth watering at the thought of a pot roast smothered in onions and of biscuits covered with gravy, he heeled the paint down the hill. He was trotting past a corral and windmill when something whistled through the air around him. A searing pain shot through his right shoulder. A rifle barked, and the paint screamed, bucking. Caught off guard, Cuno lost the reins and turned a somersault over the horse's tail, hitting the ground hard on his back.

The rifle barked again, and dust puffed at Cuno's face. His ears rang and his vision blurred as he tried to work his mind around his circumstances, only dimly aware of Renegade galloping off and furiously whinnying, heading east away from the ranchstead and the source of the gunfire.

He'd just realized he'd been shot at when he heard a man yell, "Hold it, goddammit! Hold your fire!"

Clutching his stricken right shoulder, Cuno climbed to his knees and cast his gaze around, wincing, half-expecting another shot to end it all right here.

"That's one of 'em, I think!"

"No, it's not, you fool. It's a kid. Now put that gun away before I take it from you and ram it up your ass!"

The man who'd said this last was running up on Cuno's right, from a small, square shack belching black coal smoke from its tin chimney pipe. The man was in his early forties, Cuno guessed. Medium height, with curly brown hair and a clean-shaven face. He wore a leather apron over a denim shirt. His run was restricted by his right leg, which he dragged stiffly. Reaching Cuno, he squatted with a pained effort, wincing.

"You all right?"

Cuno nodded automatically, looking warily around for the shooter.

"Let me see your shoulder," the man urged.

Cuno removed his hand, and he and the stranger inspected the wound. The seam of his shirt was torn, and there was a little blood, but not as much as Cuno had expected. His entire arm was on fire.

"Just a scratch," the man said. "You'll live—as long as you didn't bust anything in that fall from your horse."

"I'm all right," Cuno said distractedly. He was watching an elderly man with close-cropped gray hair moving toward him along the corral. The man crouched over a long-barreled, old-model rifle with an octagonal barrel aimed at Cuno. His eyes were slitted deviously, his jaws working.

The man nearest Cuno followed the boy's gaze to the old, rifle-wielding gent. Standing and moving as quickly as his stiff leg would allow, he said, "Goddammit, Nichols. I told you to put that rifle down." He approached the old man and wrenched the rifle from his gnarled hands.

"That's one of 'em," the old gent cried. "I know it—I seen him!"

A man on the cabin's stoop called, "No, it isn't. He's seein' things, Mr. Dodge."

"I know he is," the man called Dodge said, regarding the old man angrily. "And he damn near killed this boy. Nichols, if I see you carrying anything more dangerous than your pipe in the two days you have left here, it'll be the last thing you'll ever carry. Now, take a walk and cool yourself off."

The old man was several inches shorter than Dodge. His eyes flashed fearfully at the eastern horizon. "Who's gonna watch for 'em?"

"I'll watch for 'em," Dodge said. "Mr. Trumbull and Mr. Sweney will watch for 'em. Now do as I say." He gave the old man a shove, and Nichols reluctantly slunk off past the cabin, where two men and a woman had gathered on the stoop to see what was going on.

Dodge returned to Cuno. "Charlie Dodge," he said, extending his hand with an apologetic smile.

Still dazed, Cuno shook Dodge's hand. "Cuno Massey."

"Pleased to meet you, Cuno. I'm sorry again for old Nichols's welcoming volley. He's a might skittish since the stage he and these other people were on was attacked five days ago. They were left afoot until I rode out and found them. Why don't you come into the station house, and I'll tend that shoulder for you."

"Didn't realize this was a stage station," Cuno said, regarding the meek faces of the two men and the woman standing on the cabin's stoop. The men wore suits and the woman wore a fancy green traveling dress, but all costumes had seen better days. The lady's dress and the men's suits were dusty and stained and badly mussed. A broken watch chain hung from the vest pocket of the tall, bearded gent standing closest the lady.

"It is at that," Dodge said. "You're on the Parker-McRae route serving the South Platte country. Occasionally we even make a run to Denver City, given favorable Indian conditions and enough passengers, that is." Dodge clapped a hand to Cuno's back. "Come on inside. Like I said, I'll tend that shoulder for you."

"It's just a scratch, Mr. Dodge. I best retrieve my horse."

"Nonsense," Dodge said. "He won't go far. My stock tanks are the only water within twenty square miles. You can retrieve him once I've got a bandage on that shoulder and I've padded out your belly with my famous antelope stew. It's the least I can do. Where you headed?" Dodge asked as he led Cuno toward the cabin.

"Montana Territory."

"Montana, eh? That's a fair piece." Dodge halted before the stoop and regarded the three people standing there scrutinizing the newcomer with a mixture of apprehension and curiosity.

"Cuno Massey," Dodge said, "meet Louis Trumbull, Matt Sweney, and Molly Davis."

The men greeted Cuno with formal nods. The woman smiled demurely. "Pleased to make your acquaintance, Mr. Massey."

"Pleased to make yours, ma'am," Cuno said. He'd always been shy around women—especially pretty women. Molly Davis was probably in her mid-twenties. She was full-figured, and the rich hair piled atop her head was chestnut, with red glints winking in the bright sunlight. She remained standing back against the cabin wall rather stiffly, arms folded across her breasts. The collar of her dress was torn and pinned, and one sleeve had been ripped clear up her forearm. A small cut was healing on her lower lip, and her left eye was slightly swollen and discolored.

When Dodge had ushered Cuno up the porch steps and

into the dim cabin, he invited Cuno to take a seat at the long main table, where tin coffee cups sat around a large stone pot. As Cuno sat down, a girl's voice cried out, "Molly?"

Cuno looked around. The voice had come from behind a row of blankets strung across a rope against the cabin's right wall, sagging between square-hewn beams from which lanterns hung by nails.

"Molly?" the girl cried.

Instantly, the woman from the porch appeared, entering the cabin and pushing through the blankets, arranging them quickly but neatly behind her, leaving no gaps. "I'm here, Francine," the woman said gently. "Hush now, it's all right."

"Who is it?" the girl sobbed. "Who's come?" Her voice was urgent, shrill with fear.

Miss Davis's reply was too soft for Cuno to hear, and since it wasn't his business, anyway, he turned his attention to the coffeepot before him.

"Help yourself," Dodge said, returning from the kitchen with a washbasin, cloth, and several bandage strips cut from sheets or pillowcases. "Don't mind the girl," he said in a hushed voice as he sat on the bench beside Cuno. Even more softly, he said, "She's only thirteen. She had a rough time when the stage was held up. So did Miss Davis. Savages." He looked at Cuno directly and shook his head, as though the topic should not be mentioned again.

When he'd asked Cuno to drop his shirt off his shoulder and had gone to work, cleaning the shallow furrow the rifle slug had plowed about a quarter-inch deep, a possibility occurred to Cuno. "Where did this holdup happen, Mr. Dodge?"

"Call me Charlie. About six miles east of here. Why?"

Cuno winced as Dodge's rag plucked a tender nerve. "There were two holdup men, you say?"

Dodge nodded and ceased working, regarding Cuno

soberly. "According to the passengers, one was a big, red-haired hombre. The other was a wiry half-breed in pigtails. Why? You know 'em?"

Cuno's heart quickened. After five days on the trail and realizing what a big country this was, Cuno had begun to doubt his ability to find two men in it. Now, however, it didn't seem so impossible. Anderson and Spoon had indeed passed this way.

"Their names are Rolf Anderson and Sammy Spoon. They killed my pa and step-ma," Cuno said dully, keeping a tight rein on his emotions. "I'm trackin' 'em."

Cuno stared across the small, low-ceilinged room with its roughhewn chairs and tables and fieldstone hearth. He could feel Dodge's appraising gaze on him. "I've heard of Rolf Anderson," Dodge said. "You're a strapping lad. But how good are you with a gun?"

Cuno shrugged. He hadn't really considered *how* he was going to take down Anderson and Spoon, only that he was going to take them down one way or another.

Dodge studied him a moment longer, then sighed. "Well, have it your way." He wrung the rag out in the basin and picked up the white bandage strips. "But I'd leave 'em to the law, if I was you. I've done wired the sheriff in Park's View, south of here. He should be along any day now."

"He coming alone?"

"I reckon," Dodge said, looping one of the bandages around his upper arm and over the wound.

"He won't have a chance," Cuno said. "Besides, they're probably long out of the county by now."

Later, Cuno retrieved his horse and bedded Renegade down in the barn. He had supper with the others in the cabin. The others except the girl, that was, who remained on her cot behind the blankets. It was a quiet meal with a ponderous tension in the air, put there, Cuno knew, by the passengers' shared horror and survival. He could sympathize.

Dodge offered him a cot, but Cuno could not sleep with

the other men snoring and the girl waking up behind her blanket partition, sobbing until Miss Davis soothed her back to sleep. Finally, he took his blanket and headed out to the barn, where he bedded down on a hay shock. He'd just drifted off to sleep when he heard footsteps outside.

Blindly in the dark, he reached for his rifle.

6

AS THE DOOR squawked open about two feet, Cuno grappled with his rifle, trying to get his finger through the trigger guard while levering a shell into the chamber. He'd lowered the cocking mechanism but hadn't brought it back up when he heard, "Mr. Massey?"

It was a woman's voice.

Cuno froze, tried to sound calm. "Yes?"

"I heard you get up and come out here. I couldn't sleep, either. Would you consider escorting a lady on a short stroll?"

He recognized the voice as that of Miss Davis. Confused and embarrassed, he wasn't sure how to respond. He remembered how pretty she was, and his heart beat as though the barn were being stormed by rampaging Kiowa.

"Uh, of course. I'll be right there."

He tried standing the rifle against a joist but it slid off and fell into the hay with a soft thud. Leaving it, he buttoned his shirt and stomped into his boots. He picked up his hat and, smoothing his hair down, headed toward the door.

Outside, he found her standing before the barn, a thin white shawl about her shoulders, gazing at the star-dusted sky.

Hearing his footsteps, she looked at him. "I didn't wake you, did I?"

"No." He cleared his throat and stifled a yawn.

Returning her gaze to the sky, she said dreamily, "They're so lovely, aren't they—the stars? It's hard to believe this country can be at once so lovely and savage."

There was a pause while she pondered the sky and Cuno tried fashioning a halfway intelligent response. She didn't give him enough time, however.

"Well, then," she said, extending her hand to him, "shall we?"

"Sure," Cuno said, awkwardly crooking his arm so she could hook it with her own.

There was an embarrassing moment while they made the hitch. She laughed and, with a gentle tug, urged him westward down the road, passing another, smaller barn and a hay rack from which a startled cat jumped into the tall grass and disappeared.

"There's a horse trail over here," she said when they'd walked about thirty yards. "The main trail makes me nervous. One never knows who might be traveling."

"No, I reckon not."

"I suppose Mr. Dodge told you of our trouble?"

Cuno hesitated. "Yes, ma'am. I'm sorry. I hope you're going to be okay."

She shivered. "I'm not sure any of us from the stage will be okay. Not after that. Especially little Francine. She was traveling alone to her father's ranch in the Sandhills. Her mother had died of a fever back East, poor girl. Now this—what they did to her."

Obviously, she wanted to talk about it, but, while Cuno's heart went out to her, he could think of no appropriate response to the woman's travails. He wanted to assure her that

Anderson and Spoon would pay for their transgressions, but he wasn't sure how to put that into words, either.

Trying to gently sway the conversation toward less problematic territory, Cuno said, "Where are you headin', Miss Davis, if you don't mind my askin'?"

"I don't mind you asking at all, Mr. Massey. My gosh, how I've needed some conversation. The men I'm traveling with are not in the least bit conversationalists, and, while Mr. Dodge can hold up his end, he's awfully busy running this place all by himself. I'm headed for the next town on the line—Cottonwood. Thirty miles on. I'm their new teacher."

"You're a schoolteacher?"

"That's correct."

"And where are you from?"

While they strolled along the horse trail under the stars, she told him she'd come from a little town called Chambers, Illinois. She'd been teaching school there but had left for personal reasons having to do with a man. Cuno flushed at this, fearing they were once again entering problematic territory, but she didn't elaborate. She said she'd landed the teaching job in Cottonwood after answering a newspaper ad. After her "man trouble," as she called it with a self-effacing laugh, she wanted a new adventure and sought to spread her wings a bit.

"This, however, was a little more adventure than I'd counted on," she said, turning away to pensively study the velvety horizon prodded by the black silhouettes of distant rimrocks touched by starlight.

A cottonwood in the gully below rattled its leaves, and she clung to him tightly, giving another shiver. After a few minutes, they continued back toward the buildings, and she told him about her idyllic childhood in Fayetteville, Arkansas, where her father had been a judge and they'd lived in a big house and she'd often worn shiny white dresses with hoops so big they'd hardly fit through the doors. Her father had had a gambling problem, however. The family hadn't known it until the house was put up for sale and they'd had to move into a boarding house.

"That's when I went off to the teacher's college," she said as they approached the barn.

Cuno was about to respond to her story with a sympathetic remark, but before he could open his mouth, she turned to him and looked up into his face with her eyes crumpled beseechingly. "Young Cuno, would you do me a favor?"

"Of course . . ."

"Kiss me?"

He wasn't sure he'd heard correctly. "Beg your pardon?"

She smiled tenderly. "I know it's a bold request, and not at all ladylike, but I feel rather lonely and afraid just now and not one bit attractive, and just one kiss I think would help me sleep tonight." She placed a hand to her temple, massaging. "I'm afraid I just cannot get the images of those men out of my head, and I'm afraid . . . I'm afraid I'll never be able to. . . ." Her voice had faded away as it climbed to a sob.

Cuno had kissed only two girls in his short life. One had been his age and one had been a year younger. He wasn't sure how you kissed a full-grown woman, but trying not to think too much and trying to ignore his pounding heart, he lowered his head, pressed his lips to hers, which trembled slightly for a moment before they stilled and opened. She moved closer, pressing her body firmly to his.

At first, he was too nervous to feel anything but his own anxiety. Gradually, however, as she encircled his neck with her arms and as he felt her bosom swell against his chest, his enervation abated, replaced with a growing heat in his loins.

After a while, she drew her face away and gazed up at him, a dreamy look in her eyes. "You are so young . . . so good, aren't you?"

He did not know how to respond.

"You would never hurt a woman, would you?"

He shook his head. "No."

Still in his arms, her soft, pliant body radiated desire. It infected him like a raging illness, and he pulled away from her. Turning toward the barn, she took his hand in hers. Neither said a word as she led him through the still-open doors and into the shadows beyond.

She led him to his blanket and turned to face him. He felt suddenly hot and cold and nearly quaking with desire. He'd never known such a strong feeling, and it frightened him. Now that he was here, at this place he'd yearned to be for so long and had only experienced in dreams, he was not sure how to continue.

She sensed this. Her voice was just above a whisper. "Have you ever . . . before?"

He couldn't help an embarrassed grin. "No."

"Well, it's easy," she said, raising her hands to begin unbuttoning her dress. "Get out of your clothes."

Feeling shy, he stepped back in the shadows and, supporting himself with one hand on a joist, kicked off his boots. He removed his shirt and, hesitating at first, removed his jeans awkwardly, nearly falling as he tripped over them, hopping around in the hay. She laughed delightfully. A pale shadow in the barn's misty darkness, she moved to him, and he could see that she was naked.

Holding his hands stiffly at his sides, he was afraid to touch her. At the same time, he felt his exposed member grow so hard he thought the skin would crack. She moved toward him, and he saw that she'd removed her hair from its bun and had let it fall loose about her shoulders.

Suddenly, without warning, her hands were on him. Working him gently in her smooth, soft hands, she whispered soothingly, "Sh . . . it's okay. It's okay . . . we all have to have a first time." He saw her white teeth when she smiled.

She released his member, rose up on her bare toes, encircled his neck with her hands, and kissed him with a passion he hadn't known existed, taking his hand and placing it on one hard-nippled breast.

At last, they knelt together in the hay. Facing him, she ran her hands over his heavy, broad shoulders and his hard chest, down his arms bulging with the muscle he'd developed over years of freighting. She squeezed his hands in both of hers, hard, feeling the strength in them, running her fingers over the callused palms.

"You are a fine young boy," she said. "So much finer than them . . . oh, Cuno, make them go away!"

She threw herself into his arms. Kissing her, he gentled her back in the hay. Her legs opened for him, inviting him in . . .

He woke later to a horse's loud whinny. He lifted his head and looked around. He was alone under the thin army blanket he'd brought out from the cabin. Miss Davis—should he now call her Molly?—was gone. From the pearly blue light washing through the barn's small windows, he saw why: it was dawn, and not wanting anyone to know she'd slept with Cuno in the barn, she must have returned to the cabin.

The horse whinnied again, then another did the same. Hooves pounded. Blinking groggily, Cuno frowned, wondering what had stirred the team in Dodge's corral and deciding he should go see.

He was reaching for his hat when a gun popped.

Dodge's voice rose from the yard, shrill with anger. "Hey, you sons o' bitches! What the hell you think you're doin'?"

His organs surging with adrenaline, Cuno jumped up and grabbed his rifle. He was through the barn doors and out in the yard before he realized he was naked as a jaybird! Instinctively, he knew he didn't have time to dress.

He and his father had had their own problems with horse thieves, and he knew that if he didn't move fast, Dodge's team and Cuno's own paint would be gone.

Directing his gaze at the corral lit by the wan gray light, he saw two men hazing the horses out the open corral gate with their hats. Two more rode horseback outside the corral, wielding rifles. One aimed his toward the cabin. The barrel puffed smoke and fire, and Cuno saw Dodge, who was running in his awkward, shuffling gait across the yard dressed in only his union suit and hat and carrying a Winchester, drop to his knees. Cursing, the station manager lifted the rifle and returned the rider's fire, blowing the man off his horse.

Cuno ran toward the corral, no longer mindful of his nudity but only the horses. When one of the men inside the corral shot at him, Cuno dove to his right, hearing the bullet whistle past his shoulder. He brought the rifle up, shaking, his heart beating like a war drum, and fired. Clumsily, he ejected the spent shell, slammed another into the Spencer's chamber, and fired again. The rider he'd shot at didn't so much as flinch as he continued waving the horses through the corral gate.

By now, several guns were popping and men were yelling. The horses were out of the corral and one of the thieves was climbing onto his horse when he screamed and grabbed his lower back, then sank to the ground and was kicked by his own bucking mount. Cuno saw Dodge duck through the corral and shuffle toward the open gate, drop to his knees and fire four quick shots, smoothly levering the shells in his Winchester, one after another.

Cuno ran around the corral's south fence, heading for the gate. A gun popped before him, sizzling the air by his left ear and thumping into a peeled log corral slat. Cuno stopped, crouching, and saw the gunman before him, standing behind the open corral gate, extending his rifle toward Cuno over the gate, sighting down the barrel.

Cuno brought the rifle up and fired, but his shaking hands caused the bullet to plunk into the gate, a full three feet to the gunman's right. Knowing he'd missed, Cuno froze, unable to move. He felt as though death's door were yawning and a chill wind were about to blow him through. Standing there in a half crouch, his eyes wide with fear, he stared at the rifle centered on his chest, waiting for the bullet.

A gun exploded, and he jerked with a start. After a moment, he realized the shot had come from his left. Before him, the gunman stumbled back from the gate, drawing the gate toward him, blood sprouting from a neat hole in his forehead. The man fell in a twisted heap, firing his rifle harmlessly into the air, the gate swinging out over his prone body, then swinging slightly back.

Cuno looked left. Charlie Dodge stood in the empty corral, his rifle smoking. Dodge studied the man he'd just shot, then shuttled his cool eyes to Cuno.

"You all right?" he called.

Cuno licked his lips, swallowed, and nodded. His knees felt like putty.

"Well, that's all of 'em, I think," Dodge said, dragging his bad leg forward and inspecting another dead horse thief. "I only counted four. How many did you see?"

"F-four's all . . . I guess," Cuno said, his voice quaking. There was nothing like having a gun aimed at your heart to turn your bones to jelly.

"The Crater boys, from over on Washout Creek," Dodge said. "Their own water dried up, so they took to horse stealin'. This should be the last of 'em. I shot one last month.

Cuno looked around and turned back to Dodge, who was looking back at him and smiling. Cuno was about to ask him what was so funny when he looked down at himself, naked as a jaybird.

"Why don't you go get dressed," Dodge said through his grin, "and we'll run those horses down."

A minute later, Cuno was walking across the yard, ignoring the puzzled stares of old Nichols and the other two men, who'd come out from the cabin in various stages of dress to see what all the shooting was about. As he walked tenderly on his bare feet, avoiding stones and other sharp objects, he kept his groin covered with his hat. His face and ears burned with shame.

7

LATER THAT MORNING, when all the horses were back in the corral and the four dead men were buried out in the prairie, Cuno retrieved his saddle from the barn, carried it into the corral, and tossed it over the paint's back. The horse whinnied and stomped and shook its mane, still skittish from all the gunfire.

"Easy, easy," Cuno groused, steadying the saddle on the animal's back.

He hadn't been in much of a mood all morning. It had only partly to do with the humiliating fact that he'd run across the ranch yard stark naked, only partly to do with the fact that the women, including Molly, had probably seen him from a cabin window. Mostly it was due to the fact that he'd almost been killed. If it hadn't been for Charlie Dodge's quick shooting, he'd be hoofing it over the divide about now.

The experience had made him nervous and doubtful of his abilities to accomplish the task of tracking down Anderson and Spoon. He was no gunman, and he wasn't much of a tracker. But if he didn't make the two killers pay for what they'd done to his father and Corsica, who would?

He had to try. If it didn't work out, he'd at least go to his grave knowing he'd done all he could.

His jaw tensing as he imagined the two killers running free about the frontier, killing and robbing and raping to their hearts' content, probably laughing every night about the bloodbath in Valoria, he strapped the saddle tight to Renegade's back, then retrieved his rifle boot from the barn. He was returning to the corral when he heard the cabin door close and saw Charlie Dodge step down from the porch and start across the yard, heading for the corral.

Dodge had apparently fed lunch to the stage passengers. He'd invited Cuno to join them, but the boy had declined. He'd needed to get moving, he'd said, though in reality he was too embarrassed to face the others. Especially Molly. He'd wanted to say good-bye to her but he just wasn't up to it.

"Back on the trail to Montany, eh?" Dodge said conversationally as he approached the corral, working a sharpened matchstick between his teeth.

"That's right. I sure appreciate your hospitality, Mr. Dodge."

"Call me Charlie. And I sure appreciate you helping me run down those horses. Without your two good legs, it would have taken me all day." Dodge cocked his head at the cabin. "Those other three gents weren't much help."

"No problem."

"I hope I didn't embarrass you."

"I embarrassed myself, Mr. Dodge."

"If that were the most embarrassing thing I'd ever done, I'd be ridin' pretty high right now." Dodge chuckled thoughtfully, working the toothpick between his lips. He paused before continuing, shuttling his friendly gaze to Cuno. "I tell you what, though, son—and I'm going to tell you this straight because I think you're a good kid and I'd hate to see you get hurt—you got no business going after Rolf Anderson. Not with just that Spencer carbine of yours and damn little skill at shooting."

Cuno whipped his gaze to the man, his ears warming, his brows furrowing with indignance. Before he could say anything, Dodge raised a cartridge belt coiled around a gun and holster in his right hand, setting it on the corral.

"See this? This here's a single-action army revolver. Chambered to fit .45-caliber Winchester cartridges, it's commonly called the Frontier Colt or the Great Equalizer. It holds six metallic cartridges and is easily, quickly reloaded." He shucked the gun from the holster and held it up, its five-inch barrel and ejector gleaming under fresh oil. He spun the cylinder, making the clean, faint clicking sounds of a finely built revolver that had been well used—the ivory grips were worn—but also well cared for. "To my mind, it's the best revolver ever made, the most reliable and the most accurate. See?"

Dodge's hand was a blur as he swung the pistol around and snapped off a shot. The tin coffee cup that had been sitting on the seat of a nearby buckboard wagon rose high in the air with a metallic ping. At the apex of its rise, Dodge fired again, and the cup rose still higher and away. As it started falling, Dodge's Colt bucked, belching smoke with a report that renewed the ringing in Cuno's ears. The cup jerked eastward with another ping. Coming down, the cup was pierced twice more until it hit the ground, and Dodge gave it a final puncture from thirty yards away.

The cup lay gleaming blue in the sunlight, smoke threading away from its six ragged perforations.

Shuttling his awed gaze from the cup to Dodge, who still held the Colt out from his body, its clean barrel sending up a fine smoke whirl, Cuno muttered a rare curse and cuffed his hat back off his forehead. "Where'd you learn to shoot like that?"

He'd thought maybe Dodge's quick handling of the

Crater gang had been lucky shots, but there had been no luck in his ventilation of the coffee cup.

Dodge spun the pistol on his finger. "Yep, that there's the best handgun made."

"Where'd you learn to shoot like that?" Cuno repeated.

He was only vaguely aware of the stage passengers, who stepped onto the stoop to see what all the shooting was about, their faces pale and frowning. Cuno guessed their nerves were probably frayed from all the shooting and killing they'd heard and seen in recent days.

"I had somewhat of a reputation as a gunslinger in my day, boy—in the years right after the war. I didn't ask for it, but I got it. I also got this." Dodge patted his right thigh. "A gunfighter by the name of Lancaster gave me that in Corpus Christi, Texas. Shattered the bone. Never healed right. That's when I decided to take life a little easier. Makin' a long story short, that's how I ended up here."

"A shootist?" Cuno asked. "No kiddin'?"

Dodge shook his head. "It's nothin' to brag about. My life came to nothing because of it. All it did was draw unwanted attention, so even when I wanted to quit, I couldn't. Every hillbilly trailin' a reputation came gunnin' for me. Finally, one got what he wanted, and here I am, all by myself out here in Nowhere, Nebraska, workin' for a penny-ante stage company." The station manager shoved the Colt back into its holster. "This gun's yours, Master Cuno, because I know you need one for the job you have ahead. Your Spencer carbine might have held a soldier in good stead doing the war, but it's outdated and unreliable. The only payment I want is for you to spend the rest of the day here, and let me teach you how to shoot it, give you a few moves to practice on the trail."

Cuno studied Dodge skeptically. Finally, he shook his head and glanced at the gun resting in its soft leather holster. "I can't take your gun, Mr. Dodge."

"Sure you can. As a matter of fact I insist that you do. I never use the damn thing; I have a half-dozen rifles inside. It's just gonna turn to rust in my old steamer trunk. Besides, I don't like seein' it. Calls up an unhappy past. Like I said, all you have to do is stick around and let me show you how to shoot it. Somewhere, I have a case of cartridges we can pop off. Besides, Anderson already has a week on you. One more day won't make much difference. What do you say?"

Cuno studied the gun. He'd seen revolvers like it, mostly on the hips of drovers passing through Valoria, or in lawmen's holsters. He'd never dreamed he'd one day own one. Although accepting such a gift went against his sense of propriety—he knew Dodge would feel insulted if he offered to buy it from him—he could not turn it down.

Cuno shrugged and, without trying to conceal the ardor in his voice, he said, "Mr. Dodge, you made this hayseed an offer he just can't refuse."

"Good," Dodge said. "Why don't you unleather your horse, and we'll get started."

Cuno carried Dodge's case of .45 shells out behind the barn, and they spent the rest of the day shooting.

Dodge didn't show Cuno anything fancy. By shooting cans off tree limbs, chopping blocks, corral fences, and boulders, he demonstrated the best, most accurate way to fling lead. He gave him a few pointers on how to bring the gun out of its holster fast, and he even counseled the lad on shooting moving targets by swinging a rope from a tree. Cuno didn't hit the rope even once, but Dodge said he hadn't expected him to. It was just something for the kid to think about and to practice along the trail.

"Your shooting ain't half bad—I can tell you've done a share of hunting," Dodge told Cuno toward the end of the day. "But remember, Rolf Anderson and Sammy Spoon are not tin cans or white-tail deer. They're living, breathing men who can shoot back and sure as hell will, if they know you're comin' for 'em."

"I realize that," Cuno said. The sun was angling behind the barn, and the shadows here were growing too dense to shoot any longer. Using his ejector rod, he added the spent shells to the considerable pile that had accumulated throughout the afternoon.

"Well, I reckon you earned the hogleg."

"I don't know how to thank you, Charlie."

"Stop here again on your way home. And keep practicing. Even shoot from your saddle now and then. It's an undependable way to trigger lead, but you never know when you might have to do it. And remember something." Dodge paused, adding gravity to what he had coming. "When you've taken down Anderson and Spoon, go home. Don't linger. Cause if you do, others are going to want a piece of you, just so they can add the notch of the hombre who took down Anderson to their pistol butts. That's just the way it is. You don't want the kind of life I had. It'll get you this"—the station manager patted his right thigh—"or worse. Understand?"

Cuno slid the Colt Army into the holster on his hip, and looked at Dodge gravely. "I have no intention of becoming a shootist, Charlie. My only aim is to avenge my pa and step-ma's murders."

"Good," Dodge said. "Just remember that—no matter what happens. Now, I'll bet the others are grumbling about supper. Let's get back to the cabin." He cuffed Cuno's shoulder as they started walking toward the yard. "I have a feelin' Miss Molly's been missin' you somethin fierce!"

The station manager chuckled. "I saw her leave the cabin last night," he explained when Cuno shot him an incredulous look. "Saw her return . . . about five hours later."

"Oh, jeepers . . ."

Dodge laughed. "Don't worry about it, son. Out here,

you got to take it where you can get it—that's what I always say!"

Out of embarrassment, Cuno avoided Molly Davis's eyes all through supper and dessert, and left the cabin right after the meal, heading out to the corral where he fed and watered all the horses, including his own skewbald paint. Renegade seemed to be growing more accustomed to his new owner, and Cuno spent several extra minutes with him, talking to him and currying him and feeding him sugar cubes. He and Renegade had a long, dangerous trail ahead, and they needed to trust each other.

Not wanting to return to the cabin out of fear that Molly would try to engage him in conversation—he had no idea what to say to the woman after the night they'd shared—he decided to head down to the creek behind the barn for a bath. He'd seen the creek while he and Charlie Dodge had been shooting. It lay on the other side of a small cottonwood grove, which would screen him from the station yard.

He stripped down on the bank, then waded into the creek, his muscles clenching and his skin pimpling against the cold water. The creek was only about two feet deep in its highest hole, so he had to sit down to bathe. Gradually, he got used to the water and began soaping himself with the cake he'd brought from his saddlebags. He'd stood and was bent over, scrubbing his right leg, when he felt as though someone were watching.

Looking up, he saw Molly Davis sitting in the blond grass along the bank. Just sitting there, hands laced around her upraised knees, as though it weren't in the least bit peculiar—a woman sitting there watching a young man bathe in the creek.

His heart throbbed with embarrassment, and his ears heated. He just stood there, staring at her, not sure what to do. His instinct was to turn away or to cover himself, but after last night, what was the point? Her seeing him naked wasn't nearly as intimate as what they'd done together in the barn.

She smiled, seeming to be enjoying herself thoroughly, savoring the sight of his face mottling with embarrassment.

"Hello there," she finally said through a coquettish grin.

Cuno straightened, trying to ignore the fact he was naked. It didn't help that, in spite of his embarrassment, her presence had begun arousing him.

Scoldingly, she said, "You haven't said more than two words to me all day."

"I wasn't sure what to say."

"Are you ashamed?"

"No." He really wasn't. "I just didn't want the others to know."

"I guess I can accept that for a reason," she said. "I wouldn't want them to know, either. But you know what?"

"What?"

"I think we should make love again."

Cuno's heart was thumping again, but this time it wasn't because he was embarrassed. It was nice, somehow, having this woman's admiring eyes on him. "I think we should, too."

"I see you do," she said with a laugh. "May I join you?"

"The water's cold."

"It doesn't appear to have done you any harm."

Cuno looked down, and chuckled. He looked at her again. She'd stood and removed her shoes and was unbuttoning her dress, watching him with a smoky, lusty smile. He stood there, frozen in the chill water, the current swirling gently around his calves, as she pulled the dress over her head, then her chemise, which she tossed atop the dress in the grass.

She bent forward to remove her stockings, and he liked

the way her heavy-nippled breasts hung down. It had been too dark to see them in the barn last night, so he studied them closely now, admiring them, feeling his tongue swell and his heart race, wishing she would hurry. He'd never seen a naked woman before; only the one that hung behind the bar of the Pasttime Saloon in Valoria, but she wasn't real.

This one was real, he told himself now, as though trying to convince himself of the fact. She walked to him, her eyes fondly appraising, a funny little smile playing at her lips. Her hair, which she'd removed from its coils, swayed across her shoulders.

"Cuno Massey," she said breathily as she reached him, "you are a fine piece of work, my dear."

She kissed him hungrily, probing his mouth with her tongue, nibbling his lips. After a long time, she stepped back from him, gazing at him gravely, and then she did something strange, and which he never would have dreamed possible.

Slowly, she lowered herself onto her knees. She took his throbbing organ in her hands, massaging it the way she'd done last night, driving him crazy, making his breath grow shallow and his head swirl. Glancing up at him through slitted eyes, she lowered her chin, her hair falling around her face. Then she moved her hands down to the base of his penis and took the jutting member into her mouth.

He'd never known such sweet bliss was attainable on earth, standing there, the woman kneeling before him, the creek bubbling around his legs. Gently, slowly, adeptly, she freed his spirit and shepherded it off to sea . . .

8

A WOMAN'S SCREAM pierced the night.

Cuno was instantly awake. He grabbed the Colt that had become more and more a part of him since leaving Charlie Dodge's way station, and bolted out of his blankets, out of the lean-to shelter he'd erected against the rain, and ran, stumbling through the dark, toward the scream that sounded again and again.

It was followed by a helpless cry and sobbing.

The woman's voice wailed, "Cuno . . . *help us!*"

Cuno ran, tripping over fallen branches and stumps, trying to pick his way through the moonless night, seeing only vague, dark shapes, dodging looming tree trunks. His arms and legs pumped, his heart raced, his lungs grew raw. Only vaguely he was aware of a fine mist on his face, beading his lashes.

"I'm coming . . . I'm coming," he tried to yell, the words strangled by his labored breathing.

"Cuno!" the girl cried.

Suddenly, he tripped on a rock and fell belly down in cold, running water. The water was like a resolute slap to his face, offering clarity. He lifted his head and looked around, listening.

There was only the sound of the creek trickling over stones and rippling around a beaver den humping up darkly to his right. There were no more screams; there had been no screams. No real ones, anyway. The screams he'd heard had been the product of his imagination, a part of the nightmare that had included disparate effigies of violence and death and the startling image of his father playing a piano covered in blood while Corsica danced with the red-bearded visage of Rolf Anderson.

Cuno looked at the creek swirling about his arms, at the fine blue mist lending a gauzy curtain over the surrounding woods. He pushed himself off his hands, climbed to his feet, and made his way slowly back to his lean-to, under which his blankets lay dimly illuminated by his cookfire, which had died to glowing coals.

Picketed nearby, Renegade gave a curious nicker.

"It's okay, boy," Cuno said in a soothing voice. "Your master's just gettin' a little loopy, I reckon."

Cuno stood looking around for a while, feeling a keen sense of his aloneness out here, three days northwest of the stage station. The rain did not help his mood. He preferred a sky full of stars to distract him from the horrors of this world and to lull him to sleep. But even on clear nights, the dreams came, and he found himself yearning for the two blissful nights he'd spent in the clutches of Molly Davis, who had left the station the same morning Cuno had, on a stage sent out by the company. Cuno had told her good-bye the night before, and they waved cordially as the stage pulled out of the station yard.

Cuno left the station then, too, thanking Charlie Dodge again for the Frontier Colt and his hospitality, promising he'd stop again on his way home. Cuno had headed northwest along a cattle trail, toward Cheyenne. That's where Anderson and Spoon would be heading, to pick up the

Bozeman Trail, a wagon road that led through Dakota Territory to the Montana gold camps. Cuno hoped to overtake the men before they got there, however. What he'd do once he had, he wasn't sure. Somehow, with Dodge's Great Equalizer in his novice hand, he'd kill them both or die trying.

Now he rolled up in his blankets, but it took him a long time to fall asleep. Besides his loneliness, a keen fear worked at the back of his mind.

The next morning he woke with his blankets soggy from the light rain that continued falling and which made building a cookfire nearly impossible; while he'd covered his wood, moisture had penetrated the tarpaulin. After some coffee and part of a rabbit he'd eaten last night, he saddled the paint and continued riding through the forlorn, rugged country descending gradually toward the platte.

That evening he shot a small antelope on a brushy bench spotted with pines. After he'd dressed the animal, he lugged it back to his camp along a creek in a deep prairie ravine. The only trees were the pines on the benches, but the ravine offered cover from the elements as well as from Indians, for every mile took him deeper into Sioux and Cheyenne country where, it was said, the first thing you did every morning was make sure you still had your hair.

When he'd cooked a quarter of the antelope over a spit and eaten hungrily, washing the succulent meat down with coffee, he took a careful reconnaissance of the area. At the lip overlooking the creek, he could see for maybe ten miles in all directions, to low buttes and rimrocks rising from the sage-pocked prairie, which the sun turned a lovely palette of light green and salmon.

Certain that he was alone but for the meadowlarks and the magpies, he returned to the creek and practiced shooting the Colt at rocks and at bugs lighting on the water. He honed his aim, drawing quickly, not with any fancy flourishes, but only trying to get the gun out of its holster as fast as he could, aim, and hit his target.

With every rock, bug, and branch he shot at, he saw the cow-eyed, belligerent visage of Rolf Anderson, and hate bubbled in his arteries.

When the sun had gone down, he returned to the fire and poured a cup of coffee, settling back against his saddle and flipping one side of his blanket over his legs. The air had cooled considerably. The birds had silenced, and the stars pricked to life in the violet sky. From a distant ridge, a wolf howled, and he remembered the times he and his father had sat around similar fires while overnighting along some freight trail. They'd sipped coffee and talked casually or played cards while listening to the wolves and coyotes sing the last of the light from the sky.

Remembering those nights, Cuno felt another sharp pang of loneliness and grief and the sense that his father's death was only a terrible dream from which he would eventually awaken. But he also knew that he would never see his father or Corsica again, as he would never see his mother. He had no other living relatives—at least, none that he'd ever known. He was alone. The world loomed, cold and vast . . .

He'd nearly finished the coffee when Renegade whinnied. Cuno reached for the Colt he still wore on his hip. It slipped into his hand surprisingly fast. He thumbed the grooved hammer back and rolled away from the fire, as his father had taught him to do when strangers approached the camp.

Beyond the fire's circle, he gazed around at the ridges on either side of him. They were uneven black lines against the paler sky. Softly, from the ridge on his left, drifted the sound of muffled hooffalls. The night was so quiet he could hear the squeak of saddle leather and the faint jingle of a bridle chain.

"Hello the camp," a man called.

"Hello yourself," Cuno called back, mimicking his father's old reply. "Approach and light if you're friendly."

Faintly, a resonant chuckle drifted down the ridge. "I reckon I'm friendly enough."

Cuno watched the shadow of a horse and rider descend the ridge. The horse blew and kicked stones, and the leather saddle creaked. At the slope bottom, the horse snorted and quickened its pace as it splashed across the creek. Approaching, man and horse were limned by orange firelight—a tall, mustachioed man with a big Texas hat and a dun horse with a white blaze on its face and a tired but wary look in its eyes.

"That coffee sure smells good."

Cuno appraised the man carefully, but made his voice affable. "There's plenty of coffee and antelope. You're welcome to both. There's good grass yonder if you want to picket your horse with mine."

"Don't mind if I do," the man said.

He dismounted with a weary grunt and led the dun off to the grass, where the paint gave another whinny and skittered back from the strangers. Cuno had noticed the man's revolver on his hip and the Winchester carbine in his saddle boot.

"Easy, Renegade," Cuno called.

He remained sitting against his saddle, keeping his right hand near his pistol butt, while the man unsaddled and grained his horse, then gave it a hurried rubdown with grass.

"Grady Keller," the man said as he approached the fire, his chaps flapping against his denims. He set his tack down and held his hand down to Cuno.

"Cuno Massey."

"Pleased to meet you, Cuno. I'm headin' south, back Texas way, where I come from." Squatting down with a cup in his hand, he gestured at the fire-blackened pot. "Sure you don't mind?"

"Not if you don't mind six-shooter," Cuno said, referring to the coffee that was probably now strong enough to float a pistol.

"That's my favorite kind," the man said with a chuckle, picking up the pot with the leather scrap and pouring the steaming brew into his cup. Setting the pot back on the fire and squatting there on his haunches, he removed his high-crowned, broad-brimmed hat and set it on the rock beside him. "Where I'm ridin' from, it's the only kind you get."

"Where's that, if you don't mind my asking?" You had to be careful when conversing with strangers. Men on the frontier could get woolly when asked personal questions.

"Don't mind a bit," Grady Keller assured him in his slow, affable manner. "Montana. The Gallatin Valley. I've had enough of it, though. Headin' back to Texas for the simple reason I'm homesick and tired of the prickly ways o' Yankee ranchers."

"You're a drover?"

Keller nodded over his coffee cup, swallowing. He had a sun-weathered face and deep-sunk eyes. His hair was longish and brown and matted with sweat to his head. He smelled like horse and the smoke of cookfires. He also wore the unmistakable odor of cattle.

"Born in a Santa Fe whorehouse and raised in the cowcamps," Keller said. He'd torn some antelope from the quarter and was eating hungrily with his fingers. "Trailed a herd up from Nacogdoches two years ago, and stayed to work for Elmer Olson. Him and me, we didn't get along too good. Had a retired Union army lieutenant ramrodding for him. Him and me didn't get along too good, either," Keller said with a grim smile, rubbing his jaw as though it had taken its toll of punishment. "Especially after we'd gotten into the forty-rod and conversation turned to the Little Misunderstanding, as it had a habit of doing."

Keller turned to Cuno. "Speaking of which, care for a nip?"

Cuno hesitated. He'd tried hard liquor on the sly, as had every other red-blooded boy his age, but had never cared for it. He preferred beer on occasion. He felt, however, that turning down Grady Keller's offer would make him look green.

"Why not?" he said with a casual shrug.

Keller wiped his greasy hands on his chaps, and rummaged around in his saddlebags, producing a brown bottle, which he offered to Cuno. "This here's a concoction of the Silver Slipper Saloon in Julesburg. I don't promise it ain't half gunpowder and lizard tails, but it hasn't blinded me yet."

"Obliged," Cuno said, splashing a little in his coffee cup.

He returned the bottle to Keller, who laced his coffee with the forty-rod. Cuno took a cautious sip. It burned going down and gave his shoulders a shake as it set his stomach briefly aflame, but he maintained a casual expression. The light-headed feeling it instantly gave him wasn't half bad.

"Thanks for lettin' me share your fire," Keller said. "This can be lonesome country. Does a man good to flap his gums at someone besides his horse, now and then. Where'd you say you was from?"

Cuno almost smiled at Keller's indirect method of inquiry. "Valoria, Nebraska," he said. "My pa and I had a freight business there."

"You don't say," Keller gently prodded Cuno to elaborate.

Cuno told him his story and why he was here, heading for Cheyenne and the Bozeman Trail.

"Rolf Anderson, eh?" Keller said, rubbing his temple with a single finger thoughtfully. "You know, I think I seen him in Julesburg a few days back. I know I did, matter o' fact."

Cuno looked at the drover searchingly. "Are you sure it was Anderson?"

"Hell, yeah. I know what Rolf Anderson looks like. I played cards with him once in Alamosa. Once. You don't wanna cross him or let him even *think* you crossed him. I seen him staple a man's hand to a poker table with an Arkansas toothpick. You sure you wanna go after that bastard? Hell, I heard most lawmen won't even trail him. Bounty hunters learned to rein wide of him a long time ago."

"That's why I'm going after him." Cuno's voice was dull. "He's in Julesburg, eh? You know for how long?"

"Hard to say." Keller sipped his whiskey and shook his head. "He was winning at the Silver Slipper, though, so he could be there a while. His half-breed compadre, that Spoon, don't gamble, but he was on a tear with the ladies. Kept half the house awake the night I was there."

Cuno stared over his whiskey cup at the fire. He took a sip. This time the burn wasn't as bad. It gave him a good feeling, a resolute feeling that tempered his apprehension as the image of Rolf Anderson returned, dancing with Corsica while Lloyd Massey played a piano covered with blood . . .

"Well, good luck to you, son. That's all I have to say," Grady Keller said, as he poured more whiskey in his coffee. When he offered the bottle to Cuno, Cuno shook his head.

A little while later, both men turned into their blankets and tipped their hats over their eyes.

The next dawn, after coffee and reheated antelope, Grady Keller bid Cuno good luck and farewell, and gigged his dun up the southern ridge. He was a shadow against the brightening eastern sky as he kneed the dun into a lope and out of sight.

Cuno climbed atop Renegade and rode northwest, toward

Julesburg, a keen urgency to find Anderson and Spoon tensing his back till it ached. He'd ridden several hours before his thoughts returned to Grady Keller. The cowboy had seemed in a hurry to leave their bivouac. Cuno had figured the man merely wanted to get an early start; he had a long ride ahead. But that wouldn't account for Keller's uncharacteristic laconicism and the way he had sheepishly avoided Cuno's eyes.

Cuno stared straight ahead, not seeing anything, his mind racing. After a moment, he swung down from his saddle and rummaged through his right saddlebag. Not finding what he was looking for, he rummaged through the left bag, his movements growing desperate, his breath growing short.

He'd tossed nearly all the saddlebags' contents out on the ground before it became undeniably clear that the money he'd made when he sold the house and the freight business was gone.

Grady Keller, the polite, unassuming waddie from Texas, had cleaned him out.

9

"ROLF-EE," CAME A girl's singsong voice.

In a room at Miss Flora's Pleasure Salon on a side street of Julesburg, Colorado, Rolf Anderson opened his eyes. He blinked the alcohol fog from his vision, or tried to. It was a heavy, nasty fog. He cleared phlegm from his throat and let sleep wash back over him, his lids lowering of their own accord.

"Rolfy, come on now, sweetheart," a girl cooed in his ear. He could feel her warm breath on his skin. It annoyed him, like a fly buzzing around his head.

"Go 'way."

"You told me to wake you at nine-thirty, hon. Your poker game resumes at ten. Remember?"

Last night, after an all-day poker session, the girl's voice had teased him into a randy fever. This morning, however, the voice not only grated but set his head to pounding, as if a little man were wielding a big hammer just above his eyes and at the base of his skull.

He said through clenched teeth, without opening his eyes, "I told you, goddammit, to leave me the hell alone."

Charity LeFleur knew Anderson's reputation. Lying there beside him, clad in a sheer silk wrapper, she weighed the consequences of letting him sleep and missing the game against those she would no doubt incur by prodding him awake. She could simply leave and let him wake up on his own, but he would still hold her responsible for missing the game. She knew from experience that there was really no running from Rolf Anderson.

Then she let her eyes stray to the gunbelt and holster looped over the bedpost, and the big, pearl-handled Colt therein. The horn handle of a wide-bladed knife jutted from a beaded sheath. Her pulse quickened as, in her mind, she watched herself slowly, quietly, lift the gun from its holster, thumb back the trigger, and set the barrel against the big man's leathery temple. In her mind, she pulled the trigger.

Her heart gave an anxious shudder.

Who would blame her? Certainly, no one in town cared for Anderson, least of all the lawmen, whom Anderson had long since cowed. No one in the territory would blame her. Hell, Charity LeFleur could think of no one who gave a damn about Rolf Anderson. Except for Sammy Spoon, who would no doubt seek revenge as a matter of course.

Still, it was fun to think about.

The gun would make noise. The knife, on the other hand . . .

Anderson groaned, dissolving the fantasy. His eyes fluttered and he turned them to her—blue as a summer lake but somehow containing not an ounce of tranquility or tenderness. If the devil's eyes were blue, they would be the blue of Rolf Anderson's eyes. Arrogant, flat, cold, brutal.

"All right, all right," he grumbled, running a big paw down his long face and yawning, "I'm awake."

Feeling a little crestfallen at having missed her chance to kill the beast, Charity found herself truckling once again. "Would you like me to fetch water for a bath?"

He was lying on his side, his big, nude body taking up two-thirds of the bed, making her look tiny in comparison. Red-blond hair covered every inch of his pale, freckled skin. His toenails, she saw as she appraised him now, wincing slightly with revulsion, were cracked and yellow, like old seashells.

"Don't want no bath," Anderson said, working his hand into the bosom of her wrapper, jerking the garment down until a nipple appeared. "Want a poke . . . get my blood goin'. . . ." He fingered the nipple, painfully twisting. She winced again, against the sharp pain in her breast.

"Oh, honey, you're gonna be late. Are you sure . . .?"

"They'll wait for me. Come on." He rolled onto his back and patted his thigh. "Climb on top here. Work me up, girl."

Voices rose in the hall. Anderson froze and shushed the girl. A man said he'd be right back, and a door closed.

Anderson looked at the girl, squinting. "Is that Leroy Cassle?"

Charity shrugged one naked shoulder. "Leroy comes around once in a while. Why?"

"That son of a bitch!" Anderson bellowed.

Rising, he flung the girl away from him. She rolled off the bed, hitting the floor hard but not making a sound. She sat there, her wrapper down around her waist, her legs curled beneath her, as she watched Anderson quickly dress, cursing and muttering under his breath. She was afraid to move, lest Anderson take his anger out on her, as he was wont to do. You didn't want to get in the way of Rolf Anderson's temper.

When he'd stomped into his boots, he donned his hat and wrapped his cartridge belt around his waist. "See you tonight, sugar," he said quickly, clomping over her on his way to the door.

In the hall, Anderson turned right and walked to the next door down on the other side. He twisted the knob and threw open the door. The room was empty, its bed unmade, curtains closed, the smell of sex heavy in the room.

Cursing again, Anderson went to the next door, flung it open. A whore whose name he remembered as Gretta—not bad, though a little skinny, and he didn't care for redheads—was lounging face down on the bed, feet in the air, reading a magazine.

"Hey," she complained, throwing an angry look over her shoulder.

"Was that Leroy Cassle I heard in the hall?"

Seeing Anderson filling up her doorway, big Colt and knife on his belt, the girl's expression softened, her eyes growing timid.

"Leroy?" she said thinly, nodding her head. "Yeah, that was him."

"Where'd he go?"

"Went to get a cigar."

Anderson gave a snort and turned, heading down the hall to the stairs. Outside, he stalked off the front porch, hung a left down the side of the house to the back. He'd crossed the trash-littered yard and was heading across an empty lot toward the cigar store when he stopped suddenly and turned to the two-hole privy abutting a wood shed. The privy's door was shut tight.

On a whim, Anderson called, "Leroy Cassle, you in there."

"I'll be out in a minute," came the hollow reply from behind the paint-chipped door panels. "Keep your goddamn pants on."

Anderson shaped a savage smile in his beard. "Come on out here and face me like a man, you mangy mutt of a good-for-nothin' dog!"

There was a pause. Then, tentatively: "Rolf? Th-that you?"

"It's me you goddamn horse-stealin' son of a bitch!"

After another pause, the voice behind the door said, "Now, Rolf . . . c-can't we talk about this?"

"What's there to talk about, Lee-roy? You took my horse when you seen those Comanches headin' for our camp. Abandoned me afoot in the hopes those Injuns would relieve me of my oysters and leave you with all our hides—the whole two wagon loads." Anderson's voice rose like that of a poleaxed bull. "*You son of a bitch!* Come out here and meet your maker!"

"Now, Rolf, goddammit, that wasn't how it was!"

"It wasn't? Well, then step out here and set me straight. Or die behind that privy door, if that's how you wanna be remembered . . ."

Anderson paused, staring at the door of the slant-roofed outhouse. Without warning, the door burst open, and an unshaven man appeared in a cheap suit and a bowler hat and wearing two cross-draw holsters on his hips. The guns were in his hands, and his face twisted bizarrely as he triggered both Remingtons at once.

Ignoring the lead whining around his head, the hider drew his big Colt Navy, purposefully extended his arm, and fired three quick shots through the faded red vest of Cassle's suit. Cassle gave a startled cry and flew backward into the privy, taking an unceremonious seat on one of the two holes. He slumped sideways against the wall, dead. His guns dropped from his lifeless hands.

"Hold it right there, mister!"

Calmly, Anderson turned to his left, where a tall, skinny lad with a deputy sheriff's star pinned to his vest stood with his gun extended. Several townsmen and a woman in a shabby spangled dress that she'd obviously been wearing since last night stood a ways behind him, peering down the alley at Anderson.

Seeing Anderson's face, the deputy's eyes dulled and his jaw fell slack. "Uh . . ." Remembering himself and remembering the citizens gathered behind him, he tried to conjure some spine. "What the hell's goin' on here, Anderson?"

"Nothin'," the big hider said innocently.

He holstered his gun and strolled past the deputy, toward the townspeople and Julesburg's main street, heading for his poker game. "Ole Cassle just decided to take a long, leisurely shit. There a law against that?"

Cuno rode into Julesburg late that afternoon, trail-weary but with a strong purpose widening his eyes and urging his blood through his veins. He halted Renegade on the main street of the dusty little town along the Platte River, and scanned the milled lumber and adobe buildings fronting the street.

He appraised the sunburned visages of the men in canvas pants and suspenders lounging here and there, talking or staring pensively, tiredly, some with drinks in their hands. They were bullwackers, mostly, Cuno judged from their garb. He'd seen several bull trains parked outside the town. Saddle horses were bunched before the half-dozen saloons, those on the south side of the street enjoying the shade.

Cuno gigged Renegade around a train of farm wagons bearing a large, haggard-looking family, toward the Silver Slipper Saloon. The Silver Slipper's hitchrail was full, so he tied the paint across the street, in the brassy afternoon sun, near a stock tank.

His hand on the horse's rump, he turned toward the saloon, the sign on its low facade faded by the prairie sun, its windows streaked with dust. An old man sat between the batwings and the window, smoking a cob pipe.

Cuno gave the building further study, his heart beating an insistent rhythm, his mouth dry. The palm he rubbed on his pistol butt was slick with sweat.

Taking a deep breath, he waited for two horseback riders to pass, then headed across the street and mounted the opposite boardwalk. He nodded at the old man, who turned to him, squinting his one good eye.

Cuno turned and willed himself through the batwings. Before he could swing a gaze around the smoke-hazy room before him, he heard a commotion on the street, and turned back around.

To his left, on a bare patch of ground between the saloon and a mercantile, four men dressed like drovers were gathered in a circle around a girl. A man in a green checked bandanna grabbed the girl to him brusquely, and kissed her savagely. Shrieking, the girl tried to fight away from him, but he held her fast in his arms.

"Come on now, Neil—give us others a chance!" yelled a stringbean with a sharp chin and a weak jaw.

Small, slender, and dressed in worn calico, with a bonnet falling down her back, the girl jerked an arm loose and slapped the man called Neil across the face. He laughed and let her go. Two of the others promptly grabbed her, one from the front, one grabbing her breasts from behind.

"Let me *go!*" she cried again, her voice breaking with fear and exasperation, long black hair flying.

"Come on, girly, let's go find us a nice quiet place in the alley!"

"Bring her this way, Champ!"

Seeing that no one else was going to help—passersby purposefully ignored the commotion, in fact—Cuno moved to the girl's assistance. He was halfway down the boardwalk when he urged, "Hold on, hold on!"

Neil turned to him with an annoyed expression on his broad, dark face. "This ain't none of your affair, boy. Butt out!"

He turned to join the others but turned back as Cuno approached.

"Why don't you fellas do your hoorawing at someone

else's expense?" Cuno suggested, trying to retain an acquiescent note in his voice. He didn't want a fight with anyone but Rolf Anderson. "The lady doesn't look too willing."

"She's a whore," Neil said with vehemence. "Even if she weren't, it ain't none of your affair! So beat it!"

The girl gave another scream as she broke free of the others. Twisting away, she tripped and fell, pushed off her hands, and hurled herself against the adobe wall of the mercantile.

"Leave me alone!"

"What's the matter, honey?" Neil said, his voice light with mockery. "First you say you'll take all of us, then you say you won't. You know what we call girls like you where I come from?"

"Prick teasers!" the stringbean replied with a half-wit's slow guffaw.

Cuno looked around for help. The expressions of the men who'd gathered to gawk told him the girl was on her own—if he didn't help her himself, that was.

Stepping between the men and the girl, his voice came now with a hard edge. "The girl doesn't seem to want your business, so why don't you gentlemen look for another one that does?"

The men looked at him, percolating anger coloring their cheeks beneath their ruddy tans. The shortest of the bunch scowled, cuffed his floppy hat from his head, and said, "That does it, boy. I'm gonna teach you to mind your own damn business!"

Showing ragged teeth, he bolted forward and swung a haymaker at Cuno, who ducked and hit the man with a hard left jab low in the stomach. The man crumpled with a pained cry, dropping to his knees. In a moment, the others surrounded Cuno and moved in. The boy went to work with his fists, swinging furiously, ducking, feinting this way and that, dodging right, then left, then right again, and flinging haymakers, jabs, roundhouses, jawbreakers, and even something he and his father had called a Silly Willy.

An experienced sport fighter at county fairs, he had all the men down at least once, and all bloody, lips and eyes swelling, before they coordinated their efforts against him. Surrounding him like a cornered bear, some going low, some going high, they pinned his arms against his back, bulled him against a post supporting the awning over the mercantile, and took turns pummeling him with their fists.

Cuno endured the punishment for several minutes, his lights dimming, thinking more about Anderson than the men pummeling him with their fists, knowing with a keen frustration that the kill-crazy hider was only a few feet away.

But he might as well have been at the other end of the planet, for all the good it did Cuno now.

Slowly, he slumped to the ground, unable to suck a breath, the revolving world growing dark. Blood a thick coppery taste in his mouth, he passed out, slumping over on his side. Then the angry foursome went to work with their boots, kicking him over and over, until they wore themselves out.

"Where's the girl?" Neil asked, looking around, sweat and blood in his eyes.

Several more gawkers had gathered when the fight had worked its way to the boardwalk, and they watched now with amused interest, some with soapy beer mugs in their fists.

Breathless and bloody, their clothes torn and disheveled, the four drovers looked around. "Gone, goddammit. She's gone!"

With that, the short man swung around, gave Cuno another kick, then picked up his hat and headed for the saloon. Wearily, the others followed, one rubbing his jaw and groaning, "Goddamn, that kid has a nasty punch. I think he done broke my jaw!"

Cuno gave a groan, willing himself to consciousness.

He rolled onto his back and tried to work his legs beneath him, but he couldn't find the strength to push himself to his feet. For a long time he lay drifting in and out of consciousness, aware of people walking over and around him, of a horse lowering its head to sniff him curiously, of wagons and bull trains clattering by on the street, laying a fine shroud of dust upon him.

He'd opened his eyes after a time to see two horsemen approaching from the top of his vision. He blinked, felt his blood stir, and a tightening of his back. He lifted his head a few inches from the boardwalk, blinked again, and gazed at the two men riding toward him on the street.

One was a big man on a buckskin horse. A big, red-bearded man in a fringed buckskin tunic and elkhide pants, with a wide cartridge belt looped around his waist. The man riding next to him was slender and dark, his face pitted like a bullet-riddled can, and his black hair hung in greased braids to his shoulders.

Cuno's weary heart thumped; his pulse throbbed in his neck. His hand fell to his gun butt while he tried to work his legs under his body. What little strength he'd found, died. His vision dimmed again, as though a massive cloud had closed over the town, sealing off the sun.

His head drooped to the rough boardwalk, but he continued staring as the riders approached. He heard voices. Anderson and Spoon were talking boisterously, grinning. The sound of their horses' hoofbeats grew louder, and when their shadows passed over Cuno, on the lip of unconsciousness, Cuno turned his head to them slightly.

Anderson hovered over him for a moment, grinning at something Spoon was saying, his shoulders bouncing with the buckskin's trot. Absently, the big hide hunter turned his grinning gaze on Cuno, whose heart gave a horrified thump as he tried pulling the Colt from its holster. His hand was fumbling weakly with the gun, his ardent gaze on Anderson who, as he passed, bunched his lips together and spat.

Cuno tensed as the brown tobacco stream arced toward him, and splattered, wet and sticky, on his forehead. Chuckling, Anderson turned away, rubbed a hand over his mouth, and rode on.

Cuno's head fell again, and he was out, the tobacco running in a thick line down his temple to the boardwalk.

10

CUNO WASN'T SURE how much time had passed when his eyes fluttered open, but when they did, he wondered if he'd died.

He wasn't sure he could trust his aching brain, but he thought he was in a soft feather bed, naked as the day he was born, and surrounded by three scantily clad women—girls really. None of the three looked older than twenty.

Each was working on him with sponges and soft cloths.

"Is this heaven?" he heard himself ask, his voice thick and raspy.

"He's awake!" exclaimed the blonde dabbing at the cuts on his face. Her own face was cherubic and green-eyed. Her blond hair was piled loosely atop her head. The cream wrapper she wore loosely about her shoulders did little to hide her lovely, pear-shaped breasts, jostling as she worked.

"How do you feel?" asked the brunette kneeling on the bed to his right. Her rich hair hung loosely about her shoulders, brushing his knees. She was a chubby girl, with the slightly slanted eyes of a Slav.

Cuno cleared phlegm from his throat. His face had grown hot when he'd realized he was naked and surrounded by three girls. "Like I was run over by a wagon train."

"Minnie saw it all," the brunette said. "She said it was just awful."

"I'm Minnie," said the third girl.

She was a brown-eyed blond with long, straight hair—bony and slender, and clad in a man's pinstriped shirt with the oversized sleeves rolled up her arms. She wore a cowboy hat and cowboy boots, and was smoking a long cigar. Her legs were bare. The shirt, unbuttoned halfway down her chest, exposed pink, nubbin breasts. Dabbing at a gash on his left knee, she said, "I was shopping at the mercantile when I heard the commotion. I walked outside and saw a foolish young man stepping between those Rockin' R riders and some . . . girl."

"I think it was very chivalrous," said the big-breasted blonde working with a little too much vigor on a gash on Cuno's lower lip. "I'm Glory," she told Cuno, pausing her work momentarily. "There ain't many men in these parts that would risk their life for a lady," she added as she resumed cleaning the cut.

Minnie said, "Plumb silly, you ask me. One against four. Those are long odds for even a big, strappin' boy like this one here." She turned, leaning over his chest to stare closely into his eyes. "Son," she said in a slow, Southern drawl, "I don't know where you're from, but out here you gotta fend for yourself, cause there ain't but only a silly few that'll help you out of a pinch. You found that out between the saloon and the mercantile."

"Oh, Minnie!" Glory scolded the girl. "What if you'd been the girl those boys were trying to perforate with their dicks?"

"I wouldn't have expected no idiot to risk his life for me—I'll tell you that. I sure as earthly sin wouldn't have risked my neck for his!"

"I reckon next time I'll ask the girl if she wants me to intervene," Cuno said dryly through a pained scowl.

As if she hadn't heard him, Minnie continued. "Besides, I wouldn't have gotten myself in such a pickle, because when I invite four men to my crib, I don't back out halfway there! I take their money and do my job."

"How do you know she backed out?" the brunette asked.

"'Cause I heard her on the boardwalk, talkin' to the Rockin' R boys," Minnie said. "She was doin' her sweet best to work 'em into a frenzy. Next thing I know, Mr. Jesus H. Christ was tryin' to defend her honor." Minnie wagged her head. "Just plumb silly."

"Who was she?" Cuno asked, wincing against the big-bosomed Glory's overzealous ministrations.

"Never seen her before," Minnie said, going back to work on his knee.

"She was that girl whose Pa got killed back o' the Dupree House," the brunette said. She was inspecting a big, purple bruise on his thigh, inflicted, no doubt, by a swiftly kicked boot. "I reckon she'd taken to the streets, hopin' for some easy money to get her by."

"Poor girl," Glory said.

"We all have to get by one way or another," Minnie said in her dry, matter-of-fact tone, puffing cigar smoke from one side of her mouth. "Reckon turning street tricks just wasn't her way. Maybe she learned her lesson . . . at the kid's expense."

Cuno scowled at the surly, hatted, cigar-puffing girl, offended at being called a kid. Minnie appeared his age or younger.

"I wonder where she went," Cuno asked, only half-interested now, his attention compromised by the fire in his ribs and in the two dozen or so bruises and lacerations covering his body.

And by Glory's breasts, swaying this way and that within her wrapper, only inches from his face.

Reading the response in his lower regions, the brunette said, "Good Lord, this boy's comin' to life!"

"Just ignore it, Freda," Minnie said flatly. "They all come to life, sooner or later."

Turning to see, Glory giggled. "It's nice to see you're gonna make it, anyway, mister. Never mind Minnie. I think you're a true-blue hero, sure enough!" She leaned down over his face, rubbing her hand with a motherly gentleness over his head. "What's your name?"

Cuno told her, keeping his eyes off her cleavage, distracting himself with thoughts of rattlesnakes and Indian war whoops and the grotesque Mrs. Lord who'd lived near the freight yard in Valoria and who farted loudly while feeding table scraps to her chickens.

"How did I get here—wherever here is?" he asked, shoving up slightly and looking around the small, sparsely furnished room. There was one picture, a print of a black woman lounging nude in a garish rose garden, on the wall above a scarred dresser missing a drawer. His torn, bloody clothes were piled on a chair.

"Minnie came back to the hotel and told me about the fight. Well, when I heard what you tried to do for that girl, I marched right over there and got a couple of my regular clients from the saloon to haul you over here to the hotel. We sent for the doc to check you out, but he's in a surgery. I've seen enough fights, though, to know you've taken one hell of a braining, and you've got some bruised ribs. I don't think none are broken, though they might feel like it for a while."

"In other words," Minnie said, removing her cigar from her mouth and flicking ashes on the floor, "you'll live to fight another day, soldier."

"Oh, Minnie, you're a caution," the brunette, Freda, admonished, shaking her head. "Does that hurt?" she asked Cuno, probing her fingers under his thigh.

Cuno gave a start. "I'll say it does!"

Freda gave her head a sad shake. "I'm afraid you're gonna be one big bruise for a while. You'll be in bed for a few days."

"I don't have a few days," Cuno said, grimacing as much from frustration as pain, remembering Rolf Anderson's grinning mug and the wad of chew he'd spat on Cuno's forehead. "I gotta be up and at it . . . soon."

"What's the hurry?" Glory asked.

"Long story," Cuno said with a sigh. He'd been so close to Anderson. Just a few feet, a few seconds from killing the man. "Long, long story."

"Ah," Minnie said with a caustic edge. "A mystery man. Glory, close your wrapper, will you? Look at his rod. He gets much more excited, he's gonna have a stroke."

Cuno tipped his chin to look at himself. "Sorry," he said, thoroughly abashed.

"It's okay, sweetie," Glory said with a throaty chuckle, drawing her wrapper closed. "I've seen 'em before, and I'll take yours, in your condition, as a real compliment."

"I'm much obliged to you . . . all of you." He wondered how long he'd have lain in the street if it hadn't been for Miss Glory's tender heart. The looks on the gawkers' faces during the fight had told him the town didn't cotton to strangers.

Freda smiled. "Don't mention it." She added with a giggle to Minnie, "I for one am enjoying it."

"I don't suppose I could ask you one more favor?" Cuno asked Glory. "Could you send someone out for my horse? I left him—"

Glory put a finger to his lips. "All taken care of," she said. "One of the boys who hauled you up here had seen you ride into town. He remembered which horse was yours. He's stabled behind the hotel. Roderick's Hotel, for your information. Old man Roderick gives us girls his third story for a percentage of the profits." She snickered as she cleaned an ugly scrape on Cuno's shoulder. "His wife pretends she doesn't know, but she's quite aware it was our hard work that paid for that new leather buggy with the fancy tasseled canopy she's so proud of!"

"I'm much obliged to all of you," Cuno said. "But . . . uh . . . do you think I could put my shorts on?"

When Glory had stitched a deep cut on his chin, one on his lip, and one over his hipbone, she gave him his shorts. She lingered behind as the other two girls gathered up their rags, sponges, and porcelain washbowls, and left the room.

"You know, Cuno," Glory said, "you look like an awfully nice boy to be getting yourself beat up in a woolly town like Julesburg."

"Yeah, I reckon I could've picked a little nicer place to take a whuppin'," he quipped.

She frowned and crossed her arms over her breasts. "You just don't want to tell me anything about yourself, do you?"

Cuno shrugged and adjusted his position in the bed, to ease the pressure on the stitches. "What's to tell? My pa and step-ma are dead, and I'm trackin' their killer. I'd appreciate that not leavin' this room, if you don't mind."

She gazed at him, pensive, then shook her head, jostling the stray locks of hair hanging about her smooth peaches-and-cream cheeks. "I'm sorry," she said thinly. "Who . . .?"

"A jasper by the name of Rolf Anderson." He paused, noting her expression. "You've heard of him?"

"Oh, yes, I've heard of him," she said with a mirthless chuckle, which told Cuno she'd more than just heard of the man. "But I wish I never did. That man is the devil."

"You got that right."

"Oh, Cuno."

"What?"

"I know how you'd like to avenge your family's murder, but you'll never kill Rolf Anderson. He'll kill you."

He tried a smile, but winced when the stitches pulled. "I'm tougher than I look at the moment, ma'am."

"No one's that tough, and don't you dare call me ma'am. I bet I'm no older than you. How old are you, anyway?"

"Eighteen."

"See? That's how old I am. Eighteen and three months."

He wasn't sure if he should ask the next question on his mind, but she didn't seem in any hurry to leave, standing as she was with her back to the dresser, regarding him balefully, almost as though he were an old friend from an earlier, more innocent time.

"How long you been doin' this kind of work, Miss Glory—if you don't mind me askin'?"

When her eyes dropped with chagrin, he thought he'd made a mistake. But then she said, lifting her eyes to him again, "A little over a year. My father, he was a preacher." She smiled wanly. "He caught me 'sinning' with a neighbor boy—a young boy I was deeply in love with—and he kicked me out of the house. How I ended up here"—She gave a caustic laugh, glancing around the tawdry little room—"I don't rightly remember, but here I am just the same. It ain't a bad life, but don't go thinkin' I'm gonna do it forever."

"I wasn't thinkin' anything," Cuno said. "Believe me, in the past several weeks, I've learned not to judge anything or anyone but Rolf Anderson."

She stared at him. A smile pulled at her lips, and her eyes seemed to find their previous humor.

"You sure are pretty," Cuno told her.

"Why, Cuno Massey!" she exclaimed. "You're going to make this fallen angel blush from ear to ear!"

"You already are."

She turned and looked at herself in the mirror. "My gosh, I am, aren't I?" She turned back to face him. "You know what?"

"What?"

"I'm going to give you something to settle you down and help you sleep." She beamed. "For free."

Cuno felt his face heat up. "You don't have to do me any more favors, Miss Glory . . ."

"Oh, hush," she said, sitting on the bed. "You're just so sweet, I'm going to give you something special to dull the pain of those stitches. Now, take your shorts off."

"Huh?"

"You can't expect a girl to do her job with 'em on, can you?"

Then he remembered the technique Molly Davis had introduced him to. He was immediately aroused, and in spite of his sore ribs and sore everything else, he reached down to remove his shorts.

"Here, here," she said, gently shoving him back down. "Let me help. You just lie back and relax. There we go. Oh, my. That's nice. That's very nice, Cuno Massey . . ."

11

CUNO SPENT MOST of the next two days in bed. By the third day he was able to get up and move around without his knees buckling or the room spinning.

While the girls plied their trade upstairs, he spent the afternoons on the porch with old Hank Roderick, talking in a desultory way, occasionally sipping the beer Roderick brewed in his cellar. It wasn't long before Roderick had taught him how to roll cigarettes and Minnie got him smoking the cigars she acquired from the mayor, a regular client.

After a few more days, he was drinking after-supper whiskies with Miss Glory, and enjoying them. He just hoped his mother in heaven didn't see him down here, cavorting with scarlet ladies and drinking spirituous liquids with pimps.

By the end of the week, he was doing odd work for Roderick and practicing his shooting in a vacant lot behind the hotel, shooting vinegar bottles and coffee tins. He planned to leave Julesburg and get back on Anderson's trail as soon as his battered ribs would let him climb onto his horse. Part of him wasn't in a hurry to leave, however, for every night, sometimes early and sometimes late, Miss Glory visited his room with her bewitching charms.

On one such night, he lay with Glory, sipping whiskey after they'd made love. Across the hall, Minnie was entertaining a customer, and Cuno could hear the mattress singing. Suddenly, the mattress fell silent, and a scream rose from across the hall. On the heels of the scream, a man's voice lifted.

"Goddamn bitch! What'd I tell you?"

The girl screamed again.

"Teach you to laugh at me, goddamn whore!"

With one look at Glory, whose face owned a surprised, angry expression, Cuno bolted out of bed and grabbed his jeans. As he climbed into them, Glory said, "That's Vince Evans. He gets rough when he's been drinkin', and I saw him drinkin' in the Silver Slipper earlier this afternoon."

Evans's curses still rose from across the hall, but not as loudly as before. Minnie had fallen silent.

Cuno grabbed his Colt and headed for the door.

"Cuno, be careful," Glory warned behind him.

Cuno opened the door, crossed the hall, and pounded on the door of the opposite room. "What's the trouble?"

When no reply came, Cuno turned the knob and opened the door. His heart gave a shudder as he stared into the cluttered room lit by a single, red-shaded lamp.

On the bed were Minnie and a tall man with mussed, chestnut hair and long sideburns. He and the girl were naked. The man knelt before Minnie, her back to the wall, knees raised protectively to her chest. He had a handful of her hair and was pulling her head back, exposing her neck to the wide-bladed knife in his other hand.

Minnie said nothing. Her wide eyes were glazed with fear.

"Goddamn whore—I had enough of your sass! I'm gonna teach you a lesson you won't forget!"

With that, he whipped the knife back, the tip pointed toward her exposed neck.

"Stop!" Cuno shouted.

The man whipped his red-mottled face at him. His eyes narrowed briefly at the gun shaking in Cuno's hand. A grin pulled at the man's mouth, and he whipped back toward Minnie, thrusting the knife toward her throat.

His arm's forward motion had just started when Cuno's Colt bucked, spitting smoke and flames. The bullet carved a neat hole through Evans's head, just above his ear, and the tall man flew over Minnie and into the wall, folding up on the bed like a pile of white laundry.

Cuno blinked dumbly. He looked at the gun. Sure enough, it was smoking. He'd fired it. He'd shot Evans.

He looked at Minnie. She stared back at him, her eyes still bright. He was bringing the Colt down now, as though it were some foreign object he'd just discovered in his hand.

"Holy shit," Minnie said.

Throughout the house, startled voices rose, and footsteps sounded in the hall.

"Is he dead?" Cuno asked the girl. He didn't know what else to say as he broke out of his stupor.

Minnie glanced at Vince Evans. Blood trickled from the hole in his head, covering his ear and pooling on the sheet. One of his feet twitched and fell still.

Minnie returned her ardent, glassy gaze to Cuno. "Hell, yes, he's dead!"

Cuno turned when he felt a hand on his shoulder. It was Glory, looking past him into the room. She'd thrown a wrapper around her shoulders.

"Oh, my God," she whispered, cupping a hand over her mouth.

A soft confusion of startled voices had grown in the hall, and now the sound of pounding boots grew, as well.

"What is it? What's going on?" old man Roderick said

as he swung into the room, clad in a tattered green robe and with an old-model rifle in his hands.

Taking a long look at the man slumped on Minnie's bed, then at the Colt in Cuno's hand, the old man said, "Holy shit!"

"That's what I said," Minnie said dully, staring at Evans.

"That's Vince!" Roderick exclaimed, as though imparting bad news.

Minnie nodded, pensive. "It's him, all right. He was about a half second from carving out my Adam's apple when our hero here went to work with his six-shooter."

Cuno felt his lip move, and he heard himself say, as if from far away, "I reckon I should have asked you if you wanted help."

Minnie's sarcasm carved fine lines in her smooth, young forehead and sharpened the excited light in her eyes. "It's a dangerous habit you have, Master Cuno. Savin' girls that ain't worth it. I'd thank you, but I find it hard thankin' someone for committing suicide on my account."

"Oh, Minnie, hush!" Glory reprimanded the girl. She stood beside Cuno, her head coming up to his shoulder. Her face was pale and she couldn't seem to remove her eyes from the dead man beside Minnie.

Cuno was having the same trouble. He also couldn't get his knees to stop shaking or his hands to stop sweating. Funny, he'd thought Rolf Anderson would be the first man he'd kill. Spoon, the second and the last.

"Who is he?" he asked now, his wooden voice belying his angst.

"Oh, shit, shit, shit!" old man Roderick exclaimed. Awkwardly, he touched a finger to Evans's neck, as though searching for a pulse. He swung his wizened countenance to Cuno, his long face sad and miserable. "Boy, that's the son of Franklin Evans, owner of the Rockin' R ranch."

"What does that mean?"

"It means you have to leave, Cuno," Glory said, turning to him with fear etched around the edges of her pretty green eyes. "Before Evans and his men hear about this. They're a rough bunch. Outlaws, most of 'em, including Evans himself."

"Vince here," Minnie said, fingering her neck where Evans's knife had been headed, "has been beatin' up girls from way back. I figured I could handle him. I always have before."

Cuno felt himself being shoved toward the door. Looking down, he saw Glory's hand on his arm. "Go, Cuno. Now. *Please . . .*"

Cuno resisted. "The man tried to kill her. I had every reason to shoot him."

Old man Roderick shook his head. "It don't matter, son. Do as the girl says. Pack your things and leave. We'll make up a story to tell ole Evans. We'll tell him it was some stranger shot his son. Some gambler. Yeah, that's it. A gambler. Which way you headin'?"

"Toward Montana."

"Then we'll tell him you headed east. Go now. Hurry!" Roderick shoved the boy out the door.

Glimpsing Freda and three men from the hotel room below, all standing about the hall with puzzled, wary looks on their faces, Cuno went into his own room and began collecting his scattered possessions, stuffing them into his saddlebags. Glory removed his few clothes from the dresser.

His mind a nest of mixed emotions, Cuno said, "I don't like runnin'. I don't see why I can't just explain to the sheriff—"

"It doesn't matter what you say to the sheriff, Cuno my sweet," Glory said, moving to him and squeezing his forearm. "Evans will kill you. The old man and us girls—we don't want to see you hurt."

Cuno shook his head. "But—"

"But nothin'. You have to hurry. As soon as you're gone,

one of us will get the sheriff and tell him you're some gambler who rode east."

"What if he finds out you're lying? I don't want to leave you folks in the lurch."

Glory smiled. "Believe me, the sheriff is a friend." She smiled meaningfully. Getting her drift, Cuno nodded and strapped the flaps down over his saddlebags.

When he'd finished dressing and had strapped his cartridge belt and holster around his waist and had donned his hat, he turned to the door. Glory and the other two girls had gathered there, watching him with concern. Glory kissed him tenderly. Freda offered him a sisterly peck on his cheek. Leaning against the doorjamb, Minnie regarded him with a coy, sheepish expression. She'd lit a cigar and was puffing away as though nothing had happened.

However, her tone was acquiescent. "Thanks for saving my worthless hide, Cuno." She hugged him, kissed his cheek, and looked at him directly. "Keep one finger on your trigger and one eye on your back trail. Evans is a canny son of a bitch."

In the hall, Roderick shook his hand and offered him a few dollars, which Cuno refused. Hefting his saddlebags on his shoulder, he went downstairs and stole out the back door. In a minute, he was saddling Renegade in the dark barn, and then he was riding hell-for-leather down Julesburg's main drag—dark but for the light emanating from the still-hopping saloons.

He splashed across the platte, gray-dark under a moonless sky, and mounted the opposite bank. With one glance at Julesburg on the grassy bench behind him, he reined the skewbald paint around and kneed him into a gallop westward down the Bozeman Trail.

Back in Julesburg, three men in trail clothes had staggered out of the South Platte Saloon & Dance Hall to see a broad-shouldered young man in suspenders and a weathered bowler galloping down the street, as though the devil's curs were nipping at his heels.

"Well, what in the hell do you make of that?" Neil Jacobs said. "Some farm kid found diddlin' the banker's daughter?"

The other two men laughed as they stared after the kid whose dust sifted slowly over the dim street. When they'd finally gotten their bearings on the boardwalk, and had their land legs beneath them, the men headed for their horses at the hitchrail.

"Oh, Lordy," Neil Jacobs said through a yawn. "A bed sure is gonna feel good!"

"Wait a minute," Pooch Tyler grunted as he climbed clumsily into the leather. "Ain't we forgettin' somethin'?"

"What's that?" Jacobs asked.

"We're supposed to pick up old Vince at Roderick's place before we head back to the ranch."

"Oh, shit," groused the third man, Casimiro Postma. He was a sinewy Mexican with an outlandishly large mustache and sideburns. Snickering, he added, "Damn near forgot the *jefe!*"

The other two chuckled as they reined their horses westward between the dark, star-capped facades facing the nearly deserted street. "Maybe, if he's still busy," Postma suggested, "we could take the time for a little loving our ownselves, eh, *amigos*?"

"That last round left me flat broke," Jacobs said. "I reckon I'll have to get my lovin' next month."

"Here, too," Tyler said, riding stiff-backed in his saddle, blinking the alcohol fog from his deep-sunk eyes beneath the funneled brim of his sweat-greasy hat. "But I sure could use a tumble with little Miss Minnie. Howee, that girl's got fire!"

The three men chuckled as they turned the corner,

crossed a vacant lot, and pulled up at the hitchrack before Roderick's Hotel.

"The girls must be entertainin' something fierce tonight," Tyler said, dismounting. "Look at all those lights burnin'."

They were nearing the porch steps when the front door opened and old man Roderick appeared, wearing his hat and a light jacket over a green plaid shirt. He pulled the door closed and was starting across the porch when he saw the three Rockin' R riders. He stopped with a start, wary surprise arching his shaggy, gray brows.

"What's the matter, old man," Postma said with a laugh. "You look like you seen old *Diablo* himself!"

12

CUNO RODE HARD through the night, galloping the paint, then walking, then galloping again. He didn't want to overexert the horse—good mounts were few and far between out here, and Renegade was turning into a very good mount indeed—but he wanted to open as much country as possible between himself and Julesburg by morning.

When he figured he'd ridden a good twenty miles, he stopped to rest. Loosening Renegade's saddle cinch and looping a feed sack over the horse's head, Cuno sat down against a tree. He couldn't sleep. He'd never killed a man before, and the image of the limp body with the twitching foot and the bloody hole in its head kept flashing through his mind, chilling his core and making his stomach roll.

He got out his cigarette makings and rolled a smoke, still an awkward endeavor for his unskilled fingers. He was sitting there by a creek, watching the rosy dawn compose itself and smoking with his back to a tree, when he heard a twig snap. He turned his head and reached for his Colt.

Across the creek, a whitetail buck leapt a shrub and ran

through a cottonwood thicket, heading southwest, as though something downstream had spooked it.

Colt in his hand, Cuno climbed to his feet and eased a careful glance east around the trunk of the tree he'd been sitting behind. Remembering what Charlie Dodge had taught him, he opened the revolver's cylinder, thumbed a shell from his cartridge belt, and slipped the brass into the chamber he'd left empty beneath the hammer.

He closed the cylinder and was about to steal out from around the tree, when the paint whinnied and flicked its ears, turning its head to see beyond Cuno. Cuno froze, pressed his back to the tree, lifting the gun to his chest and holding his elbows tight to his sides, so he wouldn't be seen from the other side of the tree.

Softly, the sound of a light tread in weeds came to his ears. The man was walking directly toward him, slowly, one step at a time. When the footsteps neared, Cuno swung around the tree and extended his gun.

Caught off guard, the man jumped slightly and froze. He was a medium-tall man, broad through the shoulders, with a hard, weathered face. He wore a pinstriped, bib-front shirt under a scuffed and cracked black vest. His eyes widened momentarily, then narrowed, and a cunning smile touched the corners of his mouth.

He spread his legs, jerking the rifle down. Cuno triggered the Colt. The report shattered the morning stillness, scaring blackbirds from the treetops in loudly whirring wingbeats. Through the powder smoke, Cuno saw the man drop his rifle and tumble backward in the grass, a dark stain on his vest.

A shot rang out to Cuno's left, the slug plunking into the tree behind him.

Cuno turned quickly, saw the short, dark man standing about thirty yards away, and fired, missing the man and wheeling toward the creek. A shot sounded directly behind him. The bullet gave a devilish hiss as it cut the air over Cuno's head.

He half-ran, half-tumbled down the bank. He ran downstream for maybe fifty yards, then bounded up the bank, dropping to his knees and crawling behind another wide cottonwood. His heart pounding, he waited, listening.

Finally, brush rustled, and a shadow moved in the inky dawn woods to his right. To his left, in the creek bed, a boot clipped a stone and a man cursed softly.

They were trying to box him in.

Cuno hunkered low in the weeds and waited. He looked at the gun in his hand. Although his heart was pounding, his hand wasn't shaking. Killing wasn't hard, really, once you'd mastered the gun. You just had to accept that it was either you or the one trying to kill you, and block everything else from your mind.

The shadow moved to his right, and Cuno lifted his eyes over the bending weed tips. The man was moving in an arc around Cuno's position, a revolver in his gloved hand.

Cuno swallowed, thumbed back the Colt's hammer, stood, aimed quickly but coolly, and fired. The man yelled, grabbing his left arm. He tried lifting his gun again. Expressionless, Cuno gazed down the Colt's barrel and took up the slack in his trigger finger. The revolver popped. The slug puffed dust from the man's shirt, high in his chest—a kill shot.

Hearing footsteps behind him, Cuno wheeled left and ran as two quick shots rang out. He dropped to his knees in the grass and lifted his head. The third gunman's rifle barked an instant after Cuno felt an icy burn across his temple. Steeling himself, ignoring the pain, he rose to a crouch, extended the Colt, and fired. The man climbing the creek bank gave a cry and fell back out of sight.

Cautiously, Cuno looked around. The woods were still, the dewy grass reflecting the golden light of the rising sun. High up in a tree, a squirrel laughed. Cuno fingered blood from the graze on his temple as he walked toward the lip of the creek bank, and cast his gaze into the ravine.

The third gunman lay perpendicular to the shallow stream, his head at the edge of the water, his dew-soaked boots crossed almost casually on the bank's steep slope. The man's gray eyes were open, reflecting the lightening sky but seeing nothing.

Cuno stared at the man's dead eyes, confused, wondering how he and the others had gotten on his trail so quickly. Then he made sure the Mexican and the first man he'd shot were dead, taking the first man's rifle—a Winchester that fired the same loads as Cuno's Colt. He felt only a momentary guilt for taking the gun. One, the man was dead; two, he'd tried to kill him with it.

Looking around for more would-be attackers, he found three horses tethered about a quarter-mile from his resting place on Lodgepole Creek.

Unsaddling the horses, all of which bore the Rocking R brand on their flanks, Cuno turned them loose and stared after them, deciding the men must have seen him galloping out of Julesburg and tied his desperate fleeing to the killing of Vince Evans. He just hoped there would be no trouble for old man Roderick or the girls, but if there was, there was nothing he could do about it now. He was heading west.

On his way back to Renegade, he stopped, clamped his new rifle under his arm, and held his hands out before him, palms down.

His hands were shaking a little, but just a little. His stomach felt slightly queasy, but even that effect seemed to be diminishing. He'd killed four men now, and was vaguely disturbed that it seemed to be getting easier. He'd killed all three as though in a dream, cold purpose overcoming his fear.

Contrary to what Charlie Dodge had told him, it hadn't been much harder than shooting coffee tins and vinegar jars. He hoped it was this easy when he faced Anderson.

He ran down the paint, which had worked its tie rope loose during the shooting and stood in a clearing, owl-eyed and with the feed sack still hanging from its head. Cuno stowed the feed sack in his saddlebags and reset the saddle, tightening the cinch. He was reining the horse back along the trail westward when he saw something move behind a large rock about fifty yards north. The morning light limned the rock enough that Cuno could see what looked like hair whipping out from behind it.

The hair of someone hiding there.

Quickly, he dismounted, shucked the rifle from its boot, dropped to a knee, and levered three quick rounds, the bullets cracking and twanging off the rock. A girl screamed, and the figure appeared running away through the scrub on the other side of the rock.

"Oh, Jesus," Cuno muttered. "It's a girl!"

Sliding the rifle into the saddle boot, he mounted and galloped through the scrub. As he approached the running girl, he heard her sobbing.

"It's okay, Miss—I'm sorry. I didn't mean to shoot. I thought. . . . Oh, hell, quit running, will you? I'm not going to hurt you!"

He swerved the horse ahead of her, blocking her path, then swung around to face her. The girl stopped and bounded backward, falling on her butt. "Leave me be! I didn't do nothin' to you!"

He stared at her, cowering before him on the ground, as though he were some raging savage. A pretty girl, maybe sixteen, with long, coal-black hair and a delicate, oval-shaped face with ever-so-vaguely Indian features but with eyes as blue as those of any Nordic princess. It dawned on him where he'd seen her before, had heard that pleading voice.

This was the girl he'd tried to rescue from the Rockin' R riders in Julesburg.

Frowning, he grabbed his canteen off his saddle horn and dismounted. Slowly, hands spread acquiescently, he approached the girl, who had fallen silent now but who still watched him with lip-trembling, wide-eyed fear. He saw that her dress was torn and filthy and her hair was tangled and matted with weed flecks and burrs. Her arms and legs were badly scratched. If it hadn't been for the dress and her bluer-than-blue eyes, he'd have taken her for a lost, half-wild Indian.

He smiled to set her at ease, and hunkered down on his haunches. "We meet again."

She set her jaw so that her cheeks dimpled angrily. "You come one foot closer, and I'll tear your heart out with my fingernails!"

Cuno smiled. She had sand, this girl. A survivor. "I don't doubt that a bit.

"Just leave me be."

"You don't remember me."

"Why should I?" Her voice remained hard with anger and fear.

When she said nothing to this, he added, "Julesburg. I tried rescuing you from those lit-up cowpokes. I guess I should say I did rescue you. You got away while I got my ass kicked . . . if you'll pardon my French." He smiled again.

Watching her, he saw the fear in her eyes lose some of its heat. At last, she swept a lock of long, black hair from her eyes with a dirty hand. "Sorry. I was scared."

"It's okay. I didn't expect you to hang around."

Her eyes had lost their fear but they remained wary. A little sheepish, she said, "Did they hurt you bad?"

"Nah." Cuno shook his head. "What are you doin' way out here?"

The girl shrugged and glanced around pensively. "I figured I'd worn out my luck in Julesburg."

Cuno sounded surprised. "You're afoot?"

She shrugged again. "I didn't have no money, and Pa's dead . . ."

"I heard your pa was killed. How'd it happen?"

The girl's nostrils flared again with anger, but this time the anger was directed at a memory. "He left a saloon one night to use the privy, and someone knifed him and took his money, what little he had."

"I'm sorry."

The girl looked off, her black, tangled hair blowing.

"Where you headed?" Cuno asked her.

"Montana. Leastways, that's where me and pa was headed. My uncle's up there, diggin' for gold. Pa was gonna do some diggin' of his own, but he lost our wagon and all our supplies gamblin'. He always did have a weakness for cards. Ma used to say you give 'em a choice between a deck of cards and a bottle o' rye, he'd drive himself plumb mad with the decision." She shook her head, but her expression was as much fondness as disgust. "He was tryin' to get some of the money back when they murdered him."

"Who's they?"

She shrugged. "Just some border ruff in Julesburg, I reckon. Take your pick."

"So you just lit off on your own?"

"Didn't know what else to do. I couldn't stay in Julesburg without sellin'—you know—and I reckon my heart wasn't in it."

Cuno offered the canteen. "How 'bout some water?"

She shook her head.

"Hungry?"

She shook her head again.

"How you been survivin' out here?"

One corner of her mouth cocked into something close to a smile. "I'm a farm girl. I been snarin' rabbits with vines and the hem of my dress. I swiped some matches and a few other things off a bull train that drifted through a while back."

Cuno poked his hat back on his head and whistled through his teeth. "It's sure a lonely life you been livin'. My name's Cuno Massey. I'm from Valoria, Nebraska. What's your name?"

"July."

"July? That's pretty."

"July Summer."

Cuno chuckled. "No kiddin'?"

The girl was in no mood for teasing. She stared off, poker-faced.

"Well, July, you feel like ridin' with me as far as Cheyenne?"

She glanced at him crookedly, appraising him skeptically. "What you have in mind for payment?"

"The pleasure of doin' a good deed."

"Yeah," she said dryly, not believing it.

"Really," Cuno insisted. "I don't want to leave you out here all by yourself. No strings attached."

With one hand, she held her hair back from her face and looked at him again, her expression softening slightly. Quietly, she said, "I don't have a horse. I better just walk."

"You're gonna have to trust somebody sooner or later, Miss July. If you don't, you're gonna have one heck of a long walk to Montana, and I doubt you'd get there before the snow flies."

Cuno extended his hand to the girl. Reluctantly, she accepted it and stood. A moment later, they were mounted on Renegade, and Cuno spurred southwestward, toward the main trail.

Neither he nor July Summer realized that a half-mile north, two Cheyenne braves sat their horses on a low rise concealed by a gooseberry thicket. One of the braves, his cheeks brightly painted, a full quiver of arrows hanging down his back, gazed silently through a brass spyglass he'd taken from a small party of white settlers he and his companion had attacked three days ago.

Through the glass, he watched the two riders heading west, trailing a thin dust plume. The girl, her black hair blowing in the wind, rode easily behind the White Eyes. Soon, the two diminished in the distance, and the sage- and yucca-pocked prairie swallowed them from view.

The brave reduced the spyglass with a snap of his hand and turned to his companion, a meaningful smirk rearranging the painted designs on his cherry, black-eyed face.

"Another white eyes trespassing on our hunting grounds," the brave said in Cheyenne. "Tonight, we will sweep the ground around our fire with his scalp!"

"And with the girl's!" added his companion, tough-eyed.

The first brave flung an arm out brusquely, and he and his companion kneed their mounts westward along a grassy swale.

13

HEARING A TWIG snap, July Summer gasped and jerked back from the fire over which she was frying pan bread. Cuno strode in from the darkness with an armload of dead branches. Seeing him, the girl heaved a sigh.

"Sorry," Cuno said. "I reckon I shoulda warned you I was comin'."

"I'm skittish as a damn fawn these days," July said self-deprecatingly, returning to the panbread. The night had turned chilly along Lodgepole Creek, about twenty miles east of Cheyenne, and Cuno had offered her one of his blankets, which she'd draped about her shoulders.

Cuno piled the wood neatly by the fire. "Those polecats in Julesburg cause your jumpiness?"

"Them and a few others."

She didn't continue for several minutes. When she did, Cuno was sitting against his saddle and awkwardly rolling a cigarette.

"It ain't what I wanted to do," she insisted. "There just aren't many ways for a single girl to feed herself in a place like Julesburg—for a half-breed, anyway."

"Your ma was an Indian?"

July nodded. "Creek. Pa met her at a trading post when he started farming in Kansas. She died last year of a lung fever."

Cuno studied her. With her jet-black hair and expressive blue eyes, she was pretty in a hard, prairie sort of way, and it was obvious she'd grown up mighty fast. He felt sorry for her. But then, it was the rare person he'd met so far who'd had it easy—Indian blood or no.

Thinking of his own situation as much as hers, he said, "We all do what we have to do, I reckon." He scrubbed a match aflame on his boot sole, and lit the quirly. He inhaled too deeply; his lungs constricted, and a loud cough exploded from his chest.

She regarded him with amusement. "Why do you smoke those things if they choke you?"

His face warmed with embarrassment. "They don't always choke me. I reckon the tobacco's too fresh."

"How long you been smokin'?"

First he scowled, then he smiled. "Oh, about a week and a half."

They both laughed, then turned their eyes to the night, feeling suddenly easier with one another.

Later that night, Cuno woke the girl by gently touching her arm. "Come with me," he whispered.

Recognizing the alarm in his eyes, she silently obeyed, tossing off her blanket and climbing to her bare feet. Rifle in his hands, the Colt riding the holster on his hip, Cuno led the girl through the trees toward the murmuring creek.

Behind a deadfall snag, he whispered, "Wait here."

He turned and disappeared through the trees. Stealing around the camp, trying to walk as lightly as he could, stepping carefully over fallen branches, he kept the fire on his distant left while he looked around and listened. Earlier he'd heard too many birdcalls. Now, he heard nothing but the distant crackling of the fire, the quiet rustle of some small, burrowing creature.

Maybe he was getting as skittish as the girl. Maybe what he'd heard really had been night birds . . .

Something—an extra sense he'd acquired since setting off on his own—told him they hadn't been. Standing quietly by the creek and staring eastward across the open prairie capped with shimmering starlight, he poured all his energy into his hearing. After a while, gripping the Winchester before him, he walked back toward the camp, heading for the flickering orange light of the fire through the black web of branches.

When he was within twenty feet of the fire, he stopped and stood silently, watching and listening. He didn't like how quiet the night had gotten. It was an eerie, impenetrable silence so dense he could hear the persistent thumps of his heart in his chest.

Without warning, a bizarre cry rose from the shrubs on the other side of the fire, so loud it rattled Cuno's eardrums, so sinister and horrifying it froze the blood in his veins. His muscles tensed. He stood there, agape and inert.

From behind, his rifle was wrenched savagely from his grasp and flung aside. At the same moment, a wide knife appeared at his throat while the arm that had taken his rifle so unexpectedly now wrapped itself around his neck, nearly cutting off his wind.

"You fight, you die," spat a guttural voice in his ear. Cuno could smell the Indian's pungent breath and the rancid fat in his hair. "Where girl?" the brave demanded.

Across the fire, the scream sounded again, shrill and malevolent, setting the night alive with its evil. The shrubs moved as though in a sudden wind and another war-painted brave appeared, hurling himself into the clearing by the fire, crouching and jerking his head around as though looking for something.

"Where girl?" he shouted. "Where girl! Where girl!"

Clawing at the arm of the brave who had his neck in a death grip, Cuno saw the brave near the fire jerk suddenly, as if hearing something, and bound off toward the creek.

Another scream rose; this time it was a girl's scream. It was followed by a victorious whoop by the brave.

"You die, white eyes!" yelled the knife-wielding brave in Cuno's ear.

As the blade started the plunge toward his throat, Cuno flung his right hand at it, grabbing the Indian's wrist. Holding the wrist, he twisted around, popped his right knee into the brave's groin, and slammed the Indian's arm against the tree. The brave screamed and dropped the knife. Cuno lifted his knee at the crouching Indian's face, connecting with a solid smack and crunch of breaking bone.

The brave dropped to his knees, screaming. Cuno picked up the knife. Hearing July's screams, he knew he had no time to waste and no reason to spare the Indian's life. Taking a deep breath of resolve, he grabbed the raging Indian from behind and, before the brave knew what was happening, ran the knife cleanly across his throat.

A moment later he was running toward July's screams, hurdling deadfalls and ducking under low-hanging branches. He rounded a bend in the creek and saw a flicker of starlit movement on the shore of the stream. Bounding toward it, he raised the bloody knife in his hand.

As he approached the tussling shadows, he saw the Indian smack July with a savage backhanded blow. July gave a cry and hit the ground hard. The Indian dove on top of her, raging, "Little Turtle's girl, half-breed! Little Turtle's girl!"

Not wanting to cut July by mistake, Cuno dropped the knife and dove atop the Indian, then ground his feet into the sand, pulling the Indian off the girl. The Cheyenne gained his feet and swung a punch at Cuno, who ducked and jabbed the brave in his bare belly. The Indian was as big and solid as Cuno, and he shrugged off the blow with relative ease, landing a right cross high on Cuno's cheek.

Cuno stumbled back in the water and fell on his butt with a splash. The Indian dove at him. Cuno jerked to his left, and the Indian rolled off his shoulder. As the brave sprang off his knees, Cuno moved in with a hard left jab. He followed it with a right, then another left. The Indian stumbled over a rock and fell with a shriek.

Cuno pulled the Indian to his feet and went to work again with the jabs, smashing the brave's face to a blackened pulp. When the attacker was on his back again, and hanging limp in the creek, grunting and groaning, Cuno grabbed his face in both his big hands and held him under the water.

The Indian grabbed at his arms and fought wickedly, kicking, but Cuno held him down with his hands and with one firm knee on the brave's chest. Slowly, the fight in the Indian died. The hands clutching at Cuno's arms released their grip and sank down in the water. When Cuno loosened his grip on the brave, the body floated with the current.

Cuno let the Indian go and watched the body drift a few feet before catching on a tangle of roots along the bank. Turning, Cuno waded toward shore. July stood clutching her torn dress over her bosom.

"You all right?" he asked.

Her voice was thin and wobbly as she answered, "I reckon. Are you?"

"I reckon."

"Where's the other one?"

"Dead."

July staggered back as though drunk, and eased down on the bank. She sighed with all the weariness of a violent, warring world. "What if there's more?"

Cuno didn't know how to answer that, so he said nothing.

She looked at him as if silently summing up the night's events. "You fight pretty good," she said after a long time, as though trying to bolster her own spirits. "I reckon I should feel right lucky you came along."

His chest still heaving, his clothes soaked and dripping, he glanced at the dead Indian bobbing gently in the creek. Turning to July, he said, "Come on," and extended his hand. "In case there's more Cheyenne around, we best pack it up and fog it out of here."

"Wait," she said thinly, ignoring his hand. "I'm so tired."

Cuno sat beside her and took her hand in his. Her hand was soft but there was strength in it, too. He wasn't surprised. He'd sensed the strength in this weary girl at whom life had flung its worst.

He was pleasantly surprised she did not jerk her hand from his. After a time, she turned to him, leaned toward him. He put his arms around her and held her.

"Cuno?" she said quietly after a while.

"Yes?"

"I don't mean to whine, but I'm scared."

"You'll be all right. We'll be to Cheyenne in a few hours."

"Then what?"

Yes, then what. Neither of them had any money. And no friends except each other.

"Then," he said, conjuring a confidence he did not feel, against an apprehension that hung as heavy as his wet clothes. "Then I guess we'll just see."

14

ROLF ANDERSON AND Sammy Spoon strode along the shady side of Cheyenne's main drag. Approaching a bevy of teamsters standing before the Wagoners Saloon, Anderson gave one a vicious shove from behind, clearing the man from his path. The man bolted forward, beer sloshing from his glass.

Angrily, the man whipped around, his voice indignant. "Hey, who in the hell do you think you are?"

Anderson was halfway through the saloon's batwings. He turned his head to the burly teamster, his expression dully menacing. The teamster's own expression softened, his jaw dropping.

"Uh, sorry, Rolf. Didn't know it was you." Cowed, the teamster absently brushed beer from his shirt and smiled acquiescently.

Anderson blinked slowly, then headed through the batwings, the chuckling Sammy Spoon on his heels.

"Which one o' these bullwackers is Martin Wehring?" Rolf Anderson asked the barman.

The barman nodded to indicate two men—one blond and in his thirties, one dark and several years older—in battered felt hats sitting at a table at the back of the room. Both men were hungrily eating the free sandwiches and pickled eggs offered to each drinking customer.

"Martin's the older man with the beard," the barman said, going back to his dishpan.

Anderson glanced at Sammy Spoon, and the two men strolled through the tables, about half of which were occupied now at three in the afternoon, mostly by freighters waiting to head north on the Bozeman Trail. A dozen or so other customers stood around drinking on the boardwalk, trying to catch a breeze blowing through the hot, dusty town on the vast Dakota sage flats.

"Martin Wehring?" Anderson asked the bearded man holding a half-eaten sandwich in his callused brown hands.

The man measured Anderson through deep-set, brown eyes that flickered curiously at his partner. "I'm Martin."

"Name's Anderson," the hider grumbled. He didn't bother introducing Spoon. "Lookin' for trail scouts, are ye?"

Anderson had learned as much from several drivers playing cribbage in one of the wagon camps parked outside town, where women sweltered in the heat as they prepared game for supper and yelled at their kids. So far, there were six wagons in the Wehring party, captained by Martin Wehring himself.

"Might be," Wehring said now, licking cheese and bread crumbs from his cinnamon, gray-streaked mustache. "We lost three men yesterday. Sons o'bitches got tired of waiting around for the rest of my freight to get here from Kansas City. They left with the bull train that pulled out yesterday. Double-crossing bastards. Nobody has patience anymore. It's all hurry, hurry."

He glanced as though for corroboration at his fairer-skinned brother, who didn't return the glance. The brother was shuttling his narrowed gaze from Anderson to Spoon and back again.

"When's the rest of your freight due?" Anderson asked.

"Rolling in on the Union Pacific tomorrow. We should be able to pull out soon as it's loaded on wagons and the army's inpected us for contraband."

Anderson nodded. "Good. We got the trail itch our own-selves."

"Hold on," said Martin's brother, sitting to Martin's left. He washed his sandwich down with a short pull of beer from his mug, then ran his grimy sleeve across his mouth. He had a sharp face and a crooked nose; his pale blue eyes were set too close together. "We didn't say you was hired."

Sammy Spoon spoke up, eyeing the younger Wehring with mocking humor. "Who's this, Marty?"

"My brother, Rudolph," Wehring said. "We're opening a mercantile in Bozeman City." Martin frowned at Spoon, running his gaze across the half-breed's braids and ratty attire. "Who the hell are you?"

"Samuel Avila-Spoon. From Chiricowy down Mexico-way. Yeah, I'm a breed. Quarter Yaqui, quarter bean-eater, and half black-Irish. Wow!" Spoon shook his head. "Don't make me mad." Laughing, the half-breed extended his hand, grinning with exaggerated affability. Martin shook with Spoon, and then the half-breed extended the hand to the younger Wehring. "Howdy-do, Rudy. Mind if I call you Rudy?"

The younger Wehring scowled, his slender nose coloring. "Yes, I mind," he said tightly. "I use my full name, but Injuns call me sir."

Spoon's smile faded. He lowered his hand and took a step toward Rudolph Wehring.

"Hold on, hold on, Samuel," Anderson said with a good-natured chuckle. "We don't wanna offend our new employers."

"Who said you was hired?" Martin Wehring asked with growing exasperation.

"Well, we did," Anderson said agreeably. He planted a fist on the table and leaned over Martin, keeping his voice low. "And I'll tell you what, boys—we're gonna scout for free."

The older Wehring knitted his brows and said nothing for several seconds. "Free?"

Anderson glanced around to see if anyone was listening. Turning back to the table, he lowered his voice. "Not only that, but we're gonna pay you!"

Rudolph Wehring opened his mouth to exclaim, but Anderson cut him off. "Take a ride with us. We'll show you what we mean."

The Wehring brothers just sat there, looking at Anderson, incredulous scowls etching their similarly featured foreheads.

Anderson gave an impatient grunt, pulled out a chair, and sat down. Keeping his voice low, he folded his massive, freckled hands on the table and said, "You boys are headin' to Bozeman City to open your own mercantile?"

Neither Wehring responded.

"Me and my partner here can make it easier. You won't have to start the store in no tent, livin' in your wagons with your screamin' kids and pissy wives. You'll be able to build your own store right off, out of milled lumber." Anderson shaped a grin. "How's that sound?"

"I don't like this," Rudolph said, scowling at his brother. "I don't trust these two."

"Shut up," Martin snapped. To Anderson, he said angrily, "How's this miracle supposed to happen? All our savin's is tied up in freight. How in the hell can we make enough money between here and Bozeman City to afford a new store?"

"Come with us," Anderson said, "and we'll show you."

The brothers regarded each other warily. "What?" Martin grunted.

"We'll show you what we're talkin' about," Spoon said. "Easy as grandma's apple pie . . . but much, much sweeter," he added with a wet, snaggle-toothed grin.

Rudolph Wehring sneered. "You think we were born yesterday? Hell, you'll lead us off and rob us!"

Anderson threw his head back, laughing. "What in the hell do you boys have that we'd want?" He laughed again and shook his head at Spoon, who snorted with delight.

Rudolph turned to his brother, fearful. "I don't trust 'em. I say—"

"Shut up, Rudolph," Martin said, thinking it over, scowling. Finally, he pushed himself to his feet and adjusted the old-model Remington on his hip. "Let's go."

They rode northeast of town, following a series of draws. The sun beat down and the sage in the hot wind smelled of blackstrap. When they'd ridden for a half hour, Anderson reined his buckskin into a box canyon where an old, gray wagon sat with its tongue up and four mules grazed near a spring. A bear of a man in fringed buckskins sat on a campstool, whittling. Long, white hair fell across his shoulders.

He sat there as the others rode up.

"Pike," Anderson said, "break out one of those guns."

Slowly, the big man set down the duck he was whittling, sheathed his knife, and pushed to his feet. He walked over to the wagon, opened a packing crate, and hefted a rifle in his hands. He carried the rifle over to Anderson, who took the gun, examined it, threw open the trapdoor breech, and cocked it.

He snugged it up to his cheek, sighted along the eroded

canyon wall, and pulled the trigger. The hammer clicked benignly.

He tossed the gun to Martin Wehring, who grabbed it out of the air with an angry frown. "What the hell?"

"Trapdoor Springfields," Anderson said. "So new the iron's still warm. The Injuns up north'll pay for 'em in gold."

"Jesus Christ!" Rudolph Wehring exclaimed. "You know what the army'd do to us if they caught us sellin' contraband to the Indians?"

"They'd probably give you about thirty years in the federal hoosegow," Sammy Spoon said with a shrug.

"Only they ain't gonna catch us," Anderson told the Wehrings. "Cause we ain't gonna have the rifles till after we've passed the army's inspection tomorrow. We're gonna pick 'em up north of Fort Russell."

Martin Wehring sat his beefy, wall-eyed roan mare; holding the gleaming rifle across his chest. He looked owly, his thoughts a mix of contradictory impulses, his nostrils contracting and expanding. "How many are there?"

His younger brother snapped a sharp look at him. "You can't be thinkin' about—?" Martin flung out an arm, cutting him off.

"One hundred," Anderson said, a smug grin lighting his blue eyes. He spat a stream of tobacco juice on a flat rock and wiped his mouth with his hand. "We'll break 'em up and carry 'em in three or four of your wagons. We'll rig some false bottoms just in case."

"Why don't you get your own damn wagons?" Rudolph asked. He was perspiring not only from the hot ride, but from anxiety and anger. "We have our families with us—women and children!"

Anderson stared at the younger Wehring, expressionless. He was keeping his anger in check, but just barely. He needed these two. He didn't like them, but he needed them . . . for a while. He'd kill this jittery granger and his dumbass brother later, after the exchange had been made with White Bull's band of Hunkpapa Sioux. Anderson had arranged the deal six months ago, when he'd met White Bull in the Black Hills.

"Samuel and I can't haul them ourselves," he told the brothers calmly. "We don't get along too well with the army. They see us drivin' our own wagons, they'll get a might suspicious. Besides, no one travels the Montany Road these days alone, not with all the other Injuns about."

Martin Wehring was silent for a time, staring from the moronically grinning Spoon to Anderson to the rifle in his hand. He tossed the rifle back to Anderson. "Where do we meet up with the Injuns?"

"In the Bighorns," Anderson said. "They'll be waitin' for us at a prearranged spot. We just swap the rifles for the gold and continue on to Montany."

"How much we get for haulin' these long guns?" Wehring asked.

"This is your lucky day, Marty," Anderson told him. "Ole White Bull's payin' three twenty-pound gold bars. One bar at current market price is worth thirty-two hundred dollars."

He let that sink in. Martin Wehring's eyes twitched, and his nostrils flared slightly.

"Just for haulin' the rifles, Samuel and I will impart unto you and your handsome brother here one gold bar."

"One twenty-pound bar?" Rudolph asked skeptically.

Spoon said, "Ole White Bull apparently doesn't know or care how much gold is worth. He just steals it from miners in the Black Hills and trades it for rifles."

"This is plumb crazy," Rudolph said.

"Ayeeee," Spoon cried softly, grinning as he leaned over his saddle horn. "I think we got a softy here. A yellow one, sure 'nough."

"Shut up!" Rudolph cried.

Spoon removed his high-crowned black hat and slapped it across the younger Wehring's face. Wehring yelled, cowering. His horse skitter-stepped, alarming all the mounts.

"Here, here," Anderson reprimanded the half-breed humorously. "That's no way to treat our new employers, Samuel!"

"I don't like it when people tell me to shut up," Spoon seethed. "You do it again, and I'm gonna hit you with my pistol instead of my hat. How'd you like that?"

Anderson chuckled, as did the white-haired gent named Pike, looking on from several feet away and smoking a long, black cheroot.

"Rudolph, shut your goddamn mouth and keep it shut till I tell you otherwise," Martin Wehring scolded his brother. "You cause this horse to throw me, I'm gonna forget we're blood."

Rudolph's chest heaved, but he said nothing, sitting his horse in sheepish anger.

To Anderson, Martin said, "This thing foolproof? We won't be inspected later up the trail?"

"Army ain't been doin' that," the man called Pike said, smoking. "Not that I've heard of, anyways, and with the crowd I run with, if I ain't heard of it, it ain't happened."

Anderson added with a shake of his shaggy head, "The soldiers have pretty much abandoned the trail since the Injuns burned the forts."

Wehring looked at him darkly. "My god. Sellin' rifles to those savages. . . . But thirty-two hundred dollars." He whistled.

"You in?" Anderson asked.

Wehring looked at his brother darkly and set his jaw. "Hell, yes, we're in."

Anderson tossed the Springfield back to Pike. He told

the gun dealer to meet them on the trail with the rifles early tomorrow afternoon. With a nod to Sammy Spoon, he reined his horse back down the draw toward Cheyenne.

"Lord, this heat makes me thirsty!"

15

CHEYENNE BAKED IN the prairie sun as Cuno and July entered the outskirts atop Renegade.

The small settlement, with its single business street and outlying corrals and shanties, appeared more like an encampment than a bona fide town. Freight trains consisting of more than a hundred wagons and ten times as many horses, mules, and oxen were parked around it, like some makeshift stockade wall, or like a great prairie fair complete with frolicking children and dogs. The recently laid Union Pacific tracks stretched east-to-west, reflecting the afternoon light like quicksilver or slender waves rippling on a fawn-colored lake.

This was the end of the railroad line. From here, traders shipped their supplies northwest via the Bozeman Trail or, as it was sometimes called, the Montana Road.

"I don't like towns," July said behind Cuno as they rode amid corrals and feed barns and shanties. The air smelled like sage and privies and creosote-soaked railroad ties.

"No one's going to hurt you," Cuno assured her.

"I don't have any money. In towns, you need money."

"I have what was in my pocket when my roll was stolen," he told her. "That'll stretch for a couple meals and a hotel room until we can figure something else out."

"I don't want you spending any money on me. You've done enough for me the way it is. I'll get a job in a café. There seems to be plenty," she added, sweeping her gaze along both sides of the street.

The boardwalks were congested with bullwackers, and the street itself was one bottleneck after another of ranch and freight wagons and horseback riders stopping here and there to chat. Dog packs ran amok, scavenging trash heaps and barking at horses.

"Don't worry about that now," he said, pulling the tired paint horse up to the hitchrack before the Drug Emporium, which boasted a gaudy red front and several signs advertising medicinal concoctions. "Why don't you stretch your legs on the boardwalk here for a while, maybe get yourself a sarsaparilla. I'm going to do some checking around."

As the girl slid off the back of the horse, she said, "Checking around for Anderson and Spoon?"

On the ride to Cheyenne, she'd had plenty of time to learn of Cuno's quest for vengeance.

Reading the concern in July's blue eyes, Cuno said, "Don't worry. I'm not going to do anything yet. I just want to know if they're still here or if they've gone up the trail to Montana."

He dismounted and slipknotted Renegade's reins at the hitching rail, then dug in his pocket for some coins.

July scowled at him. "Hold onto your money, mister. Water'll do me fine."

He smiled and strode off down the boardwalk, gazing around at the saloons fronting the street. He went into the first one he came to and inquired with the barman about Anderson and Spoon. The barman flushed, saying nothing, and abruptly turned to pour a gambler a whiskey.

Cuno checked four more saloons, getting nothing but

shrugs and headshakes. The barman in the Wagoners jerked his apprehensive eyes at Cuno, said dryly, "Who's Anderson and Spoon?" and walked away down the hardwood.

Cuno was crossing the street when he heard someone call, "Sonny."

He turned. A short man with a horsey face that resembled ground beef, as cut and bruised as it was, stood on the boardwalk, bent forward at the waist. His right eye was swollen nearly shut. He beckoned Cuno over.

"Yes, sir?" Cuno said as he approached. The man's battered face, under the brim of a weather-beaten canvas hat with the front brim pinned to the crown, was hard to look at. The iris seemed to float in a miniature blood sea.

The man glanced cautiously around, then said in a low voice, "Heard you been lookin' for Rolf Anderson."

"You seen him?"

"I seen him." The man chuffed without mirth. "Who in the hell you think did this to my face? The other night in the Wagoners, he thought he saw me makin' eyes at the whore in his lap." The man's chapped lips pooched out and a cold light entered his bloodshot gaze.

Cuno felt a rush of adrenaline. "He still in town?"

The freighter shook his head. "Headed out five days ago, with the Wehring train."

"Where to?"

"The Wehrings are opening a mercantile in Bozeman City. Anderson and his sidekick, Spoon, are ridin' scout like they usually do this time of the year. Only they don't usually just scout. They always have somethin' goin' on the side, like sellin' whiskey to the Injuns or tradin' slave women." The man took a deep drag from the tightly rolled quirly in his fingers. Exhaling smoke, he said, "Why you lookin' for 'em? You don't look like no friend of theirs."

"I'm not," Cuno said, thinking it over. He'd missed Anderson and Spoon by five days. On a fast horse, he could make up that time in only a day or two, since Anderson was scouting for a slow-moving wagon train . . . Returning his gaze to the freighter, feeling he owed the man an explanation in return for the information, he said, "They killed my pa and step-ma."

The man nodded, pensive. "Figgered it was somethin' like that. So you're gonna try to take 'em down, eh?" The man's voice was not teeming with confidence.

"I'm gonna take 'em down, sure enough."

"That's been said about Anderson and Spoon before, son. Well, luck to ye. If you do happen to get 'em in your sights, give 'em both an extra slug for me, all right?"

"I'll do that," Cuno said coldly.

He was about to turn away, when the man said, "Here's a piece of advice. Whatever you do, don't try to trail 'em by your lonesome. Injuns are bad along the trail right now. Single riders—hell, groups of less than ten—don't have a chance. You'll lose your hair less than an hour out of Cheyenne. Hook up with a group. That's the only way."

"Thanks for the advice," Cuno said, pinching his hat brim and moving slowly back along the boardwalk. As his thoughts turned to Anderson and Spoon, he felt his insides tighten with hatred, the old images flashing behind his eyes.

On a fast horse, he could catch up with them in a day or two . . .

But then he thought about what the freighter had said about the Indians. They were a complication he hadn't, in his single-minded quest, given much consideration. He'd heard that several tribes had been a perilous hazard in these parts of late, but even after the two Cheyennes had attacked him and July along Lodgepole Creek, his primary interest had been the men who'd killed his father and Corsica. It appeared now, though, that if the freighter was right, he was going to have to take the Indian threat more seriously.

July was standing beside Renegade, patting the paint's neck, as Cuno approached. "How did it go?" she asked.

"Anderson and Spoon left town five days ago, heading north with a freight outfit." Cuno stood on the boardwalk, supporting himself against an awning post and staring pensively into the street, where an intermittent stream of wagons and horsebackers passed.

"I guess we'll be heading north, then."

He turned to look at her. "We?"

She shrugged and ran her hand down Renegade's nose. "Well, I figured we came this far, and we're going the same direction . . ."

"I'm trackin' a killer," Cuno told her. "You don't wanna be anywhere near me when I run Anderson and Spoon to ground. Besides that, it sounds like the Cheyenne and Sioux are makin' war along the trail."

"Then you shouldn't be headin' that direction, neither. Not alone, anyway."

"I don't aim to," Cuno said. "I'm gonna see about landin' a job driving a wagon for one of the freight outfits."

"What about me?"

Cuno considered the girl. She was as broke and as homeless as he was. For all her spit and sass, her wide, sky-colored eyes were afraid. He couldn't just leave her here.

"Tell you what," he said, "I'll see if I can get you on with one of the outfits, too. Can you cook?"

"Darn tootin'!" she chuffed indignantly.

"All right, then," he said with a smile. "After we've padded out our bellies, I'll make the rounds to all the saloons, see if I can find a wagon boss with a couple empty slots on his roll."

July set her full lips in a satisfied grin. "Now you're talkin'. Maybe I'll see if I can do some dishwashin' for a few nights till we leave. I'm gonna need trail clothes. I can't very well start a job in this dress." She dropped her gaze to the worn and filthy garment, a torn flap of which she'd pinned over her bosom after the Indian fight.

"Sounds like a plan," Cuno said, untying Renegade from the hitching post.

Together, they led the skewbald paint to a livery barn, where Cuno stalled the horse and ordered him plenty of oats and water as well as a good rubdown. Then he escorted July to the Bighorn Café, where they ordered steaks with all the surroundings, including apple pie with fresh whipped cream for dessert. When they finished their coffee, they parted company, and Cuno made the saloon rounds once again, this time looking for work.

Finding several wagon masters deep in their cups and not hiring, he walked out to the freight outfits parked outside town.

"I need a scout—how well do you know the country?" one man asked, holding a coffee cup in the shadows at the edge of a large fire.

Men were sitting and lounging around the wagon camp, where several deer-hide tents had been pitched. Several others sat around a folding table, playing cards. It was a festive atmosphere, with a stocky, bearded hombre strumming "The Misty Hills of Home" on a guitar. In a nearby tent, a man chuckled and a woman gave a lively shriek—probably a working girl from town.

Cuno shook his head, regretful. "I don't know the country," he admitted. "I wouldn't make much of a scout, but I've driven Murphy freight wagons since I was breast-high to a meadowlark. Conestoga mud wagons, also."

The wagon master shook his head. "Don't need another driver," he grunted, moving abruptly back toward the fire.

"What about a cook or a pot scrubber?" Cuno called to him, thinking of July.

The man shook his head and threw out a hand in the negative.

Cuno moved off in the darkness, following the powdery

trail through the sage tufts by the light of the rising moon and scattered cook fires around which shadows danced. The sounds of boisterous conversation rose crisply in the quiet night.

As he walked around a wagon, a silhouetted figure moved before him. He stopped abruptly, nearly running into the girl, who gave a soft, startled cry.

"Excuse me, Miss," he said with surprise, quickly doffing his hat. "I didn't mean to frighten you."

"That's okay," the girl said, hand to her chest, laughing nervously.

In the darkness, he could see little but her hair, the buttery light of a nearby fire limning the red-gold curls cascading about her shoulders. Her voice was both sweet and husky. "It's quite all right. You just surprised me."

Cuno hesitated, enjoying the fresh smell of her, not sure how to excuse himself. She didn't seem in a hurry to move on.

"Can I help you find someone?" she asked. "You're not from our camp, are you?"

"No, ma'am," Cuno said, surprised to hear she was from one of the wagon camps.

Upon hearing her speak, he'd immediately discounted the possibility that she was a pleasure girl. Although lighthearted, her voice didn't have that crusty edge. It had, in fact, an educated tone. He couldn't imagine an educated girl traveling with one of the bull trains.

Continuing, he said, "I was lookin' for the wagon boss . . ."

"That would be Amos," the girl said. "He's not here at the moment." He couldn't tell for sure because of the poor light, but she seemed to smile at this. "But my father is here. He's the captain of the outfit." She paused again. Cuno could feel her eyes on him, scrutinizing, wistfully biting her lower lip. "Who should I tell him is calling?"

"Cuno Massey. The name won't mean anything to him, though. I'm lookin' for a drivin' job."

The girl turned away. "Come . . ."

Obediently, still holding his hat, Cuno followed the girl past the fire, around which a handful of men lounged with plates and cups, eating beans and meat that smelled like antelope. They gave him the cautious once-over before returning their bashful, admiring gazes to the attractive girl leading Cuno toward a wagon parked under a rare tree.

"Father," she called, stopping at the covered Conestoga's rear. A lantern glowed within—a flickering, lemony light.

"Yes, Daphne?" came a man's voice.

"There's a young man to see you." She turned to Cuno, smiling pleasantly. "He wants to know if he can drive one of the wagons."

Cuno turned his gaze from hers, suddenly feeling foolish and a little annoyed. She seemed to be at once flirting with him and making fun of him.

To the wagon's back pucker, he said, "I'm an experienced driver, sir. I've been hauling freight since I was breast-high—"

"Sorry, I don't need any more drivers," came the man's voice, sounding a little bored. "Daphne, be a dear and fetch me a cup of tea, won't you?"

"Yes, Father," the girl said.

As she turned to Cuno, her slightly mocking smile was still in place. The nearby fire revealed an attractive face with a fragile nose, rosebud lips, and precocious gray eyes. Her red-gold hair was thick and wavy, falling to square, narrow shoulders. The girl wore a tight, light-blue dress with flowing skirts. Her breasts were full and high, and she carried them proudly.

She chuckled, and Cuno realized she'd caught him appraising her.

"I'm sorry," she said, in reference to her father's reply. "If it were up to me, I'd give you the job in a heartbeat."

There was the tone again, at once mocking and flirtatious. She let her own eyes linger on his chest, dropping them to his tan, corded forearms and his hammy hands clutching his shabby bowler hat before him.

"How old are you?" she asked with a bold flash of her eyes.

"Eighteen," he said, feeling a little giddy in her presence, wanting to leave but also wanting to stay. He didn't like this girl's mocking manner, and yet he felt drawn to her . . .

"That's nice," she said. "I mean it would be nice to have a younger fellow around. Most of the other gents are twice my age or older."

Cuno shook his head, puzzled. "What . . .?" He wasn't sure how to continue.

"What am I doing out here?" she finished for him with a laugh. "A girl like me?" She laughed again. "Well, it's a short story, really. Father and his brother own a big company that builds such unglamorous things as mining equipment. Since the route has become so problematic, he decided to oversee his equipment to Montana himself, and I'm along for the ride."

"This is awfully dangerous country."

"Actually, Father thought I would be safer with him and the Indians than left to my own devices in St. Louis." She gave a titter, lowering her head and squinting her eyes beguilingly. "And I wanted to come along. It's an adventure. I've always loved reading about adventure while actually experiencing very little."

Before Cuno could respond to any of this—she had quite plainly captured his tongue—she sighed. "Oh, well, Cuno Massey, I guess it just wasn't meant to be, you and I . . ."

"Daphne," came the man's voice from inside the wagon,

at once bored and chiding. "Leave the boy alone and fetch my tea."

"Yes, Father," Daphne said, giggling and giving Cuno's bicep an appreciative parting squeeze. Turning, her skirts aswirl, she bounded off toward the fire and disappeared around a wagon.

Cuno stared after her, puzzled by the girl, still feeling the thrill of her deep in his loins. It was not a comfortable sensation. Feeling chagrined but not quite knowing why, he wandered back out to the trail, heading toward the tin-panny music emanating from town.

He was walking in the darkness between two stores, stepping over trash, when gunfire broke out on Main Street. A girl screamed.

July's face flashed in his mind, and he broke into a run.

16

CUNO ROUNDED THE corner of a clothing store and ran onto Main Street, his Colt in his hand.

He slowed and stared before him, at a cluster of men and two women in the street. Neither was July, he was relieved to see. One of the men lay writhing in the street, kicking and clutching his chest. The other men stood over him, looking down. The one wearing a five-pointed sheriff's star held a long-barreled revolver, its barrel still smoking.

"Now, why in the hell did you reach for that hideout, Ernie?" the badge-toter asked, incredulous.

"When he drinks, Sheriff, he gets meaner than a Missouri mule mired in hog shit," one of the women said, a note of sadness in her tone. She shook her head and gazed down at the wounded man. "Oh, Ernie! Look what you done to yourself, hon."

Ernie lifted his head and dropped it, groaning.

"Someone get the doc," the lawman called to a group gathered nearby.

Cuno watched a man break out from the group, jog

south down the street, then turn the corner. Cuno holstered his Colt, again feeling relieved that the trouble had not involved July. It was just another skirmish, one of many he'd seen since arriving in Cheyenne only a few hours ago.

"Cuno!"

He turned to the familiar voice, and saw July running up on his right, holding her tattered skirt above her ankles.

"I heard the shooting," she said as she approached, breathless. "I was afraid you might have found those hardcases you're lookin' for." She stared at the supine man in the street, around which an even larger crowd had gathered.

"Wasn't me," Cuno said. "Just some drunk who twisted the tail of the wrong badge-toter, I reckon."

July shook her head. "This town's startin' to shoot my nerves as bad as Julesburg. A few minutes ago, some railroader said he'd give me a dime if I'd show him my titties. Sometime, I'm going to live in a town where men behave themselves."

"Good luck." Dropping his eyes, Cuno noticed July was wearing an apron, and the sleeves of her dress were rolled up her arms: "Looks like you found a job, and not one exposing yourself," Cuno said with a chuckle.

She jerked her head up the boardwalk. "I'm waiting tables over at Mrs. Haugen's Bakery down the street. I inquired after supper, and I got lucky. Her regular girl got sick."

Cuno was incredulous. "After that long ride, you're already waitin' tables?"

July shrugged. "I need trail clothes, and I told you I wasn't going to do the other thing anymore. Did you have any luck finding a driving job?"

"No, and it don't look promising." Guilt plucked at him again, remembering that he'd been so startled by Daphne that he'd forgotten about inquiring with Daphne's father for July.

"I best get back to work," July said. "I was just out getting stove wood when I heard the commotion." As she started away, she told him she'd see him tomorrow, as Mrs. Haugen had offered her the lean-to bedroom behind the restaurant for the night.

Then she hurried back the way she had come.

"July," he called.

The black-haired girl turned back around, frowning curiously. He walked to her and tipped his hat back. "I'm gonna have to say good-bye. I'm heading north on the trail tomorrow."

"No!" came the girl's startled reply. "Cuno Massey, you'll be killed by Injuns!"

"Just can't hang around here. Chances are I won't find a job with a freight team for days, maybe weeks. I can't let Anderson and Spoon get away."

She didn't say anything, just stared at him, troubled.

"You'll get by," he assured her. "Stay here until the Indian trouble's over, or until you can find a job with a big outfit." He glanced off, a little surprised to find how hard it was to say good-bye to July Summer. But then, they'd ridden the river together, so to speak, and that often brought people close. "Maybe we'll see each other again . . . in Montana." He shrugged. "You never know."

She lifted her eyes to his, nodded dubiously. "I reckon," she said. "You never know . . ."

"Be seein' you, Miss July Summer."

She tried a smile. "Be seein' you, Cuno Massey. I hope you find Anderson and Spoon and make 'em pay . . . without gettin' yourself shot."

Cuno nodded and offered a small smile of his own. "You take care, too, July."

He gave the tough-eyed girl one last glance, then headed for the livery barn, where he bedded down in Renegade's stall.

He woke several times in the night to gunfire. Unaccustomed to rough towns like Cheyenne, he grabbed his Colt automatically, then holstered it when he realized it was probably just more of the same kind of trouble he'd witnessed earlier, and had nothing to do with himself or July.

At dawn he took his breakfast at the Gay Lady Café, spending his last few coins on eggs, potatoes, a pork chop, and piping hot coffee. Somewhere along the line, he was going to have to earn money for ammunition and other trail supplies.

He still had two boxes of the .45 shells Charlie Dodge had given him. Other provisions would have to wait until after he'd found Anderson and Spoon.

Outside, he stretched and yawned on the boardwalk, then tightened Renegade's saddle cinch. As he adjusted the strap on one of the saddlebags, he heard footsteps approaching on the boardwalk, and saw July heading toward him. She appeared freshly bathed, her black hair brushed to a rich sheen.

Her ragged dress was gone. Instead, she wore a pair of boy's denim breeches and a plaid flannel shirt. On her feet she wore low-heeled boots that appeared scuffed but sturdy. She looked pretty, in a tomboyish way, but that didn't make her appearance any more welcome. He could tell by the firm set of her jaw that she intended to lecture him again about Indians.

"Damn," he groused under his breath.

"Don't curse me, Cuno Massey," she said, stopping on the boardwalk before him and crossing her arms over her breasts, like a reprimanding schoolmarm. Her freshly washed black hair winged out in the morning breeze. "I've come to make one last attempt at saving your fool, stubborn hide."

"Well, don't bother," Cuno said, annoyed. "I told you, I—"

"There he is," he heard a woman say on the other side of the street. Turning, he saw the girl he'd met last night standing under the awning before a saddle shop. Two men were at her side.

"Mr. Massey!" Daphne yelled, waving. "That's him there," she told the men.

Twirling a frilly yellow parasol, she started across the street, the ruffled pleats of her long skirt dancing about her legs. Her hair shone golden as ripe wheat, and her elegantly chiseled face owned the texture and color of cream.

Cuno was so taken by the girl's beauty that he gave the two men with her only a cursory glance before the short one dressed in a suit with a crisp bowler said, "You're Cuno Massey?" He spoke quickly and forcefully, puffing a stogie the size of a dynamite stick. His words had the edge of an accusation.

Tearing his eyes from Daphne, Cuno said, "That's right."

Curious, he returned his eyes to the blond girl. She was smiling brashly and twirling the parasol in her gloved hands.

"Cuno, meet my father, Thomas Creigh," she said. Turning to the tall gent in buckskins: "And this is our wagon boss, Amos Church."

Church nodded curtly, giving Cuno the twice-over with his deep-sunk, piercing blue eyes. He appeared Creigh's age—mid-fifties—and he had a thick, white scar on his right cheek, along his jawline, with a little curlicue on the side. It resembled dried wax, but Cuno, having seen such scars before, figured it was the result of an Indian arrow.

Daphne turned to July, her smile losing a tad of its luster. "And this is . . .?"

"This is July Summer," he said, noting the vague discomfort in July's eyes as she glanced from him to Daphne. "We met on the trail from Julesburg."

"Pleased to meet you, Miss Summer," Creigh said as he glanced at the girl briefly. "Now, Mr. Massey," he said with a sigh, biting the stogie and rising on the balls of his feet. "You came around looking for a job last night."

"That's right, sir, I did." Cuno's hope rose.

"One of my drivers was killed in town last night. Shot behind a saloon."

"I'm sorry to hear that, sir."

"Yes, yes," Creigh said quickly, impatiently, "very tragic, very tragic. So, as you might expect, I'm looking for a driver to replace him."

Cuno glanced at July, then returned his eager gaze to the short, stout Creigh, who eyed him severely. "I'm your man, Mr. Creigh."

"You say you've driven Murphys before?"

"Yes, sir. Since I was—"

"With how many yokes of oxen?"

"Well, we mainly used mules, but—"

Creigh shook his head. "No mules here, Mr. Massey. Ox teams. A minimum of four yoke to a freight wagon."

That was a lot of pulling power. Cuno asked, "What are you haulin', anyway, Mr. Creigh?"

"Boilers and quartz-stamping machinery," Creigh replied. "Twenty-six wagons' worth. I'm heading for Alder Gulch. As of last night, I have twenty-five whackers and five scouts, all under the leadership of Mr. Church. We'll be pulling out at noon in the company of two other outfits. What do you say, Mr. Massey? You're a big, strapping lad. Can you manage four yoke of oxen? The pay is one hundred fifty dollars, half up front, the other half when we reach Virginia City."

Creigh turned the stogie in his mouth, drawing on it and smiling around it shrewdly at the width of the lad's shoulders—a teamster's shoulders.

Cuno had opened his mouth to reply when July elbowed him. He glanced at her, saw the cheeky expression on her face. Turning back to Creigh, he cleared his throat. "I'll take the job, sir, if you think you can find work for Miss Summer here. I'd hate to leave her here by herself."

He saw Daphne glance at July and slightly cant her head critically under the parasol.

"Together, are you?" Creigh said, giving July the up-and-down with his impenetrable brown eyes. "Amos, you think we can find work for this girl?"

Church pursed his lips and nodded dully. "I reckon the cook could find somethin' for her to do."

"All right, I'll offer you twenty-five dollars, Miss Summer. That's more than what an Indian girl could make around here—at a respectable job, that is. Take it or leave it."

"I'll take it," July said, ignoring Creigh's offhand insult.

Taking charge, Amos Church said, "Both of you be at the team in half an hour, and we'll get you set up."

With that, he and Creigh turned and started back across the street. Daphne stood there, smiling her peculiar, brassy smile, as if waiting for something.

"I guess you put in a good word for me," Cuno told her. "Thanks."

"Oh, it was nothing at all, Mr. Massey. Father and Amos needed a good driver, and I sensed you could drive just about anything you pleased." Her eyes turned smoky. "I'll see you later."

Without so much as a glance at July, she wheeled gracefully and followed her father and Church across the street. Cuno saw more than one man's head turn to watch the lovely girl's slender fanny sashay within her dress.

July cleared her throat.

Cuno turned to her with a pleased smile. "Well, I reckon we're headin' north."

"I reckon," July said. "And headin' into a whole lot of trouble."

"With an outfit that size, we shouldn't have much trouble with the Indians."

"I'm not talkin' about Indian trouble," July said, shuttling her gaze to the blond Daphne Creigh retreating along the opposite boardwalk, leaving a bevy of head-turning men in her wake.

"You mean Daphne?"

July shook her head fatefully. "Anyone in their right mind can see the kind of trouble that girl courts. But then, you aren't in your right mind. I saw the way you were lookin' at her."

"I have to admit," Cuno said with a sigh. "That girl strikes a pretty pose."

July rolled her eyes. "I have a feelin' it's going to be a long trip to Montana. What is it with men and titties?" She gave a caustic chuff. "Well, I'll go say good-bye to Mrs. Haugen and get my stuff. Meet you back here in a half hour?"

"What's that?" Cuno said, distractedly watching Daphne disappear around a corner. "Oh, yeah," he said with a jerk, coming around. "Sounds good."

With another eye roll and head shake, July wheeled off toward the bakery. "Trouble," she muttered. "Just plain trouble . . ."

17

"INJUNS!"

The cry reached Rolf Anderson on the wind. The hider swung a look northeast, where a lone horseback rider was galloping, bent low over his horse's head, the brim of his Stetson basted against his forehead. Behind the man, about a hundred yards out, more riders appeared, galloping out from behind a low, rocky butte.

They, too, were riding hell-bent-for-leather, screaming like devils.

"Injuns!" the scout exclaimed again as he approached the wagon train.

Anderson hipped around in his saddle, yelling to the drivers, "Corral the wagons! Pronto! Corral the goddamn wagons!"

As Anderson drew his Henry rifle from his saddle sheath, he couldn't help smiling. He hadn't killed an Indian in months, and he'd been itching for the chance. Killing white men was one thing, but killing an Indian—especially one on the warpath—now, that was something that tickled your loins but good, made all the trail boredom and toothless whores worth the time and effort.

He gigged his buckskin past the oncoming scout and peered through the rider's dust at the fast-approaching Indians. It was a party of about fourteen, Anderson quickly counted, and they were all painted for war, their long hair and braids dancing about their shoulders. Several wielded lances while several others nocked arrows.

A reflection off something metal in one of the savage's hands bespoke a rifle. It was never good to see an Indian with a rifle, but Anderson only vaguely matched the hazard to the fact that he'd been selling fireams to Indians for years.

Lifting the Henry to his shoulder, he squeezed off several quick shots before the Indians' arrows started falling perilously close. Reining the buckskin around, he galloped over to the circling wagons, lifting his neckerchief against the dust churned by the hundred or so mules and oxen. There were several emigrant teams in the Wehring party—about thirty wagons total—and he could hear women screaming and babies crying.

The drivers and scouts yelled to each other, cajoling and warning, ducking now as the arrows reached the train spread out over half a mile. A few of the scouts closest to Anderson had dismounted and were laying down some fire. One man bucked back off his knees and fell with an arrow through his heart. The other scouts got up and scrambled toward the wagons corralling in scattered clumps.

Anderson grinned. "Dirty red niggers! This is a handful here, sure enough!" he yelled to Sammy Spoon, who had dismounted and was now taking cover behind one of the wagons.

Spoon threw his head back and gave a loud, boisterous war cry—as eerie and hair-raising as anything the full-bloods were sending up. Then, propping the barrel on a wagon wheel, he started levering his Winchester while

Anderson galloped his buckskin behind Wehring's Conestoga.

Sidling up to the wagon, he jerked Rudolph Wehring from the driver's box. Cursing, Wehring hit the ground and stumbled to his knees. Anderson climbed onto the driver's seat, shouting to Wehring, "Steady the goddamn mules!"

Standing on the driver's box, Anderson started jacking shells at the Indians—Hunkpapas, he could tell from their face paint and horse gear—who rode in from the northeast at an angle. Screaming, hooves thundering, they dashed in close enough to loose a few arrows and dodge a few bullets, then circled back out and back.

There were five wagon companies in Anderson's immediate party, spread at least a hundred yards apart to avoid eating each other's dust; it was Anderson's group that took the brunt of the attack. When the hide hunter had emptied his sixteen-shot repeater, he swung it out like a club, dismounting a Hunkpapa who had stormed in close, hoping to pierce Anderson with an arrow from a few feet away. As the fallen warrior's horse galloped off, wildly shaking its head, Anderson jumped off the wagon, ran to the Indian as the young renegade was climbing to his feet, shaking the stars from his eyes.

"Die, you son of a red bitch!" Anderson raged.

As the invective rose from his widespread lips, the red-bearded hider ran his bowie knife under the warrior's jaw, opening a gash that immediately geysered liver-colored blood.

Dropping the writhing brave, he pivoted in time to confront another horseman galloping toward him. The Indian loosed an arrow that sang two inches right of Anderson's left ear. Not so much as flinching, the hider unsheathed his revolver and blew the savage over his horse's rear.

Anderson jerked around in a half crouch, ready for another onslaught. No more Indians were in shooting range, however. In fact, the Indians—what few remained on their horses—seemed to be breaking off the attack, heading back the same way they'd come. They left seven dead attackers in the sifting dust behind them.

"Ay-eeeeeeee!" cried Sammy Spoon, still crouched behind the wagon wheel, the barrel of his Winchester smoking. "Now, that was some fightin', Rolf!"

Anderson laughed as he gazed around at the bloody, crumpled bodies. He holstered his revolver and was mopping sweat and dust from his forehead when Rudolph Wehring, stepping out hesitantly from his wagon, said, "I think I see one moving!"

"Don't kill him," Spoon yelled to Anderson and the other four drivers within hearing.

His rifle in his hand, the half-breed ran out to the Indian, who was slowly climbing to his knees. Spoon clubbed the brave back down with his rifle butt and yelled, "Thunder, bring your women up here!"

One of the scouts, a Crow named Spring Thunder, remounted his brule war horse and galloped back to a cluster of stalled wagons about fifty yards behind. Soon, the scout returned with a rickety farm wagon clattering behind him. An Indian woman, who looked a hard forty years old at least, was driving. An Indian girl sat beside her. Both were dressed in bright calico, raven hair pulled back in buns.

"Who in the hell are they?" Anderson asked Spoon.

The other wagons were coming on from behind. The babies and a woman were still crying. The men's voices rose with excitement.

"Thunder's woman and daughter." Spoon smiled, showing all his teeth, black eyes dancing. "They'll make short work of this Hunk-poppy here."

The scout called Thunder spoke in Crow to the two women, who smiled as they cast their evil leers on the Sioux warrior kneeling before Spoon, blood running from a bullet graze on his temple. The wife slammed the brake home and climbed down from the seat, the girl close behind.

The two spoke excitedly as the woman opened a box behind the seat and removed a hide bundle from which the handles of skinning knives protruded.

"Oh, Lordy," Anderson said, chuckling and shaking his head.

"I don't get it," Rudolph Wehring said, glancing curiously from Spoon to Anderson. "What are they going to do?"

The Hunkpapa's eyes had found the women now. They shone bright with fear. He spat a stream of words, then tried gaining his feet. Spoon clubbed him back down, then knelt to hold the brave's arms behind his back.

"They're gonna make it so's the man's ancestors won't be able to recognize him in the next world," Anderson said. "The Crows and the Sioux—they never did get along."

The other wagons pulled up and formed a ragged circle around the fallen brave.

As the women went to work on the Indian struggling in Spoon's arms, the wagon drivers gathered around to see what was happening. It didn't take long for word to spread to the most outlying wagons, and for the children to come running against the protests of the women.

"What in the hell is going on here?" Martin Wehring asked angrily as he pushed through the crowd. Seeing for himself, and hearing the animal-like wails, he turned to Anderson, as though the hider were responsible.

"Jesus Christ! Why don't you make them stop?"

Anderson shrugged. "Stop? Hell, they're just gettin' started!" Watching the Crow women working deftly with their knives, their hands and arms awash in blood, he said through a chuckle, "Oh, ladies, not his . . . his . . . oh, *mercy*—that has to *hurt!*"

Long before the Crow women were done with the Hunkpapa brave, most of the wagons had drifted off to form a night corral along a creek curving through the low hills in the west. The grisly exhibition was even too much for the scouts to take, and they too had ridden off to set up a camp and to start cook fires.

That went for Anderson and Spoon, as well. They were sitting around their own fire as the sun sank, tipping back a bottle, when they saw the rickety farm wagon, captained by the two Crow women, climb a knoll above the creek.

Dragging behind the wagon was the Hunkpapa's body. Or what was left of it. Through his spy glass, Anderson saw only a headless torso so caked in blood it could have been a red blanket bouncing and fishtailing behind the wagon's clattering wheels.

"Nope," the red-bearded hider said with a fateful sigh. "You never wanna cross an Injun gal."

"'Specially a Crow," Sammy Spoon said through a grin, lifting the bottle to his lips.

"Where in the hell you s'pose they're headed, anyway?" Anderson asked the half-breed as he watched the wagon.

Spoon brought the bottle down and filled his red clay pipe with *shongsasha*, a potent Indian concoction that, combined with the whiskey, often made him as wild as a Texas twister. "They're gonna leave him up there in the buttes," he said with an oily smile, "as a little message to his people. Diddle with us and lose your oysters . . ."

"Now, why didn't I think of that?" Anderson said, belching whiskey and raising the bottle.

A while later, the hider climbed to his feet and clapped his hat on his head. A little wobbly after the whiskey, he walked away from the fire, disappearing in the darkness that had come down like a black glove.

"Where you goin'?" Spoon asked him. The half-breed was nibbling a rabbit he'd shot and cooked over the fire.

"None o' your friggin' business, Samuel," Anderson growled.

Holding a hunk of charred rabbit to his mouth, Spoon smiled knowingly.

Anderson moved between the wagons and pushed through the stock corralled within the circle—oxen, mules, horses, and cattle. There were half a dozen fires within the circle, around which the men and women from the train had gathered to talk and eat, the giddiness in their voices owing to the fact that the Indian attack hadn't been more severe. Only two whites had been wounded.

Three wagoners were greasing the wheel hub of a Murphy, laughing uneasily as they recounted the Crow women's treatment of the Hunkpapa brave. Several children ran around the wagons, flinging spindly lances whittled from cottonwood branches.

Anderson ignored all this. He cast his gaze searchingly among the wagons humping up darkly around him, white canvas stretched over ash bows. Finding the one he was looking for, he stepped up to the open tailgate upon which lantern light laid a wan sheen from within.

He peered into the wagon, his eyes narrowing. A woman lay inside, in a narrow alley amid the household goods heaped to the bows. A rusty railroad lantern and a small picture of the crucified Jesus stood on a footstool beside her. Her head propped on pillows, she read a small, leather-bound Bible.

Her thin, colorless lips moved as she read. She scowled, as though making an effort. She was pretty, but not as pretty as she'd been five years ago, when she'd been selling herself in Coffeeville, Kansas. Her face was pale and drawn, and there were lines around her eyes.

Nevertheless, Anderson remembered her wiles. He bet she still had a few tricks up her skirts . . .

"Psst!" he called, grinning.

She lowered the Bible instantly and peered over the open tailgate, wide-eyed, her face bleaching with alarm.

"Who's there?" Lilly Larsen cried, obviously still stricken by the Indian attack.

"Bonito Senorito."

Her expression changing little, she said with an urgent rasp, "Rolf! Go away! I can't be seen with you!"

"Bullshit," the hider groused as he climbed onto the tail-gate and crawled into the wagon, smiling lasciviously.

"Rolf! Please! I'm married now. If Jerry ever found out . . ."

Anderson laughed. "You mean ole Jerry don't know you were a soiled dove before he met you?" Jerry was the farmer she'd married and with whom she was traveling to the Gallatin Basin in Montana.

"No, he doesn't, and if he ever found out—"

Anderson crawled up beside the woman, running his eyes over the thin sheet covering her body on this warm summer night. "Where is Jerry, anyway?"

"He's playing cards with some of the other farmers in our group. But he could be back anytime, so you have to go. Please, Rolf, go. *Now!*"

He ignored her feeble attempts at pushing him away. Lifting the sheet and peering beneath it, he said, "Ah hell, if Jerry does like he's been doin' since we left Cheyenne, he'll be up drinkin' an' playin' cards till midnight. That means we got us a couple hours, Lilly, my flower. Just you and me."

He nuzzled her neck. She struggled against him.

"If you don't leave this second, I'm gonna scream! I mean it!"

His face mottling with sudden anger, Anderson grabbed his bowie from the beaded sheath on his belt. "Oh, no you ain't, Lilly, my flower," he spat through clenched jaws, his blue eyes aflame, the cords standing out on his freckled neck. He grabbed the back of her head with his right hand and laid the bowie's razor knife blade to her throat. "Cause if you do, I'll cut your goddamn head off!"

The girl fell silent, stiffened, the muscles in her face going slack. She rolled her fearful eyes at Anderson, whose own eyes burned into her like those of an enraged demon.

"Understand?" he said, his voice hard.

Stiffly, she swallowed, nodded.

"Good," he said, and slammed her down.

18

"DOIN' ALL RIGHT up there, girl?"
"Doin' all right, Mr. Stamper," July Summer called back over her shoulder to the cook reclining in the chuck wagon's box. July drove the two-mule team, a wide straw hat keeping the sun from her eyes.
"Handlin' the mules all right?" the cook asked.
"Handlin' the mules all right."
"No sign of Injun trouble?"
"No sign of Injun trouble."
Stamper had made the same inquiries five times in the past two hours. July wondered why, if he was so darn worried about her competence as a driver, he didn't just take over the driving himself, instead of dozing most of the day in the hollow he'd carved out of the foodstuffs behind the chuck box.
But then, she knew the reason. All three nights since they'd left Cheyenne, as soon as his cooking duties were completed and July was busy washing dishes and keeping the coffee hot, Stamper had started tipping back his homemade applejack and didn't stop until he'd emptied

the bottle. He hadn't turned into his bedroll beneath the wagon until long after midnight, and when he woke the next morning he looked as though someone had drained all the blood from his veins, leaving a liberal dollop in each eye.

"Well, let me know if you see any Injuns, for godsakes," the cook said. In his prime, he'd fought Indians in the army, and was more jittery out here than even July was. "I'm gonna sleep a little longer."

"You got it, Mr. Stamper." She had a mind, just to alleviate the boredom, to wait until Stamper was good asleep, and then cry, "Injuns!" She wouldn't do it, however. The man might have a stroke, and then July would do not only all the driving but all the cooking, as well.

With a devilish snicker at the thought, she returned her gaze to the trail over the mules' ears, lifting the bandanna over her mouth and nose against the dust kicked up by the long stream of wagons ahead of her, and snugged the floppy-brimmed hat on her head.

The hat and her trail clothes had been a gift of the woman she'd cooked for at the bakery in Cheyenne. They'd belonged to her son, a cowpuncher who'd died in a stampede. July had been grateful for the gift, but now she found herself envying the prissy little dresses Daphne Creigh wore—a fresh one every day, complete with matching parasol and hair ribbon. Maybe if July wore something like that, she'd attract Cuno's notice the way Daphne did.

Not that that would mean so much, or that July couldn't get along without it, but . . . oh, hell. She might as well admit it to herself. She was head over heels in love with Cuno Massey, and every time he made eyes at Daphne Creigh, July's heart wilted like a tomato plant set out too soon in the spring.

But she had a hard time seeing herself in such silly, frilly garb, no matter whose attention it attracted. If Cuno didn't like her for who she was—tomboy half-breed and all—then she'd just have to forget about him.

Soon the wagon boss, Amos Church, rode his black gelding around to all the wagons, informing each driver that they would be stopping on the banks of Antelope Creek for the night. The creek appeared a few minutes later, in a line of trees at the base of a low jog of silvery hills. When July had stopped the wagon and set the brake, she saw Cuno turn away from his own wagon—an enormous Murphy freighter with iron wheels as tall as Cuno and pulled by three yoke of long-horned oxen burly as buffalo. Cuno winced against the west-angling sun and slapped his hat against his thigh—a new but dusty cream slouch hat for which he'd traded one of the outriders a Barlow knife.

July's heart warmed when she saw him moving this way, donning his Western hat and adjusting his gunbelt on his lean hips. "Well, that wasn't a bad pull," he said, conversationally. "How's everything goin' over here?"

"Just fine," July said coolly. It didn't pay to sound too eager around a boy you were fond of. Indifference was always best.

"We must have made a good twenty-five miles," Cuno said, helping July down from the wagon.

"Must have," she said casually. "No sign of any other trains, though."

Cuno knew she was referring to Anderson's train. "No, but we're making better time than he is. That's what the scouts are saying, judging from the tracks of his outfit. That means we're probably moving faster. It might take a couple weeks, but we'll catch up to him, probably well before we hit Montana. Well, if you don't need help with anything, I best tend to my team."

He started turning away when he heard his name called.

Looking over the sweat-shiny backs of the two mules hitched to the chuck wagon, Cuno saw Daphne standing by her Dearborn. "Cuno, could you help me fetch some water when you get a chance?"

Flushing, Cuno glanced at July, who favored him with a mocking, cockeyed expression. To Daphne, he said, "Be over soon as I've unhitched my team."

"You'd think the little prairie rose could fetch her own water," July said with a caustic grunt, turning abruptly away to wake the cook, still asleep in the chuck wagon's box.

"Her pa won't let her go off alone," Cuno explained to July's retreating back.

It was a weak explanation, he knew. The girl simply liked giving orders and being doted on, and Cuno didn't like the fact that her heavenly beauty compelled him to make a fool out of himself. Wheeling with annoyance, he headed for his ox team, which he unhitched, watered, and turned loose in the big open area surrounded by the wagons. Then he walked amid the pungent tar buckets and wagon jacks and the cook fires, over which the cooks from each freight team prepared their mulligans and fried their game in long-handled iron skillets.

He avoided July's gaze as she sliced potatoes in a pot, and stopped at Daphne's Dearborn. The wagon, with its fine spruce top and running gear of high-quality Wisconsin oak, looked ridiculously small and refined amid the burly freight rigs.

He called the girl's name at the wagon's rear flap, and Daphne stuck her blond head out, smiling and holding a book. "Oh, you are a dear. Father refuses to let me walk down to the creek alone, and he's off with Amos."

"That's all right," Cuno said, feeling like a rube but enjoying the way the girl's lustrous hair curved over her shoulders and licked at the low neckline of her dress.

Daphne glanced at July working stiffly at her chore, intentionally not looking this direction.

"Quite a little workhorse, isn't she?" Daphne said as she entwined her left arm in Cuno's right.

He retrieved the wooden water bucket hanging beneath the wagon's frame, and began leading the fashionable girl toward the creek. As he walked he nodded greetings to the other teamsters gathered around their wagons to talk, smoke, drink coffee, and inspect their wheel hubs and axles. Cuno had come to know several of them well. They were a burly, rowdy bunch, but they were good men, and after dark, when the endless stream of chores had been finished, he often joined a cribbage or poker game played for matchsticks.

"She's a good worker, that's for sure," Cuno said, meaning July. "She pulls her own weight and about half of Stamper's."

"Mr. Massey, are you saying I don't pull mine?" Daphne turned to him with a mock-hurt expression, frowning her gray-green eyes and pouting her cherry lips.

He returned her gaze, baffled by this puzzling girl, but before he could say anything, Daphne laughed her high laugh, canting her head toward his arm. "Oh, don't worry. I know I don't pull my own weight, but why should I have to? Father has enough money and men to pull it for me. Besides, someday I will give it back to all of you with a wonderful book about my travels."

"You're gonna write a book?"

"Indeed, I am."

"Like the one you have in your hand there?"

She lifted the book as if surprised to find she'd held onto it. "Oh, no," she said. "This is *Jane Eyre* by Mr. Currer Bell, who, I've heard via one of my teachers at finishing school, is none other than a young English minister's daughter. It's a wonderful novel—my favorite, in fact—but my first book will be about my own trials and triumphs in the West."

"Well, let's hope we don't have many trials," Cuno said as they walked through the tall grass along the creek, startling a coyote from the brush across the water.

"Yes, but many triumphs," she said in an intimate voice, placing her other hand on his arm as well, and canting her head against his shoulder. "I fully intend to include you, Mr. Massey."

"Me?" he said with a laugh, turning to her.

"Of course," she said, regarding him boldly, running her brassy eyes across his chest. "How could I not include such a fine specimen of an earthy young man as yourself? A young man who has, quite literally, stolen . . ."

There was a rustle of brush behind them, the rattle of hurried footsteps. Cuno swung around in time to see one of the freighters rushing toward him—a young man Cuno's age named Jimmy Bigelow, his face pinched in anger.

"Get the hell away from her, Massey—you hear?" Bigelow gave Cuno a vicious shove. Unprepared, Cuno stumbled back several steps.

"Jimmy!" Daphne cried. "What do you think—?"

Bigelow faced Cuno as he spat, "I know what he's up to, Miss Daphne, and don't you worry. I ain't gonna let him do it!"

"Do what?" Daphne asked. "He hasn't done anything."

"I know his kind. He's tryin' to come between us. Has been ever since we left Cheyenne."

Angered by the attack, Cuno shot back, "Make your fight or get scarce, Bigelow. I'm tired of your lip-flappin', and you won't shove me again unless you want your tail jerked."

"Oh yeah?" Bigelow cried. He was slender and quick-eyed, with dirty chestnut hair falling to his shoulders. "How do you take to having your lousy block knocked off?"

With that he swung a haymaker. Cuno easily ducked

under it and came up with two quick jabs to Bigelow's solar plexus, followed up with a stout right cross to Bigelow's chin. Bigelow went sprawling over a deadfall log, cursing.

"Hey, break it up over there!" It was the wagon master, Amos Church, running in from the south.

Cuno stood with his feet spread and fists raised. Bigelow was climbing to his feet and looking ready to swing another punch when Church ran between them.

"Hold on here!" Church ordered. "Break it up. What the hell's got your horns in a twist, anyways?"

Neither Bigelow nor Cuno said anything. They stood regarding each other angrily, fists raised, but the gray-bearded, buckskin-clad Church held his ground.

"Speak up or I'll have you both bullwhipped. I don't allow fightin' in my camp, damn your hides!"

"Just a little misunderstandin'," Cuno said, wanting to keep this between him and the other freighter. "Ain't that right, Jimmy?"

"Yeah," Bigelow said tightly, his angry eyes glued to Cuno. "Just a little misunderstanding's all, Mr. Church."

Church regarded Daphne shrewdly. "It wouldn't have anything to do with Miss Creigh now, would it?"

Daphne looked down, at once sheepish and coy. Cuno would have sworn she was enjoying the display.

"I thought so," the wagon master said with a fateful sigh. "Well, boys, like I said before, I don't allow fights between my drivers—over women or anything else. It happens again, you'll both take a bullwhippin'. That clear?"

"Clear as rain to me, Mr. Church," Cuno said.

"Me, too," Bigelow agreed, though his eyes made it a lie.

Church ridged his gray brows at Cuno. "Massey, you turned out to be a right capable driver, but don't make me regret hirin' you on." To Daphne he said, "Miss, maybe you better walk back to camp with me. You two split up right here and now. Skedaddle back to your wagons. Don't let me catch you within a hog toss of each other again."

"Of course, Mr. Church," Daphne said innocently. She swung a coy, parting glance at Cuno, then took the wagon master's arm as she walked with the tall gent through the brush.

"I'll carry your water to your wagon, Miss Daphne," Bigelow called to her, truckling, and grabbed the bucket. He filled the bucket in the creek, then turned to Cuno.

His voice low but menacing, he said, "You stay away from that girl, you hear? She's mine. Been mine since Nebraska City, and I won't have you buttin' in."

"Oh?" Cuno said plainly. "That's funny—she didn't mention anything about you to me, Jimmy."

Bigelow jutted a finger at him warningly. "Just stay away, Massey. I have friends." He grinned without humor and swung around and, water bucket sloshing, trailed Church and Daphne back toward the camp. Several other teamsters had come down to see what all the commotion was about, and, satisfied the trouble was over, they turned and went back to their wagons and cook fires. Several of the men were grinning, some murmuring and shaking their heads.

Cuno lingered at the creek, feeling like an idiot. Only his fourth night on the job, and already he was fighting over a girl. He deserved that bullwhipping Amos Church had threatened. He didn't want to appear to be kowtowing to Jimmy Bigelow, but he decided to give Daphne Creigh a little wider berth. That should make July happy, anyway.

Later that night, he played poker with several other freighters, on a folding table one of the men had packed for just that purpose. He was given some good-natured ribbing for his scuffle with Bigelow.

"You stay clear of that girl," Calvin Burdine said around the quirly in his mouth. "She's trouble."

"What kind of trouble?" Cuno said, trying to fill in a straight.

"Just take it from me," Burdine said, "she's trouble, and leave it at that."

"Ah, he just wants a piece of her himself," Jeb Foster said, elbowing Burdine in the ribs. "He's been freightin' so long, he sees a pretty little redhead and he starts feelin' eighteen again!" Foster chuckled and hacked phlegm from his throat.

Ignoring the burly Foster, Burdine crinkled his coyote eyes at Cuno, his face looking even more leathery than natural in the umber light of the nearby cook fire, near which one of the scouts strummed an out-of-tune guitar. The night was quiet and the stars had come down. Distant snores drifted on the breeze.

"Don't worry," Cuno told the old-timer. "I intend to."

"That's good, 'cause that Jimmy Bigelow ain't any less trouble than she is. And neither are his friends."

"Oh?" Cuno said. "Who're his friends?"

"A couple drivers with that outfit from Kansas City, parked over yonder. That Cajun named LeBoix and that scrawny redhead named Tangen. They're all bad. In fact, there's paper on 'em, I heard."

Cuno sucked his quirly and glanced at Burdine. "They're wanted?"

"That's just a rumor," Foster told Cuno, leaning across the table with a conspiratorial air. "I wouldn't doubt it if ole Burdine here started it himself."

"The hell!" Burdine rasped. "There's paper on those owlhoots, sure enough." He sat back and scrutinized his cards, holding them out from his farsighted gaze. "Leastways, I know I'd steer clear of them and the girl. Whatever you do, don't say I didn't warn you, Cuno me boy."

A few minutes later, Amos Church strolled by and ordered the fire out and for them all to go to bed. As Cuno headed for his bedroll, which he'd spread beneath his wagon, he saw a figure in the darkness. He paused, dropping a hand to the polished butt of his Colt.

Then he saw the silvery starlight glistening on red-gold hair.

"Daphne?"

19

DAPHNE EXTENDED HER hand. Reluctantly, self-consciously glancing around to make sure they were alone, he took her hand in his.

"I wanted to apologize for that Bigelow boy's behavior," she whispered above the snores of a wagoner beneath a nearby Murphy. "I don't know why he thinks I'm his property. Why, I've hardly said more than two words to the boy!"

"That's all right," Cuno said. "I reckon he fancies you." He smiled in spite of himself, noticing how her sleek wrapper molded to her womanly curves. "Can't really blame him."

She offered a pleased smile and squeezed his hand meaningfully. "Come along, sir," she whispered seductively.

"Where to?"

"The Dearborn."

"What?"

"Sh. Come." She tugged his hand.

He resisted, remembering his decision to give her a wide berth. She may have been beautiful, but she was trouble. "No. It ain't right, I . . ."

She turned to him, moved to him, rose up on her toes, and planted a soft, moist kiss on his lips, gently nibbling the lower one as she pulled away with a flirtatious little smile. "Oh, come on," she pleaded in a little girl's voice. "Just for a little while?"

The kiss was like a tonic. In a moment, wordlessly, he felt himself being pulled along to her wagon. She climbed the back ladder through the tie flap, turned, and beckoned him inside. He hesitated, glancing at her father's wagon looming nearby, the domed canvas showing pale against the star-filled sky.

Feeling the pull of this beguiling waif even when she didn't have a physical hold on his hand, he placed both hands on the ladder and climbed. He felt giddy, his feet weightless.

Inside, she gestured in the light of a flickering lantern, and he sat on her bed, which was surrounded by books, tablets, and note cards. Ink bottles lay everywhere, as did pens and nibs and chewed pencils. Lacy underwear and the pale blue dress she'd worn earlier hung from a line strung from a corner in the wagon's front to the opposite one in the back. More clothes spilled from a dresser and from open steamer trunks.

"You travel well," he heard himself remark with humor as he raked his gaze around.

"A girl must be prepared for anything, mustn't she?" Daphne said, sitting close enough beside him that their hips touched.

He turned to her, finding her a distraction he could not ignore. She looked up at him now, her eyes shining, a lusty smile spreading her mouth. "Cuno, I don't mean to be bold, but I don't see any reason to beat around the bush. If you want, I can make you feel . . . good." She ran her pink tongue across her red lips, her eyes fairly smoking. ". . . Like a man."

His mouth opened but his voice had left him. Finally, it

returned. Clearing his throat, he said, "We haven't known each other long, Miss Daphne," Cuno managed to say, keeping his voice as low as he could and still be heard. The last thing he wanted was to wake her father. He wasn't sure how Mr. McCreigh would feel about finding one of his drivers in his daughter's wagon, but he had a feeling he'd probably be bullwhipped and set afoot.

Daphne smiled as she gave her head a single shake. "You're resisting me, Cuno. Why is that? Don't you think I'm pretty?"

"I think you're about the prettiest girl I've ever seen," he managed, glancing at the tent flap through which a few stars could be seen. He wanted to leave, but his muscles would not comply. The memory of Molly Davis's sexual miracles would not let him leave, although he knew he was risking his job and even his chance at finding Anderson and Spoon if he stayed.

She leaned close, whispered in his ear. "Do you want to make love to me?"

He looked at her. His mouth was dry, his tongue swollen. "What I want and what I should do—"

He stopped as she set her hand on the swelling in his pants. A thrill went through him like a lightning bolt. She didn't move her hand, just left it resting there. He could feel the warmth of the hand through his denims.

"Cuno, I do not pretend to be a nice girl. When I see a young man I like, I go after him. Women, you see, have needs just as men do. I know it isn't proper to say so, but I've always said proper could go diddle itself. I see no reason why I should eschew physical pleasure when I know so well how to receive it . . . as well as to give."

She smiled reasonably.

"Maybe we should just cease this nonsense straightaway," she added. Rising, she turned and faced him, stepping between his knees.

She spread her wrapper wide, let it fall down her

shoulders. She wore something sheer and lacy beneath it, with tiny straps clinging to her fragile shoulders. She slid the straps over her shoulders, let them slip slowly down her arms.

Cuno watched the straps' slow descent. When they fell past her elbows, the garment dropped low on her breasts, caught on her pink nipples for a moment, then slid over them and onto the floor. The lamplight danced on the full, firm breasts jutting toward him, only inches away from his face.

"Kiss them," she whispered.

He did, slowly, giving into his young man's passion and need, forgetting about her father and his purpose for being here in the first place. The feel and slightly salty taste of the swollen nipples enflamed him, and he rubbed his cheek against them, until she knelt before him and said quietly, "Take your pants off."

Dizzy with desire, his chest swollen, he stood and kicked out of his boots. He hastily removed his cartridge belt and gun, and set them aside. Then he unbuckled his pants and dropped them over his hips. She knelt before him, staring at him admiringly.

Lifting her eyes to his, she said, "You are going to have a very special place in my book, Mr. Massey."

He swallowed, winced against the sweet pain of his desire. His annoyance with her power over him lingered just beneath the surface of his lust. He rasped, "I don't want no place in no book."

"Have it your way, love," she snickered, wrapping her hand around him. "But you've certainly earned a place in my bed."

Meanwhile, outside, amid the dying fires, sleeping wagoners, and milling livestock in the wagon corral, Jimmy Bigelow made his way toward the Dearborn. Before him he clutched a bouquet of wildflowers, their delicate, bell-shaped blossoms drooping groundward.

Stumbling on a wagon tongue, he moved around Mr. Creigh's Conestoga and approached the Dearborn. He paused, a smile shaping itself across his blocky face, glad to see a lantern on in the Dearborn's box.

He walked a few more steps, and stopped, frowning. The wagon moved slightly, the canvas drawstrings dancing a little, as though in a breeze. But the night was as still as a held breath.

Listening hard, he heard murmuring within.

His frown turning to a scowl and his adrenaline burning in his belly, Bigelow moved around to the wagon's rear. He listened again.

Sure enough, he could hear the muffled but distinct sounds of a woman sighing, as though in the throes of passion. A man cleared his throat, swallowed, sucked air through his teeth.

Dropping the flowers, Bigelow grabbed the ladder and carefully, quietly climbed. Removing his hat, he peered through the small, round opening in the flap. His eyes narrowed and his nostrils flared. His pulse jerked a vein alive in his neck.

He stood there, watching and listening, grinding his teeth. Finally, he moved slowly down the ladder, donned his hat, and stole off in the darkness.

Under his breath, he rasped. "You just dug your own grave, Massey, you son of a bitch!"

The next afternoon, the Wehring team stopped near a spring to replace a cracked wagon wheel. There were about seven wagons in the team, with the rest of the outfit either ahead or behind. The country was scarred with rocky ravines, and more than one of the wagons had been delayed by cracked wheels or axles or by trouble with one of the oxen or mules.

While the Wehring brothers helped the driver of the damaged wagon, Anderson and Spoon sat down against a cottonwood tree, crossed their arms over their chests, and pulled their hat brims over their eyes for a snooze.

Meanwhile, Jerry Larsen checked the off rear hoof of one of his mules.

"Shoe's on good and the hoof's trimmed good," he told his wife, sitting in the driver's box. "Mighta just picked up a stone. Worked it out now, though."

He dropped the mule's hock and turned to his wife, who had not spoken to him all day.

"What's the matter up there?" Larsen asked harshly, tired of Lilly's sullen demeanor. "Cat got your damn tongue?"

She was seldom this quiet. If anything, Larson's wife of eight months was overly talkative. Why, when she got going, she could talk the hinges off a barn door. And she wasn't no Lutheran's minister's wife in bed, either! At least, she hadn't been before last night. When Larson had crawled into the wagon after his card game and had placed a hand on her shoulder, she went tight as a wagon jack and turned away.

He'd figured it was just her time, but that didn't explain her silence today.

Her silence continued now as she stared off to the west, over the wagon the Wehrings were working on and beyond the Wehring children playing kickball on the other side of the spring.

Beside himself, Jerry Larsen moved toward the wagon and thrust an angry finger at his wife. "Goddammit, Lilly. What on God's green earth is the matter with you? By God . . . hey, what's that on your lip?"

Larsen squinted and canted his head to see the left side

of Lilly's face—the side she seemed to be trying to hide from him. He hadn't noticed the cut on her lip, for she'd been wearing a neckerchief over her mouth as they drove, but he was sure that was what it was, all right. A cut.

"Woman, how did you cut your lip?"

"Jerry, please leave me be." Her voice was small and brittle. He'd never heard it so brittle before.

"Turn and face me, dammit. Listen to me, ye hear?"

She sobbed and slowly turned to him. "Oh, Jerry, please, it's nothing. I just cut myself on a tree branch. Let it go. Please, Jerry."

He moved to the driver's box and stared up at her. She flinched from his view, glanced away, her lower lip trembling. The movement opened the scab slightly, and blood gleamed in the sunlight.

Larsen squinted his eyes. It was no scratch, he could tell. It was a cut like what you'd get if something blunt split your lip. Something blunt, like a knuckle. Someone had hit her. She wouldn't be acting this way if she'd only cut her lip on a tree branch.

A memory occurring to him, his suspicion plucking at him, Larsen stalked around to the back of the wagon. He reappeared at the front a moment later, a small, bone-handled Barlow knife in his hand.

"I found this in the wagon box this morning," Larsen told his wife scoldingly, displaying the knife in his open palm. "I thought you might have found it around the camp, but now I'm startin' to wonder. Lilly, was someone else in the wagon last night?"

Lilly stared at her husband darkly, her eyes fearful, her face pale. She said nothing. Larsen stared back at her, puzzled and angry.

He was about to ask her again where the knife had come from, when, by the tree about twenty-five yards away, Anderson yawned loudly. His and Spoon's ground-hitched horses tore buffalo grass just beyond them. Hearing the yawn, Lilly jumped, startled, and lifted her frightened gaze to the hider, who lounged there with his arms and ankles crossed casually.

Larsen turned to the hider and his half-breed sidekick. When he shuttled his gaze back to Lilly, his eyes were slitted suspiciously. Lilly jerked her gaze away, as if to erase the moment from her mind.

Larsen looked away from her again, turning full around to Anderson who, still dozing, moved his shoulders as he scratched his back on the tree. Slowly, Larsen walked toward the man, staring at him, holding the knife out in his open palm, as though it were an offering.

He paused near Anderson, stood staring down at the snoring hider. Larsen's sparrow chest rose and fell as his breath grew labored. His face was hot, sweat popping out on his forehead. As his mind worked over the connection between the knife and his wife's split lip and silence, an angry red haze formed before his eyes.

He knew Anderson's reputation as a killer, but he wasn't thinking about that now. He didn't care. If the man had done what Larsen thought he'd done to his wife, the man would pay.

He gave Anderson's boot a kick. "Hey," he said.

Anderson gave a little start and a snort, and relaxed again, whistling a snore.

"Hey," Larsen repeated, giving Anderson's boot another kick.

"Wha-wha?" Anderson grunted, blinking his eyes and poking his hat up on his head.

Seeing Larsen standing over him, Anderson frowned curiously. Then he saw the folding knife in the farmer's big, callused hand.

"Oh!" Anderson exclaimed, a surprised smile spreading his red beard as he climbed to his feet. "You found my knife!" He chuckled as he plucked the knife from Larsen's hand and flipped it in the air. "I thought that was gone for good, sure enough. Thanks a heap, Lars."

He clapped the farmer's back, pocketed the knife, and walked north past his and Spoon's grazing horses.

Behind him, Larsen glared at his back, his face red with exasperation, his hairy nostrils contracting and expanding. Finally, he wheeled around and stalked back to his wagon, where his wife sat, regarding him fearfully.

"Jerry, what are you doing?" she called in a tremulous voice as her husband disappeared behind the wagon.

"Jerry!" she called. "Jerry!"

When Larsen didn't say anything, Lilly climbed down from the driver's box. She was running toward the wagon's rear when her husband reappeared, this time clutching a big Patterson Colt revolver to his chest. His eyes were wide and wild.

"Jerry, don't!" Lilly cried, stopping before him, impeding his path.

"Out of my way, woman," Larsen barked, tossing her out of his way with a simple but powerful shove.

"Jerry, he'll kill you!" Lilly sobbed.

She pushed herself off the wagon and ran to her husband, pleading with him to stop and grabbing his arm, trying to turn him around.

"Goddamn ye, woman," he barked again, "stay out of it!" With that, Larsen gave his wife another powerful shove backward. Stumbling over her skirts, Lilly fell beside the wagon, sobbing.

"Dammit, Jerry!" she cried.

Ignoring her cries, Larsen turned stiffly and walked past his mule team, toward Anderson standing off in the sun-dappled, breeze-rattled woods, his back to the wagons. He was relieving himself, Larsen could tell, one hand before him, a twinkling yellow stream appearing between his legs.

Larsen's pace increased as he neared the hider, and he raised the big Colt in both hands.

"Anderson!" His voice boomed through the woods.

The farmer broke into a long-legged, lumbering trot toward the hider. *"I'm gonna kill you, you son of a bitch!"*

With an annoyed look on his face, Anderson turned around, one hand still aiming his dribbling member. "Jerry, what in the hell are you talkin' about? Put that gun down before you hurt yourself."

Fifteen feet from Anderson, Larsen stopped, leveled the heavy revolver, thumbed back the hammer, and canted his head as he peered uncertainly down the quivering barrel.

"Jerry, you fool, put that gun down," Anderson scolded.

"You goddamn pig!" the farmer raged, ignoring the pleas of his wife, still on the ground by the wagon. "I'm gonna kill you!" With that, Larsen pulled the trigger.

The big Colt boomed, smoke and flames geysering from its barrel. Anderson winced as the slug whistled over his left shoulder and plunked into a wagon box behind him, setting the mules to screaming and rearing.

Larsen cursed as the mules sped off with the unattended wagon, and lowered the Patterson to recock it. Before he could level it again, Anderson drew his own Colt in a flash, casually extended it, shook his head with disgust, and blew a neat, black hole through the farmer's forehead, exactly two inches above his nose.

"Jer-ryyy!" Lilly screamed as the farmer's head flew back, his feet clumsily following, stumbling. He took three steps, dropped to his knees, sat there for several seconds, chin up as though looking at the sky for guidance, then fell face forward in the grass.

By this time, the other men, including the Wehrings, were shouting and moving this way. Lilly climbed to her feet and came running. Sobbing, she dropped to her dead husband, crying his name.

Anderson holstered his Colt and turned to Sammy

Spoon, who was still sitting by the tree, arms crossed over his chest. He was grinning, showing all his brown, scraggly teeth.

"Stupid granger," Anderson groused.

While the other men gathered around Larsen and the weeping Lilly, Anderson buttoned his pants and turned toward the runaway wagon disappearing in the distance.

Shaking his head with annoyance, Anderson said, "Now, who in the hell's gonna run those mules down?"

20

CUNO'S COMPANY RATTLED and squawked across the prairie rising gradually to the rumpled apron of the Big Horns. They were a scattered collection of Conestogas, army ambulances, Murphys, and rudimentary farm wagons, composed of five different outfits, all thrown in together for safety against the red man.

Cattle bawled, mules brayed, the oxen plodded in their hang-headed fashion. Amos Church rode back and forth along the serpentine line, sometimes strung out for over a mile, encouraging the drivers and scouting for Indians.

Nearly every day, somewhere along the trail, the train witnessed evidence of recent disaster—graves marked by poorly chiseled stones or crosses, burned-out hulks of wagons, bleached human bones dug up and scattered by scavengers, and the gaunt ruins of army outposts burned a year ago by the Sioux and Cheyenne when the army abandoned the trail in the wake of the Fetterman Massacre.

The arid, bloody Bozeman now belonged to Sioux Chief Red Cloud. As the train traversed the two-hundred-mile stretch of desert between Cheyenne and the higher pine country to the north, Cuno realized only too well that the sage-peppered buttes, yucca-tufted sand hills, and sun-baked rimrocks could hide a thousand warriors.

His sixth day on the trail, he slouched in the driver's box of his lumbering freighter, boots propped on the footrest, trace ribbons in his hands, neckerchief shielding his mouth and nose from the adobe-colored dust. Renegade trailed on a lead rope behind the wagon. At once bored and impatient, Cuno gazed along the trail, which followed ancient water courses northwestward, toward snow-mantled peaks. His mind was on Indians, but it was also on Anderson.

The train had lain over yesterday on the banks of Crazy Woman Creek, to wash and mend clothing and to repair wagon beds pounded incessantly by their heavy cargoes. Blacksmiths worked at their portable forges, reshaping wagon wheels and stock shoes, while the scouts and several drivers, including Cuno, hunted for antelope and deer, which they jerked that night by cook fires.

It was a delay Cuno hadn't counted on, but it appeased him to realize that Anderson's crew had probably made at least one such stop so far itself. Most trains stopped for maintenance every couple of weeks, no matter how large or small or what they were carrying.

Also tempering his impatience was the mesmerizing Daphne, whose sexual wiles were always creative and astounding. He'd thrown himself into the nightly trysts like a thirsty nomad into a cool mountain stream. While trying to be as discreet as possible, he no longer worried unduly about getting caught. Daphne helped him forget about the horrors he'd witnessed back in Valoria, helped him even to forget about Anderson for one blissful hour or so each evening.

His nights, for now, were heaven. He had a feeling they wouldn't be heavenly much longer.

A week and a half out of Cheyenne, the wagons took their nooning along a deep barranca littered with bleached bison bones and ancient arrowheads, in a shallow valley between rimrocks. That evening, they traveled until six-thirty, for the summer nights were long in the northern latitudes, the light lingering until well after ten o'clock. The teamsters bivouacked on a bald mesa near the ruins of a small army outpost overlooking the south fork of Clear Creek.

When the spanning of the wagons had been accomplished and the stock rope-corraled along the creek, Daphne flashed her mirror at Cuno. Nonchalantly, he made his way across the mesa, pausing when he spied July Summer talking with one of the drivers—a lean, affable man in his late twenties, Steve Casebolt.

July stood with her back to the chuck wagon, chatting with the man, who stood before her, hands in the pockets of his denims. He was laughing at something, shrugging his shoulders while he regarded July flirtatiously. July smiled and shook her hair back from her head. As she did so, her glance found Cuno, who gave a self-conscious start and continued on his path toward the mesa's edge.

He brooded as he walked. Obviously, there was some sparking going on between July and Steve Casebolt, and something about that just didn't set right.

He let the concern pass from his mind as he caught up with Daphne behind a boulder halfway down the mesa.

She kissed him hungrily. "You kept me waiting," she said with an air of good-natured chiding.

He smiled. "Sorry."

"You'll learn that Daphne Creigh waits for no man, Master Cuno."

"Then I reckon Daphne Creigh better find herself someone to court her besides a lowly bullwacker."

"Oh, I reckon a lowly bullwacker will have to do . . . for now," she said, tilting her head coquettishly. She frowned as she studied him. "What's wrong?"

He returned the expression. "What do you mean?"

"Something's on your mind. What is it?"

He shrugged. "Nothin'."

Her smile returned, vibrant as ever. "Nothing except me, you mean."

He flashed her an appeasing smile. "Of course."

He took her hand and led her down the trail toward the creek, where they shed their clothes, hurriedly bathed the sweat and dust from their bodies, and coupled with animal passion on a sandbar ribbed with driftwood and sheltered by saw grass.

An hour later, Daphne left the creek while Cuno lingered, smoking. They didn't want to show up back at the encampment together, lest someone should get suspicious of the forbidden tryst between a common teamster and the boss's daughter. When Cuno finally made his way back toward the mesa's top, he stopped suddenly, hearing a quick rustle in the ravine to his right.

He turned that way as Jimmy Bigelow's sneering countenance appeared around a boulder at the ravine's lip, a .36 Colt Navy aimed squarely at Cuno's middle.

"Unh-unh," the hardcase said, shaking his head as Cuno's hand dropped to his pistol butt.

Cuno moved his hand away as two more men appeared behind Bigelow. One was a scrawny redhead with sharp eyes. The other was a stout young man with a cap of tight, brown curls and a large black wart on his left nostril. They were both dressed in rough trail garb. Both had well-cared-for pistols in their hands, and they looked like they knew how to use them.

"Meet my friends, Zip Tangen and Louis LeBoix," Bigelow said, grinning with cunning humor.

Cuno studied the three. He'd been expecting a move from Bigelow after the prior incident involving Daphne, and the hardcase had played it well. He'd taken his time until Cuno had nearly forgotten about him and had let his guard down.

Cuno said, "Heard about you boys. Nice to finally make your acquaintance."

Bigelow said, "Shut up and flip your gun out of that holster, nice and gentle, and toss it on the ground."

"This is hostile country. An unarmed man is a dead man—ain't that the saying?"

"In your case, you stay armed one more second, we're gonna blow holes in your hide." It was the Cajun, LeBoix, who spoke dully and with little expression on his dark-eyed face.

Cuno doubted they'd do it. The shots would draw men from the camp. But then, he didn't know these three and really had no idea what they were capable of. Reluctantly, he lifted the Colt from his holster with two fingers, held it out away from his body, and dropped it in a sage tuft.

Waving his pistol and stepping to his right, Bigelow said, "In the ravine."

"What's in the ravine?"

"That's where we're gonna whip the livin' shit out of you, boy," Tangen said. His thick, peeling lips stretched back from his teeth.

"Get in there," Bigelow said, giving Cuno a hard shove.

Cuno whipped around to face the young hardcase, squeezing his hands into fists, his anger burning.

"Unh-unh," Bigelow taunted with a belligerent smile, raising his Colt Navy.

The scrawny redhead laughed. "He don't like bein' pushed, does he?"

"I don't give a shit what he likes," Bigelow spat. He raised his revolver higher, pointing the barrel at Cuno's forehead. "I'm gonna show you what happens to sons o' bitches who trespass on my territory. Now, get into that ravine or die, hayseed."

Cuno glanced at the revolvers bearing down on him. Restraining his anger, he shrugged, turned, and headed down the ravine's crumbling bank, grabbing shrubs to break his descent. One by one, the three gunmen followed him down and stood facing him, positioning themselves so that the falling sun was behind them, in Cuno's face.

"Now what?" Cuno said. "You gonna fight me one at a time, like men, or all at once, like cowards?"

"I can handle you all by myself, hayseed. Just take me a minute," Bigelow said, eyeing him darkly. He shoved his gun into his holster, removed his belt and holster and thrust the load at LeBoix with a brusque, "Hold onto that," and doffed his hat.

He approached Cuno, raising his hands. Crouching, he bolted forward, faked a left jab, then landed a right. Gaining a false confidence, Bigelow moved in fast. Cuno blocked his shoulders, pivoted from the hip, and landed a deft haymaker at Bigelow's nose, which burst like a blood-filled tick.

Bigelow staggered, grabbing his bloody nose in both hands. Awed and exasperated, he bolted toward Cuno sloppily. With a methodical combination, each fist complementing the other, Cuno punched him to his knees.

When Bigelow had shaken his marbles back in line, he glanced at the two men flanking him. "Get that son of a bitch!"

LeBoix and Tangen quickly lost their guns and hats and, loosening their shirt collars and cuffs, moved in with their fists raised. Two minutes later, Cuno had dropped LeBoix, but Tangen was whipcord tough and fast. He was nearly Cuno's match, and, working with LeBoix, he was a handful.

When the bloody Bigelow shook off the pain of his broken nose and plunged back into the fray, it was three against one. It wasn't long before Tangen and LeBoix each had one of Cuno's arms and Bigelow was working on his face with one savage punch after another.

"You gonna keep your goddamn hayseed paws off my girl?" Bigelow raged, blowing blood off his lips.

Before Cuno could say anything, he heard a shell levered into a rifle breech. "You throw another punch, mister, I'm gonna blow a hole through your noggin."

Bigelow whipped his glance up the ravine slope, as did Cuno. July stood there, Cuno's rifle in her arms. She wore a straw hat under which her raven hair whipped around her cheeks in the breeze.

Bigelow raised his hands, palms out, appeasing. "Hey, easy now, girl," he said. "That thing could go off."

"It *will* go off, if you don't hightail it out of here pronto."

Tangen dropped Cuno's right arm. "It's that damn half-breed girl travelin' with the Creigh cook."

July sneered. "You should study for the law, you're so damn smart." She raised the heavy rifle in her arms, as though she'd raised one before, and sighted down the barrel at Tangen. "I ain't gonna say it again."

A rifle cracked, and Cuno's three attackers jumped. It was not July's rifle that had barked but another off in the distance.

More shots sounded, and July turned her gaze northward. "Oh, my God!" she cried, her face going pale, the rifle sagging in her arms. "Someone's makin' off with the stock!"

21

"SHIT!" LEBOIX YELLED, dropping Cuno's right arm. As Cuno sagged to the ground, he saw the sheepish, frightened look on Jimmy Bigelow's face and knew he and his compatriots were supposed to be guarding the bosque in which the stock had been corralled.

"You fools," Cuno groused, wincing against the pain spiking his bruised cheeks and jaw.

As the others quickly gathered their weapons and scrambled up the ravine wall, Cuno knelt in the brush and sand, spitting blood from a gash in his mouth. July was watching him, not sure what to be more concerned about—him or the stock.

Taking a deep breath, Cuno heaved himself to his feet and pulled himself up the ravine, using the same shrubs that had broken his descent.

Turning a look northeastward, he saw a dust fog rising behind the cottonwoods and willows on the other side of a broad bend in the creek. Through the fog he saw horses, oxen, and mules, and the occasional bare-chested Indian on a short-legged bronc. An intermittent volley of shots lifted—probably from the scouts who'd been patrolling the camp perimeters. Alarmed yells and commands rose from the encampment at the mesa's crest. Men spilled down the ridge, pistols and rifles in their hands.

Down the grade, below Cuno and July, Bigelow and his two compatriots were hoofing it toward the creek, yelling and cursing, realizing they'd probably made the biggest mistake of their lives when they'd abandoned their stock-tending duties to settle their own personal score with Cuno.

"Christ!" Cuno spat, no longer feeling his bruises, adrenaline pounding in his veins. "They get the stock, we're all stranded out here. Those jackasses!"

He grabbed his rifle from July and saw Renegade standing about twenty yards behind her, saddled and tied to a shrub.

"I was out gathering wild onions for stew," she explained, casting her hand-shaded gaze back toward the creek, where the Indians' ululating cries rose amid the intermittent cracks of gunfire. Cuno always offered her Renegade for such chores.

Saying nothing, Cuno picked up his pistol from the sage tuft, grabbed Renegade's reins from the shrub, and mounted.

"Be careful," July called.

Cuno spurred the horse into a wind-splitting gallop, soon overtaking Bigelow and the others. He barely slowed as he splashed across the creek, then gigged Renegade up the other side. Close ahead, the thinning dust sifted. The gunfire and Indian cries faded eastward, around another, distant cottonwood copse.

He galloped toward the trees, keeping his head down over Renegade's neck, holding his rifle tightly in his right hand, ready to bring it up when an Indian came into range.

As he split two low buttes and traversed a saw-tooth game trail around a third, he saw three of Amos Church's scouts galloping a hundred yards ahead of him and tracing a gradual arc to his left.

Casting his glance leftward, he made out four or five Indians pulling their heavy, salmon dust cloud toward a knoll, behind which they soon disappeared. As the three scouts approached the knoll, one man lurched back in his saddle, grabbing at the arrow jutting from his chest. His horse reared, and with a startled cry, the scout rolled off the horse's left hip.

Heeling Renegade into an even faster gallop, Cuno saw the Indians peek out from behind the knoll, arrows nocked and aimed. As the projectiles arced toward the two mounted scouts, the men swerved their horses right and left, the frightened beasts screaming at the sudden onslaught.

"Jeb, get down!" one of the scouts cried to the other.

As Jeb's horse fell with an arrow in its side, the scout bounded out of the saddle, rifle in his arms, and dove behind a rock. The other man reined his skewbald to a sliding halt, jumped free of the leather, and dropped to a knee, bringing his rifle to bear on the knoll. He levered his entire magazine at the knoll, then dropped the rifle and grabbed the six-shooter from his hip.

He raised the revolver but paused when he saw Cuno galloping up behind him, about twenty yards to his left.

"I'll circle around!" Cuno yelled.

The scout fired another round at the knoll. His partner ran up on his right, the man's Henry rifle barking in his hands, and together they sprinted toward the knoll, keeping the Indians pinned down with gunfire.

Meanwhile, Cuno galloped Renegade past the knoll, keeping about thirty yards between him and the Indians crouching there, spread out behind the rise, their black, windblown hair visible above the tawny grass and sage clumps.

Counting five savages, all armed with bows and arrows, Cuno slid out of his saddle and slapped Renegade's rump.

As the horse ran bucking off, dragging its reins, Cuno dropped to his knees and lifted the Winchester to his shoulder. He'd always been a decent shot with a long gun. Aiming down the barrel, he saw two of the Indians release arrows at him. One dropped at his boot; the other arced over his head.

Steeling his nerve, Cuno planted a bead on the brown chest of one of the Indians and squeezed the trigger. He didn't wait to see if he'd hit his mark, but swung the barrel on the Indian beside the first and fired. As the Indian blew back in the grass, the two scouts appeared atop the knoll, both men firing into the remaining Indians, twisting the savages around with their shots and dropping them like wet wash from the line.

Cuno stood quickly and ran toward Renegade, who'd stopped to graze about a hundred yards away. He sheathed the rifle and mounted. Seeing a thick dust veil rising from a cut between buttes, he heeled Renegade into another ground-eating gallop.

Sporadic gunfire still sounded. Glancing to his right, Cuno saw that less than an hour of good light remained. His gut flooded with bile as he pondered the result of the Indians getting away with the wagon stock. The train would be stranded out here, at the mercy of the same savages who'd raided their remuda.

Also, with a searing burn in his gut and a stiffening of his spine, he couldn't help thinking of Anderson and Spoon getting away, scot-free, his father's murder unavenged.

When he'd ridden a good mile, tracing a winding route

through hogbacks, he reined the horse to a halt. Peering at the dust plume, he realized the Indians were hazing the herd in a slow eastward arc, on a course that would soon take them back south.

Hoping no Indians were waiting in ambush, he spurred Renegade up a hill and onto the benchland carpeted with purpling bluestem and brome. He gave the horse a brief blow, then spurred him straight east, hoping to cut the Indians off as they headed south.

Pulling up after a hard, twenty-minute ride, he gazed into the ravine before him. Mules barreled by in a cloud of pungent alkali dust. There was no sign of the oxen, which had probably long since been left behind, unable to keep up the breakneck pace.

Something whistled past him as he hunkered down beside a boulder. Whipping his gaze toward the arrow's source, he saw an Indian, his skin wildfire red in the crimson glow of the falling sun. The brave was riding and hazing the herd and also trying to nock another arrow.

Planting a bead on his chest, Cuno blew the Sioux out of the hurricane deck.

Levering another round, he positioned another Indian in his Winchester's sights and fired, missing the brave but frightening his mount, which bucked, unseating the startled rider. The brave scrambled to his feet just in time to be knocked flat by a bevy of screaming mules, his body kicked to a bloody, ragged pulp.

As the herd thinned, passing southward, Cuno heard the gunfire of the pursuing scouts and saw several more horseback Indians go down. He'd accounted for two more when one Sioux—a big man with a wide face marked with swirls and slashes of paint—galloped up the ravine's wall.

Cuno jumped back, dropping his rifle and falling on his butt.

With an ear-piercing cry, his eyes bright as a devil's, the

painted man glared down at his quarry and extended the bow, drawing back the arrow. He was so close that Cuno could hear the squeak of the ash and the creak of the gut sinew pulled taut. The man released the arrow with a loud snap.

Cuno jerked to the side at the last second, the screaming arrow carving a shallow furrow along his right side and pinning his shirt to the ground. Pulling himself free, Cuno clawed his Colt from his holster and fired.

The big Indian jerked backward over his horse's rump but held fast to the reins. The animal shied at the shot, pivoting to the right. The Indian fell left, hitting the ground with a grunt. Groaning, he clawed at the ground and pushed up on his knees, his eyes even wilder than before as he grabbed for the knife on his beaded sheath.

Still sitting, Cuno lifted the gun and blew two more holes through the Indian's painted chest, and added a third just to make sure. When the man was down and still, Cuno climbed to his feet and turned to the ravine.

He saw no more Indians. Two scouts passed, then a third, reloading his Winchester as he rode with his reins in his teeth. Seeing Cuno, the man took his gun under his arm, slipped the reins from his mouth, and sawed back on the bridle, halting the tired roan.

"You hit?" he called.

"I'm all right," Cuno returned.

"You cut 'em off right smart. The others hightailed it northward." The scout jerked a thumb to his left. "Gonna take us till mornin' to run down these damn mules, though."

The man spurred the roan into a trot and disappeared around a bend.

Cuno got up, retrieved his rifle, and walked after his horse. In a minute, he was heading down the ravine, intending to help haze the runaway stock back toward the camp. Realizing that his knees had turned to putty, he wondered if he'd be able to catch up to Anderson before the Sioux caught up to him.

It was beginning to seem like just a matter of time before the Indians, as the veteran teamsters put it, dressed him out and stretched his hide.

22

EVEN WITH MOST of the men helping, it took nearly all night to round up the stock.

At nearly four the next morning, Cuno rode his horse back to the camp, where the coffee fires were tended by the handful of women in the train and by the few men left behind to guard them. As he passed Daphne's Dearborn, he saw that the wagon was dark, the back pucker flap tied. The girl was asleep while the other women tended the fires and kept watch for more raiders.

"Massey."

Cuno halted the paint and turned to his right, where the lean, rugged form of Amos Church sat his steeldust mare, a withered quirly in the dark gash of his mouth. Cuno rode over.

"Bigelow, LeBoix, and Tangen were supposed to be guarding the bosque when those redskins salted our herd. What I wanna know is, as far as you know, were they?"

"Were they what?" Cuno said, playing dumb.

He'd seen his three assailants out in the buttes, desperately hazing the stock back toward the camp, looking sheepish and scared, no doubt knowing that their leaving the bosque unattended was a crime punishable by a severe bullwhipping. They may have deserved it, but Cuno wasn't a snitch.

"Were they guarding the bosque, like they claimed?"

"I reckon, if that's what they claimed," Cuno allowed with a shrug.

Church regarded him with a skeptical tilt of his head. "Where you get those bruises on your kisser?"

"These?" Cuno said, fingering his puffy lower lip. "I was sleepwalking and tripped over a rock."

Church gave a grunt, blowing cigarette smoke through his nose. "Risky business, sleepwalkin'."

"Don't I know it, sir."

Church chuffed again, gave an ironic half-smile, and reined his horse away. "Get some sleep, Massey."

"I intend to, Mr. Church."

Cuno kneed the paint over to his wagon and crawled out of the saddle. He slapped his hat against his thigh, beating the dust off, then tossed it aside and began unsaddling the horse. His mood soured as, the more he thought about it, the more he couldn't help feeling partly responsible for the raid. It hadn't been his turn to watch the bosque, but it had been because of him that Bigelow, Tangen, and LeBoix had left it.

Because of him and Daphne, that was, who now slept in her well-outfitted wagon, snug as a bug in a rug.

He set the saddle in his wagon box. Hearing grass crunch nearby, he looked up. A female silhouette moved toward him, holding a cup steaming in the faint glow of the false dawn.

"Coffee?" July asked.

"Thanks."

"How'd it go?"

"We lost a scout but got most of the stock back." He sipped the coffee, thoughtful. Death was everywhere these days.

"Could've been a lot worse, I reckon," July said. "You all right? Those boys were workin' you over pretty good when I came up."

He shrugged. "Just bruised. I guess you rescued me."

"Wasn't nothin' you hadn't already done for me."

"Where'd you learn to handle a rifle like that?"

"I hunted back on the farm, but all I did was aim it. Hell, even your miss spiffy-dresser can aim a rifle, I bet." July paused. Cuno wished he could read the expression on her face, but it was too dark. "I best go see if Mr. Stamper's back yet."

She turned and walked away.

"July," he called.

She stopped and turned.

"Thanks for the coffee," he said, though it wasn't all that he'd wanted to say.

"You're welcome," she said, forming a pensive smile. Slowly, as if she didn't want to, she turned and moved on.

They laid over that day to rest the men and animals. In the early afternoon, Cuno was napping under his wagon when someone touched his shoulder. He looked out from under his hat brim to see Amos Church squatting beside him, the wagon master's face looking impossibly leathered behind his thin, gray beard.

"Got a proposition for you, Massey."

"What's that?"

"Seein' as how you're so good with a gun and a horse, how 'bout ridin' scout? We lost a man last night, and one more, Tom Devlin, took a bullet in the thigh. He won't be able to sit a saddle for several weeks. I'd like you to replace him, and he'll drive your wagon."

Cuno had spent several years driving a freight wagon, but it no longer interested him. His place was on a horse.

"You know this is my first time out here," he warned Church.

The wagon master shook his head. "You don't need to know the country. You'll just be outridin', keepin' an eye out for Injuns and callin' a warnin' to the wagons you see so much as a sun flash."

"You got it."

"Don't you wanna know what the pay's like?"

"I don't care," Cuno said. "I'll take the job."

Church studied him, his deep-sunk blue eyes sharply probing from their rawhide sockets. "It's fifty dollars more. Hazard pay. It's risky."

"Can't be much riskier than drivin' this slow pile of boards through Injun country."

Church studied him again. "Where did you learn how to shoot? You don't look like the desperado type."

Cuno looked off and shrugged a shoulder. "It's a long story, Mr. Church. Just know that I'll take that scouting job, and I'll be damn good at it."

"No more sleepwalking," Church said.

"No more sleepwalking, sir."

Church studied him. "What is it about you, kid?"

"What's that?"

"Damn peculiar. You mix well enough with the others, but you're not one of them. You aren't now and, I don't care if it took us ten years to reach Virginia City, you never would be. You got a look about you. There's a darkness under all your honey and wheat. Damn peculiar." He rubbed a gnarled hand down his jaw. "I'd be damn interested to know what you're up to, what you're doin' here, but I know it ain't none of my business." He extended a hand. "Welcome to the scouts. Be mounted and ready to ride in the morning at four."

"You got it, sir." Cuno paused. "Someone killed my old man and step-ma. I'm hunting them, and when I find them, I'm gonna kill them."

Church stared down at him soberly. "I had a feelin' it was something like that." Church gazed back at him, the lines around his leather eyesockets deepening. "Remember," he said finally, "you have a job to do."

"I won't fail you, Mr. Church."

Church nodded, then turned and ambled off like a man who felt about as much at home walking as he did standing on his head.

The next evening, Cuno and three of the other scouts were gathered around their cook fire, drinking coffee and smoking. The sun was nearly down and the meadowlarks gentled their solemn cries across the meadow in which the wagons were spanned, the stock grazing within the circle.

Church and another scout, Rod Kettleson, rode up on their sweat-silvery mounts. "We spotted another wagon train ahead about ten, eleven miles," Church said. "We should overtake them in a day or so. Might be a good idea to join up."

"The more the merrier," Jeff Bingham said beside Cuno, drawing deep on his quirly. Cuno knew he meant that the more whites in a group, the less the odds of the Indians attacking. The Sioux and Cheyenne were many things, including some of the best light-horsemen the world had ever known, but long-odds players they were not.

"All right then," Church said, and rode off, probably to relate his nightly report to Mr. Creigh.

Dismounting, Kettleson said conversationally, "Looks like we'll be seein' some new faces in a couple days."

"Not a minute too soon for me," Bingham said. "I'm so damn tired of your ugly mugs I'm ready to hang myself from the nearest cottonwood."

Playing solitaire on a flat rock, Bob Clement chuckled. "You're just hopin' there's gonna be some pretty gals in that outfit."

"You can't blame me," Bingham drawled. "The only good-lookin' women in our group is Miss Creigh and that half-breed girl helpin' the cook. To get to Miss Creigh, you have to get past her father. And I tried sparkin' that half-breed girl, and she'll talk to you, but she just don't seem interested."

Clement hooted a laugh as he slapped down a card. "Imagine that!"

When Clement's laugh boiled down to a simmer, he turned to Cuno with a conspiratorial air. "Come on, Massey. Fess up. How'd you do it?"

Cuno had been lost in thought, thinking about the wagon train Church had spied two days ahead of them. That would be Anderson's train. It had to be . . .

Trying to get a handle on his thumping heart, he turned to Clement. "How'd I do what?"

"Rumor has it," Kettleson said as he dropped his saddle on the other side of the fire, fanning the low flames, "you been sparkin' Miss Creigh. Miss Daphne Creigh, the pride and joy of Mr. Thomas," he added with mock formality. "How in the hell did you get past the old man?"

Getting past Daphne's father had been no trouble at all, since she had the pugnacious old gent not only wrapped around her little finger but believing she was as pure as mountain snowmelt. But Cuno said, "I have no idea what you boys are talkin' about. Me sparkin' Daphne Creigh?" He chuffed mirthlessly. "That's crazy. I've hauled water for her a time or two, sure, but . . ." He wagged his head. "Hell. . . ."

"Yeah, hell," Jeff Bingham said lazily. "There's been all kinds of rumors about her. Bound to be when a girl looks like that an' you got a wagon train full of horny saddle tramps and mule-skinners." He chuckled. "And then you get guys like Jimmy Bigelow spinnin' yarns about how he was doin' the mattress dance with her as far back as Fort

Robinson!" Incredulous, Bingham tipped his head back and blew a stream of quirly smoke.

"Now that half-breed girl," Clement said, considering the cards laid out before him. "I might just have to—"

"Her name's July," Cuno said, his voice pinched.

Clement looked up with surprise. "What's that?"

"She has a name," Cuno told him. "It's July. And she's off-limits, understand?"

Clement gave Cuno a long look, a slow frown shaping itself on the scout's sun-seared features. A cunning look grew in his brown eyes. "Who says so?" he asked tightly, sliding his hand to the butt of the Remington holstered on his hip.

Cuno's own hand dropped to his Colt. "Think about it, Bob," he warned. His mind was awash with contradictory emotions having to do not only with Daphne and July but also with Anderson and Spoon. It had all come to a boil. "Think about it real hard."

The other men fell silent.

The tension around the fire drew taut as remuda rope.

Finally, Clement blinked and relaxed his hand on his gun. "Okay," he said, trying to sound casual. "Hunky-dory with me if you're sweet on the girl. Just try gettin' anywhere with her." He grunted a humorless laugh and returned to his cards as though nothing had happened.

The others sighed and snorted and turned away. Cuno flicked his cigarette into the fire, heaved himself to his feet, and stomped off in the darkness, as angry at himself as at Clement. He never should have said anything about July, but the words had come of their own accord, and there was no way to retrieve them now.

As he walked through the darkness between the fires and lounging freighters, his mind turned from Clement and July to Anderson. He stopped and peered north, beyond the ragged slopes of the Big Horns looming in the west. Owls called above the breathy snaps of the fires and the muffled, desultory conversations around the wagons. Coyotes wailed from a scarp somewhere in the east.

In the north was Anderson. In a couple of days, their wagon train would merge with his. What would happen then, Cuno had yet to decide. Maybe Anderson would recognize him. If so, the hider would make it easy. Cuno would kill him in self-defense. Then Spoon would no doubt want in, and Cuno would kill him, too.

Cuno frowned and gave a little grunt. It sounded easy, talking to himself out here. Just a little Sunday-go-to-meeting. It would be far from that. Cuno had gotten handy with a six-shooter, but Anderson had been handy with a gun for probably as long as Cuno had been alive.

Bringing the hider down wasn't going to be easy unless Cuno took the coward's way out and backshot him, which wasn't an option. Cuno wanted the man to know who he was, and why he'd been hunted all the way out here. Why he was going to die. What's more, Cuno wanted to see the fear of death in the bastard's eyes, just before he expired . . .

Cuno hadn't realized he'd wandered into a grove of pines on the eastern edge of the encampment until he heard a girl's laugh followed by a young man's.

Cuno looked around. Two figures took shape about twenty yards ahead and to his right, between two tall pines. The girl stood with her back to a tree, the young man facing her. But then Cuno realized that the girl wasn't standing. The young man was holding her up with his arms, her legs wrapped around his waist.

As the starlight shone faintly on their pale bodies, Cuno knew the girl was naked and that the boy was naked from the waist down.

Jimmy Bigelow wore only his shirt and hat.

Daphne laughed again. It was more of a squeal.

"Shut up," Bigelow admonished, breathing heavily.

She laughed again, and Bigelow slapped a hand over her mouth.

Cuno turned away, crept slowly back through the trees, walking quietly, finding himself smiling and then laughing softly.

"Who's there?"

It was July's voice rising before him. She stood beside her deer-hide tent, a bucket in her hands.

"Cuno."

"What's so damn funny?"

He shrugged. "Everything."

She watched him silently, a puzzled expression on her face.

"You have any whiskey?"

"Whiskey?"

"Yeah."

She canted her head to one side. "Just so happens I might. What do you want it for?"

"Why does anyone want whiskey?"

"I never knew you to get drunk."

"Well, it so happens I just figured out I been sparkin' the wrong girl, and I'd like to get drunk and forget about how foolish I've been."

The girl didn't say anything for a long time. "I don't have any whiskey for that," she said quietly.

He walked to her quickly, took her in his arms, held her tightly, tipped her head back, and closed his mouth gently over hers. At first she was stiff, resisting, but then her body relaxed, and her lips opened. They were soft and smooth and moist, and he liked the way she tasted, the way her slender body felt in his arms. Supple and warm and womanly and good.

With difficulty, he turned away. The time was not right for them. "Good night, July."

Her brows beetled with confusion. She didn't want him to leave. Finally, she said quietly, "Good night."

Cuno turned away. He never should have kissed her. His life was getting too complicated. He needed to simplify. He needed to think of only Anderson and Spoon . . .

Remembering why he'd sought July out in the first place, he stopped and turned back to her. "There's another wagon train, one, two days ahead. I'm betting Anderson's in it."

She sighed and nodded slowly. "Don't do anything *loco*, Cuno. Please?"

"Don't worry. I'm gonna think it all out beforehand." He turned and walked away.

23

THE NEXT MORNING, about ten o'clock, Cuno lifted his neckerchief over the lower half of his face and squinted his eyes against an onslaught of sand swirling in from the north. He tipped his hat over his eyes and lowered his head.

"Here we go!" he grouched, having expected the storm for hours. He reined Renegade over to the wagons, in case the storm got so bad he couldn't see the train.

"You doin' all right?" he asked July, who was driving the chuck wagon again while the cook slept in the back.

"If one more man asks me that," she yelled through her own bandanna, "I'm gonna get out Stamper's gun and start shooting!"

"Hold your fire, pilgrim!" Cuno shot back, keeping his horse close to the chuck wagon in case the mules started to bolt.

Over the next hour, the storm impeded their progress, whipping half of western Dakota through the wagons and ripping at the canvas coverings. The stock threatened to stampede, and the scouts and teamsters had their hands full keeping the wagons on the trail. Gradually, the train broke into separate outfits of varying degrees of speed. Thirty-two wagons composing Creigh's team, at the head of the broken column, took their nooning in a long, slender hollow among the prairie hogbacks, with only one wind-battered cottonwood offering shelter.

There they waited out the storm, which relented finally around three-thirty in the afternoon. The teamsters, including July and the hungover cook, spent the evening sweeping out wagons and repairing canvas. Walking away from the camp to tend nature, one of the teamsters found a fresh grave with a headboard inscribed JEROME LARSEN, 1835–1867. As if in afterthought, someone had scratched below: SHOT BY R. ANDERSON.

When Cuno, along with several other scouts, saw the inscription, his organs flooded with adrenaline, and his fingers tingled. He found himself nodding automatically, feeling both anxious and eager. Anderson was near. Maybe only a few miles ahead.

"Well, I'll be a son of a bitch," Amos Church grunted. He stood across the grave from Cuno, beside Mr. Creigh, who puffed a long, black cheroot, which had a sweet, molasses odor.

Creigh lifted his somber gaze from the grave to Church. "What is it, Amos?"

"R. Anderson. That's Rolf Anderson, sure as shit," the wagon master said, glancing around fearfully, as if he half-expected Anderson to appear out of the sod.

"Who's Rolf Anderson?" Creigh said.

"Bad hombre," one of the drivers, Steve Casebolt, said with a grunt.

"Bad hombre, indeed," Church said. "I was hopin' we wouldn't run into him out here. He's a buffalo hunter, but you'll find him out here most years, running whiskey or rifles to the Injuns. Sometimes he runs women he's taken off farmsteads—good-lookin' young girls he sells to the Injuns for gold or safe passage or both. He's a friend of Red Cloud's and White Bull's. White Bull is the red bastard, I suspect, whose raiding parties I've been keeping an eye on."

Church lifted his haunted gaze to the buttes pushing up around them and from which the monotonous buzz of grasshoppers rose. "They're close and getting closer all the time."

"Too damn close for me to get much rest," Bob Clement agreed.

"You think White Bull is gonna make contact with Anderson?" Cuno asked Church.

The wagon master shrugged. "Hard to say, but I don't like it. We got Anderson ahead of us, and White Bull all around us."

Creigh was darkly interested. "If this Anderson is as bad as you say he is, maybe we shouldn't be so eager to catch up with his train."

Cuno bit his cheek. He wanted very much to catch up to Anderson's train, which was why his stomach relaxed when Church said, "I doubt his whole train's in cahoots with him. Probably just a few in his immediate outfit. That's how he usually works it. Talks some poor farmer in to hauling contraband for him, for a cut the poor man never sees."

Church blew cigarette smoke. "I say we try to catch up to his outfit and keep an eye on him. If he supplies White Bull with whiskey or rifles, there's gonna be hell to pay for us and every train behind."

"Those Indians don't already have rifles?" Creigh asked.

Church nodded. "Some, but mostly old blunderbusses or war-model, single-shot Spencers. Those Indians steal gold from the miners in the Black Hills and use it to buy repeaters from renegades like Anderson, damn all their hides to hell and back!"

Church glanced sheepishly around at his scouts, all of whom nodded absently and returned their gazes to the grave. That they all feared Anderson was evident by their expressions, and it gave Cuno another apprehensive chill.

Could he take down a man like Rolf Anderson?

As he turned back to the encampment with the others, he knew he was only a few days at the most from finding out.

That night, well after dark, Cuno sat on a rock away from the corralled wagons, taking his revolver apart and setting the parts on a blue bandanna beside him as he cleaned them. He was snapping the gun back together when he saw Daphne moving toward him around the other wagons and the water barrels, stepping over tongues. Her hair was down, and she wore a light shawl around her shoulders.

"Hello there," she said, stopping before him and gazing down.

"Hidy," he said, not looking up at her but continuing to put together his Colt.

"I haven't seen you in a while. You've been ignoring me. Why?"

Cuno shrugged. He didn't want to tell her about his finding her with Jimmy Bigelow. There would be no point. Obviously, she felt nothing for Cuno, just as he felt nothing for her besides a basic sort of animal need.

"I reckon I been busy."

"Too busy for . . ." She gave her hip a little coquettish swing to the side. ". . . what we do together?"

He twirled the revolver in his hand, holstered it, and sighed as he lifted his bewildered gaze to her. She smiled down at him condescendingly.

"Oh," she said, suddenly frowning. "Cuno, you didn't think there was something . . . something actually between us . . .?"

He shrugged. "I don't know what I thought."

"Cuno, you and I," she said, haltingly, "we come from entirely different worlds."

"I'll say we do," he said. He ran his eyes down her slender, opulent figure, his bruised innocence turning to goatish need. "How close is your wagon to your old man's?"

She studied him, uncharacteristically baffled. Slowly, a soft light gleamed in her eyes. "Too close, I'm afraid. He's been worried about Indians."

"Where?"

"Where what?"

He stood and faced her, feeling both a careless need and a defiant anger. "Where should we do what we do together?"

She glanced behind her at the wagons, which were silhouetted against the several fires guttering in their midst. At two of the fires, men talked lazily. Most of the teamsters, however, had been asleep for a couple of hours, exhausted from the sandstorm and knowing they'd be pulling out at the first hint of dawn.

"Why not right here?" she said, indicating the high grass around the stock he'd been sitting beside.

"Why not?" he said, stepping toward her, grabbing her brusquely and pulling her toward him. He kissed her roughly, and she hung in his arms, totally unresisting, like a rag doll in the embrace of a deviant child.

"Wait," she said finally, wrestling out of his grasp.

She stepped back, ran the back of her hand across her mouth, and stared at him with a peculiar expression on her face. Her eyes lit deviously as she kicked off her slippers, unbuttoned her dress, and lifted it over her head. She wore nothing under it. Shaking her head, her hair danced about her shoulders, partially hiding her face. Her eyes were dark with lust as she gazed at him through the tangled strands of her hair.

"Do you like what you see?" she asked in a hard whisper.

When he didn't answer, she stepped forward and slapped

him resolutely across his left cheek. She grinned malevolently. She was about to slap him again when he grabbed her hand, pulled her to him, kissing her with more violence than passion, then eased her down and lowered himself on top of her, working his pants open with one hand.

He was working away on top of her, her ankles crossed behind his back, when he sensed rather than saw someone nearby. Someone gasped. He jerked a look to his left and saw July stumbling backward, as though she'd been slapped in the mouth. Turning quickly, she walked briskly back toward the wagons.

"July!" Cuno called, rolling off Daphne and grappling with his pants.

"Oh, leave her!" Daphne said, laughing. "Cuno, come back . . ."

But he was already on his feet, hurriedly buttoning his pants and grabbing his gunbelt, and then he was jogging away toward the wagons. He followed July around the chuck wagon and stopped. She stood facing him, her back to her tent, the cook's Spencer rifle in her hands, aimed at Cuno's belly.

"Get away from me," she said her voice taut with hard emotion. Her lips trembled and her black hair curtained around her eyes.

Someone smacked his lips and spat, and Cuno saw the portly Stamper sitting beside the dying cook fire, a tin cup in one hand, a bottle in the other. Drunk as a lord, he swayed from side to side as he lifted his head at the sudden commotion. "What is it?" he asked thickly. "What the hell's goin' on? Injuns?" He squinted through an alcohol fog.

Ignoring the man, Cuno said, "July, please, put the gun down. We gotta talk."

"I said get outta here or I'll perforate your worthless hide!" She broke down, sobbing, the rifle barrel dropping slightly and jerking with her convulsing shoulders. She dropped her head, openly crying now and cussing like a veteran teamster.

"July," he said, and took a step forward. She stiffened instantly, backed up a step, and swung the rifle up. "Get away from me!" she screamed.

"Hey, what the hell's goin' on?" one of the teamsters called from his bedroll under a wagon.

Not wanting to awaken the entire camp, Cuno swung around and walked away, heading in the general direction of the outriders' fire. A white shape appeared before him, stepping out of the darkness.

Daphne.

He stopped, his heart thumping, his head spinning as though he'd just awakened from a dream or a three-day drunk. She threw her arms around his neck. "Come on, Cuno, we were just getting started."

She was like a fly buzzing around his ear. He pushed her arms down, shoved her away. "Leave me alone," he grumbled, and headed for the umber coals of the outriders' fire.

"You bastard," Daphne called behind him, just loudly enough for him to hear clearly in the quiet night.

Near the fire, Bob Clement was rising for his night watch shift. "Go back to sleep, Bob," Cuno told him, picking up his rifle. "I'll take your shift."

As he headed away from the fire, Clement said, "Hey, Massey."

Cuno turned. Looking sheepish, Clement said haltingly, "Sorry about what I said about Miss Summer a few nights back. Steve told me you two came in together."

"Forget about it," Cuno grunted, turning and walking off.

He took his position on a hogback two hundred yards west of the wagons and spent the next two hours blocking out Daphne and July and everything else that cluttered his mind, refocusing his inward eye on Anderson and Spoon. He had been wasting his time on unimportant things, but now Anderson was near and he needed a clear head, a steady hand.

When Steve Casebolt walked out to take over his watch, Cuno returned to the fire and rolled up in his blankets, willing himself to sleep. Tomorrow could very well be the biggest day of his life . . .

"Ah shit," he grumbled around ten o'clock the next morning. He sat his horse on a pine-studded bench half a mile from Creigh's outfit. The teams had held up when one of the wagons belonging to a preacher from Cincinnati, who intended to start a church in Big Timber, Montana, had cracked a wheel. It wasn't the broke-down wagon that bothered Cuno now, however.

It was the three riders heading this way—Jimmy Bigelow in the lead, one hand on his pistol, an acrimonious smirk on the knife slash of the young hardcase's mouth.

24

"MASSEY, I HAVE a problem. Maybe you can help," Bigelow said as he drew rein.

Bigelow's two amigos, Tangen and LeBoix, flanked him, staring hard at Cuno. They too had their hands on their pistols.

"Maybe." Cuno offered a neighborly smile but felt a liberal dose of apprehension. It was obvious they'd ridden out here when they'd seen him alone. They wanted him alone.

"I went over to Miss Daphne's wagon last night"—Bigelow grinned toothily and rubbed his unshaven jaw as he rolled his eyes at LeBoix—"to deliver some flowers, you understand."

LeBoix snickered. "Flowers—that's right."

"Anyway," Bigelow said, his eyes hardening again, "She wasn't there. When I asked her where she was this mornin', you know what she said?"

Cuno shrugged. "Mighta said she was with me. I reckon you're not enough for her, Jimmy." Cuno smiled icily.

Bigelow stared back, his eyelids funneling. He appeared to have stopped breathing, the cords standing out in his neck. "You wanna die, I reckon," he growled, barely moving his jaws.

Cuno shrugged again. "Not me."

Bigelow swiped at the two grasshoppers clinging to the brown hair curling over his right shoulder, dislodging only one. "You sure as hell must, since you were doin' the mattress dance with my girl last night."

Cuno gave a caustic snort. "Your girl? Hell, Jimmy, she's there for anyone's taking, don't you see that? Don't you see this is all part of her conniving style—pitting two beaus, if you can call us that, against each other? Probably giggles as she writes about us in her diary every night."

Staring hard at Cuno, as if not hearing a thing, Bigelow swiped at the other grasshopper, missing it once again. "She's mine, Massey. I thought I done taught you that. Reckon I'm gonna have to start all over."

"Not this time, Jimmy. But if you're gonna claw that hogleg, then claw it or get your hand away."

Silence yawned. The sun beat down, canting shadows over the faces of the three hardcases, reflecting off the sandy hairs along Bigelow's jaw. The corner of his right eye twitched, and then his hand jerked, clawing at the butt of his .36.

It was out and leveling when Cuno's gun popped and bucked in his hand.

Bigelow's head and shoulders jerked forward as the .45 slug struck low in his chest. His cheeks puffed a surprised grunt. Cuno shot him again. Bigelow was rolling out of his saddle when Cuno, sensing as much as seeing LeBoix claw iron, blew a hole through the Cajun's flat right cheekbone.

"You want some of this?" Cuno asked Tangen, who sat stiffly in his saddle, his face paling beneath his tan, holding both hands belly-high, palms down.

LeBoix hit the ground with a thud and a grunt. His horse fiddlefooted as it turned and ran south toward Bigelow's.

Tangen looked at his two friends lying dead and bloody on the ground.

He returned his gaze to Cuno, who sat his saddle, jaws taut, vaguely amazed at his own calmness and skill with the Colt. As Charlie Dodge had pointed out, all the target shooting in the world would not prepare you for an actual contest with living, breathing men only a few feet away. His success here made him a little giddy.

As Tangen continued staring, the shock began leaching from his gaze, replaced with a darkly defiant cast. With slow deliberateness, he set both hands on his saddlehorn.

Cuno nodded and holstered his Colt. He, too, set his hands on his horn. The two men's gazes locked. Neither of them looked toward the wagons and the men approaching on horseback to find out what the shooting had been about.

Tangen's right hand whipped from the horn to the butt of his Colt Army. Cuno followed suit. Tangen had his gun out a split second after Cuno aimed his own weapon off Renegade's right shoulder. Holding the horse's bridle taut with his left hand, Cuno triggered lead with his right.

Tangen gave a yell as the bullet split his breastbone. The hardcase fired his own Colt in the air as he flipped off the back of his horse, which turned, lowered its muzzle to inspect its fallen rider, then, dragging its reins, drifted off to crop a foxtail tuft.

Cuno holstered his Colt as four of the outriders approached at a gallop, hands on their holstered pistols. Amos Church was in the lead, his cheeks and eyes ablaze with anger.

"What in the Sam H. Hill is going on here, goddammit!"

"They drew first," Cuno said mildly, glancing down at the three crumpled bodies.

Church looked around at the dead men, befuddlement and outrage plain in his eyes. He shot a skeptical look at

Cuno from under his broad hat brim. "You mean to tell me you shot all three of these boys fair?"

"I had a good view of the last shooting, Mr. Church," Rod Kettleson said. "Tangen made the first move."

Church was not appeased. To Cuno, he asked, *"Why?"*

"I'd rather not go into it, Mr. Church."

Church studied the dead riders again, and shook his head with frustration. Returning his cold blue gaze to Cuno, lips pursed within his gray-white beard, he said, "It's about Miss Creigh, ain't it?"

When Cuno didn't say anything, Church said, "I knew it was a mistake—Mr. Creigh packin' along that . . ." He paused meaningfully, wrinkling his nose. ". . . daughter of his. Bound to be trouble."

"I'll understand if you're quit of me, Mr. Church," Cuno said, "but I won't take a bullwhippin'. They were first on the draw."

Church looked at him hard. "Young man, I would kick your ass off my outfit if I didn't need every hand I got. Now, goddammit, I'm gonna have to have two of my outriders drivin' wagons, which means the scouts are gonna be shorthanded." LeBoix had not been a wagon driver, but a blacksmith and wrangler. "Goddamn your hide!"

Cuno held the wagon master's angry glare, did not turn away. He waited for his sentence to be read.

"Well, get a shovel and start diggin' graves," Church told him. "You're on your own. We're movin' out. To hell with you." He cursed again and reined his horse around.

Cuno said, "You want me to drive a wagon when I'm done?"

Church didn't look at him. "You ain't drivin' no wagon—not with the way you can shoot. But you'll take a double watch every night from here on in, and if you get in any more trouble, no matter who sparked it, you'll be cut so fast it'll make your head spin."

With that, Church gigged his skewbald into a gallop toward the wagons.

The other riders remained facing Cuno, puzzled looks on their faces. "Where in the hell did you learn to shoot like that?" Rod Kettleson asked, spitting a stream of chew and wiping his mouth with a gloved hand.

"I had a lot of time on my hands back in Nebraska," Cuno said, purposely evasive.

"You must have," Jeff Bingham said as Cuno crawled off his mount and grabbed the collapsible shovel off his saddle.

The other two riders rode after Church, but Bingham remained with Cuno. The scout gave a soft curse and dismounted his gelding. "I'll give ye a hand."

Cuno was looking around for soft ground conducive to grave digging. "I can handle it."

"No problem," Bingham said. "It's the least I can do for the hombre that finally rid us of those three ring-tailed stripe-backs."

The next morning, Rudolph Wehring stood by the breakfast fire, sipping coffee from a tin cup and staring thoughtfully across the dawn prairie capped in low, gray clouds. A chill wind blew, and the smell of rain was in the air. Wehring wore a homespun cardigan over his shirt, his cloth watch cap pulled low on his head.

His Spencer rifle, which he had used while fighting for the Union as a Kansas volunteer, protruded from under his left arm. Last night he'd spent a good half hour cleaning and loading the weapon, preparing it for his grim task, which he intended to carry out this morning.

"The bacon will be finished in a minute, Señor," the Mexican cook said, forking the bacon around in his long-handled pan. Around him, other drivers had gathered for coffee, blinking sleep from their eyes. From across the circular encampment rose the cries of a small child and the angry protests of its mother.

"Ain't hungry," Wehring said absently.

He tossed the dregs of his coffee in the fire, dropped his cup in the grass, shifted his rifle to his right hand, and walked over to his brother's main wagon. Underneath, three of Martin's five children still slept, curled in sheets and quilts, faces pink and puffy, hair tangled.

Rudolph paused near the back end, frowning. The sounds of lovemaking issued from the box.

Rudolph scowled, considered postponing his visit with Martin. But he had little time to lose. He wanted to get the job done this morning, so he wouldn't have to continue thinking about it, worrying himself into a tizzy.

"Martin," he called softly, stepping up to the open back end.

Glancing inside, he saw Martin's wife, Mariette, straddling the prone Martin while the baby fussed quietly on a pile of quilts in a corner. Mariette's nightgown was bunched around her waist, leaving her legs and heavy, pendulous breasts bare. Her hair was down and hanging toward Martin's doughy chest.

Mariette continued laboring over Martin, sighing and throwing her head back while Martin grunted beneath her, his pudgy hands clutching her hips, bucking against her.

Glancing discreetly away, Rudolph cleared his throat. "Uh . . . Martin. I need to talk to you."

He hadn't finished the sentence before Mariette gave a startled shriek. Glancing inside the wagon, Rudolph saw the woman roll off Martin and quickly cover herself with a sheet, pulling the sheet past her head, turning away, cowering with embarrassment.

"Rudolph, for chrissakes!" Martin complained, doing nothing to cover his own nakedness. "What the hell . . .

can't you see I'm busy?" His pudgy face with its pug nose and small, brown eyes was mottled red from exertion and frustration. His thinning, receding hair glistened faintly with sweat.

"Sorry, brother, but this can't wait," Rudolph said with gravity. Leaning over the tailgate, he beckoned Martin with his arm.

"Oh, for chrissakes!" Martin said, heaving himself onto his knees and scuttling over to the tailgate. "What the hell is it?"

"I know you don't want no part o' this, but I had to tell ye anyway. The boys and me"—Rudolph glanced at the other drivers watching him warily beneath their hats—drew straws last night. I got the short one. I'm takin' 'em down this mornin'—Anderson and Spoon."

Martin Wehring sighed and ran a stubby paw down his face. "Ah, Jesus, Rudy. Can't you wait till after we've exchanged the rifles with the Injuns? Hell, they're the only ones know where to find ole White Bull."

"I was gonna wait," Rudy said, staring grimly into his brother's eyes. "But that was before Spoon pawed my middle girl last night, down by the seep when Grace was tendin' nature. He was *loco* on that crazy weed of his, and she got away, but by God I won't allow them to mess with my girls. You were out on watch, but me and about ten of the other drivers agreed they had to die. They sure as hell won't scare or vamoose just cause we told 'em to."

"You got the short straw, eh?"

Rudolph nodded, tried swallowing down his fear, but it wouldn't go. "They already raped a woman, killed a man. How much we gonna put up with, anyways?"

Martin shook his head and glanced back at his wife, staring at him wide-eyed above the sheet held up to her chin. Turning back to his brother, he said, "It's crazy business, Rudy. They'll kill you."

"I'll get the drop on 'em. They sleep in late every

mornin'. I'm headin' for their camp right now. You with me?"

Martin looked at him, incredulous. "Hell, no!" he half-rasped, half-barked. "They'll kill me. They'll kill us both. Wait till after we've sold the rifles, then I'll chance it."

"It ain't gonna be no easier after we sell the rifles," Rudy said. "I'm goin' over there right now—get shed o' those two varmints."

He started away from the wagon. Over the tailgate, Martin said, "Rudy, don't!" He kept his voice down so he wouldn't alarm the camp. "Stop, you crazy fool!"

But Rudy kept walking toward his saddled horse tied to his main wagon, beside which his wife was changing the diapers of their baby on a folded quilt. Their second youngest stood nearby, still sleep-mussed, blond curls floating in the chill breeze. The woman looked up as Rudy passed and untied his horse from the wagon. Rudy only glanced at her. The baby cried and waved its arms, kicking its legs.

"Rudy, goddammit!" Martin yelled now, both hands gripping the tailgate. He would have run after his brother if he hadn't been naked. Looking to the other drivers shuttling their gazes between Rudy and Martin, he said, "Someone stop him. He's gonna get himself killed." He didn't care how loud his voice was now.

The drivers ignored him. They watched Rudy darkly.

To Rudy's wife, Martin said, "For Godsakes, woman—stop him!"

She turned to Martin. "Why?" she said blandly. "He's the only man in the family."

Rudy booted his rifle, climbed heavily onto the beefy dun, and rode toward a cut of hills rising in the southwest.

25

RUDOLPH WEHRING APPROACHED the trees nestled at the base of the hills twenty minutes later. Dismounting slowly, smelling woodsmoke and boiling coffee, he shucked the Spencer from his saddle boot and tied the dun to a slender cottonwood. The horse lowered its head to crop the waving blond grass.

The sun was climbing slowly into the purple rain clouds, giving little light. Birds chirped and the wind made a rushing sound in the leaves in the treetops. The noise should cover any that Rudy made as he approached Anderson and Spoon's camp.

They always camped a distance away from the main group, ostensibly to keep a secluded watch on the camp. The real reason, Rudy knew, was because they were afraid one of their own teamsters, tired of having their women ogled and insulted, would shoot them in the back.

Quietly, holding his breath, Rudolph levered a shell into the Spencer's breech, squeezing the stock as though trying to wring water from a rag. Taking a deep breath, he began walking west through the trees growing in a shallow swale that collected runoff water from the hills. Dew-beaded wheat grass, bluebonnets, and pokeweed dampened his square-toed farmer's boots and trouser cuffs.

He walked for fifty yards, then paused beside a broad elm bole, casting his gaze ahead, where a low fire sent up a wispy smoke thread. A blackened coffeepot hung from an iron spider over the fire. Just beyond, two ground-hitched horses grazed beside their saddles and bridles. To the left of the fire, Rolf Anderson lay on his side, his back toward Wehring.

Just beyond Anderson, lying flat on his back, his boots crossed on the trunk of a beaver-felled tree, lay Sammy Spoon. Spoon's arms were crossed behind his head, and his feathered hat was tipped over his face. The snores of both men rose above the wind muttering in the treetops.

His heart pounding, Rudolph Wehring lifted the rifle to his shoulder. First he'd take out Anderson, then Spoon.

He adjusted his stance, snapping a branch.

Instantly, Sammy Spoon lifted his head, shoving off his hat with his right fist. The half-breed bolted to his feet, grabbed his knife off his cartridge belt, and, spreading his feet and crouching, slung it end over end toward Wehring.

Rudolph heard the whistle of the blade cleaving the air. At the last second, he recoiled, turning and dropping his rifle. The blade whipped by so close he could feel the air puff against his neck. It plunged into the tree with a *whomp*.

Wehring gave a cry, tripped over a deadfall, and fell on his butt. He saw Spoon walking toward him, grinning. Anderson was awake now, too. His gun was out.

Wehring was more frightened than he'd ever been, nearly paralyzed with fear. Grunting and wheezing, he climbed to his feet and ran stumbling back through the trees.

Boots pounded the ground behind him. Spoon squealed a laugh. The half-breed's labored breathing grew louder in

Wehring's ears. He was nearly to the edge of the woods when Spoon, diving, grabbed his ankles, and he went down.

"Stupid granger," Spoon said, laughing. "What in the hell you think you're doin'?"

"I-I . . . let me go."

"Let you go, hell." It was Anderson. Twisting around, Wehring saw the big, blond hider staring down at him, hard-eyed but grinning bemusedly. He held his six-gun low at his side.

Wehring panted, staring at them fearfully.

Spoon was kneeling. "Stupid granger was tryin' to bushwack us. What should we do with him? Kill him?"

"Nah," Anderson said. "We need him to drive his wagon. It has twenty of our rifles in its false bottom."

"What then?" Spoon said. "Can't just let him go. Want me to carve an eye out, chop a few fingers off?"

"Nah. Take him too long to heal. How 'bout we give him a good old-fashioned hide-tannin'?"

Spoon smiled a chipped-tooth smile. "Sounds good to me."

"What? No—wait," Wehring protested.

"Get his pants down, Samuel."

"Come on, Rudy—hold still!" Spoon ordered, clawing at the granger's pants.

Wehring struggled, tried to stand, but Anderson gave him a hard kick in the gut. That took the starch out of him, and, clutching his ribs, he fell back and tried to suck air back into his lungs. In the meantime, Spoon jerked his pants and undershorts down his legs while Anderson, kneeling at Wehring's head, held his arms.

Wehring's cries and protests and leg-licks were futile. Anderson and Spoon got his pants down to his ankles and turned him face down.

"You want the honors, Rolf?"

"Go ahead."

Spoon gave Wehring's exposed white derriere a sharp slap with his open palm. The pain seared up Wehring's back and locked his jaws.

"Achhh!"

But that was nothing compared to the wallop Anderson gave him.

"Ahhh-owwww!"

The screams continued as Spoon and Anderson took turns pummeling Wehring's exposed ass. The two were having so much fun that they didn't hear the four riders approaching through the trees until a horse blew loudly, only a few feet away.

"Well, I'll be goddamned," Spoon said, holding his hand in midair. "We got company, Rolf."

Anderson looked at the four men who drew rein around him, regarding him and Spoon and the cursing Wehring with mute interest.

Cuno Massey's heart pounded, but his face was implacable, washed of emotion. He sat his saddle stiffly, one hand on his thigh. Taking even breaths, he moved the hand slowly toward his six-shooter.

26

CHURCH SAW CUNO moving his hand toward his gun, and gave him a look.

Cuno froze. His hand slid back to his knee. As tempting as it was, a shootout here might get innocent men killed. Besides, he didn't want to kill them unawares. When he killed Anderson and Spoon, he wanted them to know exactly why they were dying. The right time would reveal itself soon, when he could calmly explain to Anderson and Spoon exactly why their lives were spilling out of their bodies, and why their souls were on their way to the devil.

"What the hell is going on here?" Church asked, staring dubiously at the man whose pants were down around his knees and whose ass had turned red from the pummeling. Panting and cursing, the man lifted his desperate eyes at the newcomers.

"What's it look like?" Anderson said. He shoved his hat off his forehead, sweaty blond hair curling beneath. There were dust and seeds in his thick, red beard. "We're givin' this man a thrashin'. He's been bad. Very, very bad." Shaking his head with mock gravity, Anderson smiled.

Spoon guffawed, but his eyes were on the newcomers while one hand rested on his pistol butt.

Church said, "I see," and glanced at the others. Kettleson and Casebolt looked vaguely amused; Cuno alone did not. He found nothing about these men amusing.

Meanwhile, Rudolph Wehring took advantage of Anderson and Spoon's distraction to scramble awkwardly away and pull his trousers up to his waist. He frantically notched and buckled his belt, climbed to his feet, and ran back through the woods behind the newcomers.

"Ah, he's had enough," Anderson said to Spoon, who returned his gaze to Church and the others, his eyes flattening, losing their humor. "Who in the hell are you, and what in the hell you think you're doin', sneakin' into a man's camp unannounced?"

"We're from the Creigh train, about three miles back," Church told him, his voice tight, one hand on his knee, the other holding his horse's reins chest high. "We were riding toward the train yonder when we heard the commotion. What did that man do, anyway?"

"Tried to shoot us," Spoon said with a chuckle.

Church stared at him skeptically, nodded.

"I didn't catch your names," Anderson said.

"I'm Church, wagon master for the Creigh party. These two on my left are Kettleson and Casebolt. This on my right is . . ." Church paused, glancing at Cuno darkly.

"Morgan," Cuno said.

Anderson and Spoon's gaze shifted to the young man on the buckskin. The hairs along Cuno's neck prickled and he steeled himself for a fast draw. But no light of recognition appeared in either man's eyes, and after a moment they turned back to Church.

Anderson lifted a shoulder. "All right, you're with the team behind us. What in the hell you want from us?"

"Figured to join you," Casebolt told Anderson. His voice, as had Church's, betrayed his distaste for the two men before him.

"You did, did you?" Anderson said. "Well, we ain't lookin' for company."

"Why's that?" Church said. "You don't believe there's safety in numbers?"

The humor had left the half-breed's savage face. His wide, deep-set eyes were black. "No," he said slowly. "We don't."

"What Samuel's sayin'," Anderson said, "is skedaddle your asses outta here. Vamoose!" His voice boomed above the wind in the trees. A couple of the horses gave starts, jerking their necks and shuffling their feet.

"That ain't very neighborly," Cuno said.

"It's all right, Morgan," Church said reasonably. "If they don't want company, they don't want company." He was still staring at Anderson and Spoon, who stared back, hands on their pistol butts.

Finally, Church reined away. "Come on, boys."

The other three, including Cuno, were reluctant to leave. They sat their mounts, giving the hardcases their cold, challenging gazes.

"I said come on, boys."

Casebolt and Kettleson backed their horses out of the trees. Only Cuno stayed where he was. He couldn't help raking his gaze over Anderson's face one more time. Since they'd found the hider and Spoon, his heart had been walloping his ribcage while images flooded his consciousness—images of Corsica being carried out of her bedroom, her dead eyes pinning Cuno with a sightless stare. Images of Lloyd Massey dancing to a hail of lead, sprawling across the blood-washed piano, sinking to the floor.

Images of two sun-washed gravestones standing in a hushed country cemetery . . .

"Do I know you, boy?"

Anderson was regarding him now, head cocked slightly to the side. Spoon stared as well, parted lips revealing a mouthful of chipped, crooked teeth the color of old tobacco juice.

Cuno smelled death on these two, as heavy as that in any boneyard.

"Don't reckon," Cuno said flatly.

"Now that I think of it, Rolf, he does look familiar." Spoon frowned and canted his head. "Where you from, boy?"

Cuno's fur was up. "Don't call me boy, you—" He let his voice trail off, restraining himself.

Spoon laughed. "Listen to this kid, Rolf!"

"No cause to get touchy," Anderson said, adding, *"son."*

"Morgan!" It was Amos Church calling through the trees. "Get your ass out here pronto."

"Your momma's callin' you, boy," Anderson said, grinning his humorless grin.

Ears warm with anger, his right hand sweat-pasted to his thigh and twitching slightly, Cuno reined his horse back through the trees, keeping his eyes on the two laughing killers behind him.

"We'll see you later, boy," Spoon yelled with a whoop.

"You bet you will," Cuno muttered. He swung around to see Church and the other two riders waiting at the edge of the trees.

Church's eyes glittered with fear. "I told you, Massey—no trouble."

Casebolt turned to him. "So what are we gonna do, boss? Think they're carrying?"

"They're carrying, all right," Church said grimly. "Damn their hides."

"What are we going to do about it?" Cuno asked.

He knew what he wanted to do. He wanted to ride back

into the trees, introduce himself, and shoot both hardcases through their foreheads with Charlie Dodge's Colt. If it hadn't been for Church, he would have told them his real name when they were trying to place him. He'd savored the moment long enough.

"We'll catch up to them tomorrow," Church said after thinking it over. "We'll camp within a half-mile. If any of the wagons break away from the main group, we'll shadow them." He jerked his steeldust around and gigged the horse back toward their own wagons. "If it looks suspicious, we'll stop them . . . with bullets."

That night, about eleven-thirty, Cuno was making his patrol rounds atop Renegade. He passed within sight of July's tent, the interior of which glowed with a lighted lamp. Cuno considered stopping to talk. But she hadn't spoken to him for two days, and he doubted she wanted anything to do with him now. Not after finding him between Daphne Creigh's legs the other night.

But he missed July's company more than he'd expected to, no matter how hard he'd tried to put her out of his mind.

He rode Renegade down a depression in the dark prairie capped with stars and was reining up the other side when several shots rang out. Halting the horse, he clawed his pistol out, and whipped his head around, listening.

More shots cracked. Cuno gigged Renegade north, sucking air through his teeth when he heard the unmistakable thunder of pounding hoofs.

Soon, men from the camp were yelling and running, dark shapes amid the wagons and guttering fires. Circling back around the encampment, Cuno cursed and put Renegade into a gallop toward the creek around which the stock had been rope-corralled.

Guns popped, the muzzle flashes flickering in the northeast like fireflies. Curses and shouted orders rose.

Beyond the creek, in the light from the climbing, buttery half-moon, the herd was moving south, the light slick on their shifting backs and on the horns of the lumbering oxen.

As the creek and its buffer of willows neared, Cuno saw a man down on his right. The man's horse was galloping and buck-kicking eastward.

Reining Renegade to a sliding halt, Cuno slipped from the saddle and crouched over the man. It was Kettleson. On his hands and knees, he clutched his belly, dark and slick with blood and protruding intestines.

"Rod . . ."

"Sons o' bitches," the scout groaned. "They're . . . makin' off with the stock."

"Easy, pard, easy."

"Water!"

"No."

"Jesus God, I'm thirsty!"

Cuno eased the man onto his butt, then helped him lie back in the bluestem near a gopher mound. He could smell the man's insides and knew he was done for. Returning to his horse, Cuno snatched his canteen off his saddle, popped the cork, and gentled it to Kettleson's lips.

The scout no longer wanted it. He shook his head. "Through . . . I'm through. Go after 'em. Take 'em down for me." His head dropped to the grass; he gave an immense sigh and lay still.

"Damn it all!" Cuno corked his canteen, ran to Renegade, mounted, and rode after the fleeing herd.

The animals had scattered beyond the creek and out of sight, and now Cuno was following the sounds of the intermittent gunfire. He saw several men lying in the tall grass, but he did not stop to see who they were. He had to run down the stock, without which they were all doomed.

He'd ridden across the broken prairie for twenty minutes before he realized the shooting had ceased. He slowed

Renegade to a walk. Low ridges rose on either side of him. Above, stars. Dust sifted, marking the stock's recent passage. The unmistakable smell of mules and oxen lingered.

Silence.

He rode for a few more minutes then reined up suddenly, gazing ahead, bringing his rifle to his shoulder. A figure moved toward him—a man on foot. As the man stumbled closer, Cuno recognized the gray-bearded Amos Church. The wagon master was hatless; the tails of his shirt were out. His gun was not in its holster.

Church stopped about twenty feet in front of Renegade. Church stared for several seconds, working his lips as if searching for words. He stood stiffly, as if a rod had been rammed up his spine.

"Anderson . . . Spoon," he rasped. "About eight redskins."

He fell face forward in the grass. Jutting from his back was an Indian war lance.

Cuno scrambled out of the saddle, hunkered down beside Church. "Mr. Church!"

Church sighed, cleared his throat. "It was . . . diversion. They're after . . . the women!"

With that, his face hit the dirt, and he died.

July flashed in Cuno's mind. Daphne, and the half dozen other women in their outfit—women as well as children.

Cursing, Cuno left Church and climbed back into the saddle. Reining the horse around, he gigged him back the way he'd come, galloping hard, eating up ground.

It had been the women they were after. Church had said Anderson and Spoon traded white women to the Sioux . . .

Cuno hunkered low over the horn and put the steel to Renegade, slapping the horse's rear with his gloved left hand. He had a sick feeling it was a futile effort—he was too far away—but he had to try and get back to the camp before Anderson and Spoon made off with the women. If not, there was no telling what horrors lay in store for July and the others.

Approaching the camp, twenty minutes later, his stomach turned hard and his pulse pummeled his temples. He found July's tent collapsed. The cook lay dead near the chuck wagon, a rifle nearby, blood glistening on his head from which his scalp had been cut. The curly gray mat hung atop the war lance protruding from his gut.

27

JULY WAS NOWHERE to be found. Neither was Daphne. The Dearborn was empty, its mussed interior showing signs of a halfhearted struggle. Lying nearby, half in and half out of a dead cook fire, lay Thomas Creigh, two bullet holes in his face.

Searching the camp for survivors, Cuno found none. All five of the elderly men who had stayed behind were dead, as was one of the women, Mrs. Langley, the stout young wife of a former harness maker. She'd been stabbed and shot, her face badly bruised.

None of the wagons was missing. The women must have been carried off on mules or horses.

Running out across the dark prairie, Cuno desperately searched for fresh sign, casting his gaze this way and that. To his right, hooves thudded, and two riders approached. Cuno drew his Colt.

"Identify yourselves!"

"Mills and Jefferson," came the shaky reply. It was two of the wagoners. "We brought back five of the mules but the rest are scattered from here to Sunday."

"We got bigger problems than scattered stock," Cuno told the men, who reined up before him now, their mounts blowing with exhaustion.

"What you mean?" Mendel Jefferson asked, fear edging his voice. He was the only black man in the camp. A bachelor in his late forties, he was heading for Virginia City to mine for gold. Now he looked around the dark encampment, quiet as a graveyard. "What happened?"

"Running off the stock was just a diversion. Anderson and Spoon and about eight Indians, according to Church, came for the women. They got 'em."

"Oh, Jesus, Mary and Joseph!" Bryan Mills exclaimed, reining his horses over to the wagons.

"See any of the other men out there?" Cuno asked Jefferson.

"'Bout five of 'em tryin' to turn stock back toward camp." Jefferson's worried gaze was on the wagons and collapsed tents. "Seen a whole lot more dead men than live ones, though, includin' Mr. Church."

From the encampment, Bryan Mills's voice rose, calling for his wife, Sarah. Cuno and Jefferson looked that way and exchanged glances. Cuno shook his head in the negative. Jefferson bunched his lips angrily but said nothing.

Probably half of Anderson's group had hazed the stock away from the camp and ambushed the men who'd ridden after them. The other half had invaded the camp.

"What are we gonna do?" Jefferson asked Cuno at length.

Cuno cursed, his face creased with frustration. "We can't track 'em in the dark. We'll head out at dawn." With Church and the other scouts dead, he'd take over command of the train—what was left of it. That meant that before they could do anything else, he'd lead a contingent after Anderson and Spoon. Church should have let him kill them earlier, when he'd had the chance.

Cuno turned and walked away, his eyes cast groundward

on the off chance he'd pick up some sign. It was no use. In the dark relieved only by stars and a dull half-moon, there was no way to distinguish Anderson's tracks from the myriad of those around the encampment.

Finally, Cuno sat against a rock. He watched as several more riders returned to the camp and scurried around frantically, finding the dead men and futilely looking for the women.

Trying to forget about what horrors July and the other women were going through, Cuno willed himself into a light doze. He'd need to be fresh tomorrow to track Anderson and Spoon and the eight Indians with whom they rode toward their rendezvous with White Bull.

Although it was only a couple of hours before dawn, it seemed like a long night. Cuno dozed restlessly. At the first wash of dawn, he was standing by the breakfast fire, swilling coffee and hastily eating jerky and hardtack.

Fifteen wagoners had returned sporadically throughout the night, having recovered about twenty of the mules and oxen. The only scout at the coffee fire that morning was Cuno Massey. The others lay dead on the northeastern prairie along with half of the wagoners.

Cuno and the other survivors would bury the dead later. At the moment, they had to worry about getting the women back.

Finishing his hasty breakfast and leaving half the surviving wagoners with the wagons, Cuno and the seven others spread out looking for tracks. A half-mile from camp, Cuno cut the sign of three mules and ten horses, two of which were unshod. The morning sun climbed into a clear sky, drying the dew in the bluestem.

"Here!" he yelled to the other riders fanned out around the camp, eyes glued to the sod. He fired his Colt in the air, two swift reports. "This way!"

With that, Cuno reined Renegade through a cut through the hills, forded a shallow creek, and trotted along a wash, keeping his eyes skinned on the tracks the renegades had done nothing to obliterate.

Rolf Anderson reined his buckskin to a halt in a valley peppered with pines and junipers. A stream trickled to his right beyond some willows. The bright sun dappled the water, shone on the boulders humping up from the stream.

"We'll take a blow and water our animals here," he told the men coming up abreast of him.

Directly behind him, the five captured women were tied to two horses. A blonde in a frilly, soiled, white gown rode the first horse, keeping her head down as if deathly afraid of the sun. Behind her rode a dark-haired girl in men's trail garb. On the following pinto were two more women, in their late twenties, early thirties. Sandwiched between them was a curly-headed child who couldn't have been much over twelve.

Sammy Spoon rode behind him, followed by the two Wehrings trailing five pack horses carrying the rifles, and the eight Sioux warriors who had met Anderson, Spoon, and the Wehrings on Eagle Creek last night. The Indians had been sent to direct the white men to White Bull's camp on a remote stream called Hell's Fork by the mountain men who once trapped this country.

On the way, they decided to raid the neighboring pack train, see what kind of women they were trailing.

"Samuel, why don't you help the ladies down to the creek. They look thirsty."

"Sure thing!" Spoon whooped. He slid down from his saddle, strode over to the first horse, and cut the ropes tethering the buxom blonde and the half-breed girl to their saddle.

He jerked the blonde off the horse by her arm. The girl hit the ground hard, screaming.

"Please, oh please, oh please!"

"Please, oh please," Spoon mocked. *"Shut up!"*

The girl lowered her head to the dirt, sobbing.

Spoon stared down at her, expressionless. "This one's louder than a damn coon-dog bitch, but she sure is purty, Rolf. How much do you think she'll bring?"

Anderson shrugged. "A hundred dollars, at least. White Bull's partial to blondes."

Spoon still stared at the crying blonde. "I don't know whether to beat her or fuck her."

The Indians had all dismounted. One brave with swirls of red paint under his fierce eyes ran up to Spoon and pushed him. Angrily, he pointed at the girl and lectured Spoon in Sioux, which neither Spoon nor Anderson understood.

"What's he goin' on about?" Spoon asked Anderson.

The leader of the Indian contingent tossed his horse's reins to another brave. Walking up behind the first Indian he said to Spoon, "Splashing Water says you must be careful with girl. White Bull not accept damaged girl. No fuck. No more slap."

"No fuck, no more slap," Spoon said. "Well, how 'bout this one here?" he asked, regarding the willowy half-breed dressed in blue denims and a blue chambray shirt. She sat the horse with a fierce expression. "Can I fuck and slap this one?"

"Keep your goddamn hands off me, you filthy savage!"

"Savage?" Spoon intoned, indignant. "Why, hell girl, you got as much Injun in you as I do. Why don't I just drag you off into the trees an' dick you right, take some starch out of your drawers."

"Just try it," the girl shouted, her voice cracking with fear and exasperation, "and I'll cut your savage balls off!"

"Why, you little—"

"No fuck, no more slap!" the Indian railed, grabbing Spoon's arm.

Spoon turned to the Indian, his own brown face turning black with fury, his eyes narrowing.

"Samuel, you heard the man," Anderson said. "No fuck, no more slap." Anderson laughed. "Listen to the man. These females are probably worth a whole gold bar. You mark 'em, they'll be worth half that."

Spoon stared at the Indian, who stared back, one hand on a big knife on the belt wrapped around his naked waist. At length, Spoon relented. "Ah, hell," he groused, jerking his hand free of the Indian's grip. He brusquely grabbed the half-breed girl off the horse. "Get your ass down here!"

Later, when the horses and women were watered and the canteens had been filled, Anderson sat on a log and rolled a smoke. One of the Indians kept watch on the trail while the others lay in the grass for short naps. They'd had a busy night with no sleep.

The women sat near the water, the two older women consoling the younger one, who was crying again hysterically, as she'd been doing off and on since the raiders had taken her from the wagon camp. The blonde in the fancy dress kept her own counsel, sitting off from the others, staring at the water.

The half-breed also sat off by herself, facing the land, an angry cunning look on her pretty face, shuttling her gaze from the snoozing Indians to Anderson and Spoon. She was trying to figure a way out of this mess. Anderson grinned as he sucked deep on his quirly. She'd make some redskin around White Bull's council fire a very happy savage indeed.

The two Wehring brothers stood near their horses drawing water from the creek. They were having a private conversation, worried expressions on their faces.

Anderson was half-finished with his quirly when the blond girl turned to face him. A wistful look entered her eyes. Slowly, with studied grace, she climbed to her feet. She ran her hands through her disheveled, red-gold hair. Then, holding her skirts above her white leather boots, she strode toward Anderson. The smile on her face was manufactured; she had trouble keeping it there. It did not reach her eyes.

Anderson could see the shape of her long, slender legs through the folds of the cream skirt, the nervous heave of her pronounced bosom. He smiled and blew smoke.

"Hello there, Missie."

The girl's lips twitched as she widened her smile. "I-I'm afraid I didn't catch your name."

Anderson sucked the quirly and said nothing.

"My name is Daphne," the girl said. "Daphne Creigh."

Anderson just stared at her, grinning thinly, eyes on her heaving bosom, the cleavage of which was only partially hidden behind fine, pink lace.

The girl watched him for nearly a minute. Running her hands through her hair, she said, "You don't really want to turn me over to those . . . those savages, do you?" She hesitated, moistened her lips with the tip of her pink tongue. Taking a deep breath, she continued. "I . . . could be yours, if you wanted."

"Mine?" Anderson asked. "What do you mean?"

She knelt. Haltingly, she placed a hand on each of his spread knees. She looked at him meaningfully. "I could mean anything you wanted, if you keep me from those savages. I-I've heard what they do to white women."

Anderson studied her through slitted eyes. Sticking his quirly in his mouth, he leaned forward, planting his elbows on his knees. Reaching his right hand out, he turned it palm out to her, and shoved it down her dress, cupping her left breast, squeezing as if testing a cantaloupe for ripeness.

Her breath caught in her throat. She stiffened.

Anderson grinned. "Nice teats. I like a pig with nice teats. Maybe you're right. Maybe I do wanna keep you around—as long as you please me, that is. I have a feelin' you'd bring even more money down south, on the Staked Plains."

He removed his hand from her dress, puffed the quirly. "We'll see."

She let out her breath, closing her eyes with relief.

Anderson stood. "Everbody mount up," he yelled. "Time to vamoose. Don't wanna keep White Bull waitin' now, do we?" Grabbing the girl's wrist, he jerked her over to his horse and threw her up behind the cantle.

Spoon said, "What're you doin', Rolf?"

"She's ridin' with me. Wanna feel her titties against my back."

28

RENEGADE'S REINS IN his hand, Cuno Massey stood in the narrow valley and studied the hoof-pocked ground.

"They stopped here to water their horses," he told the six riders coming up behind him. " 'Bout an hour ago."

"We must be catchin' up to 'em," said Mendel Jefferson. "They're takin' their time."

"Yeah, they're cocky."

Jefferson cursed. "Must think we don't have the oysters to fog after 'em."

Cuno turned to the creek. "We'll give our horses a quick drink, then change their attitudes."

At the head of his column, Anderson rode through yet another, deeper valley with a stream trickling on his left.

He enjoyed the feel of the blond girl's pert breasts against his back as he rode and fantasized about spending White Bull's gold in Mexico this winter.

Allaying the fantasy, the two Wehrings rode up on his right side, worried expressions on their sweat-beaded faces.

"Anderson," Martin Wehring said haltingly, riding abreast of the hider. "Rudy and me—we want out."

"You do, do you?" Anderson grunted.

Wehring nodded. "We didn't know you was gonna ambush that other train, take these women. We ain't in it for that."

Rudy added, "The rifles is one thing, b-but we didn't know you was gonna kill white men and kidnap these women. We won't have no part in that."

Anderson reined his horse to a halt, and the entire column slowed to a stop behind him and the Wehrings. He studied the two nervous men, then shrugged. "You want out, get out."

Martin glanced at Rudy. "Well, we figured we should get somethin'. You know—for hauling the damn rifles all the way from Cheyenne."

"W-why don't you let us keep a dozen of 'em," Rudy suggested. "That sounds fair, don't it?"

Anderson's upper lip curled, and he shook his head with disgust. He stared at the men darkly, silently. With a sigh, he drew his Colt and thumbed back the hammer. The girl behind him gasped.

"Wait," Martin Wehring cried, throwing up his arms to shield his face. "You can keep the goddamn rifles!"

Anderson drilled him through the chest, and the German tumbled out of his saddle.

Rudolph Wehring stared at his brother. Whipping his shocked, horrified gaze back to Anderson, he screamed, "No!" He reined his horse around and gigged him toward the creek. Anderson aimed and fired. Rudolph sagged in the saddle as his horse splashed across the creek.

Behind Anderson, the women screamed. The blonde's breasts shivered against his back.

Rudy Wehring's horse stopped on the other side of the creek, side-stepping, turning around. Wehring lifted his head, clutching his left shoulder with his right hand. He saw Anderson raising his Colt again. His mouth opened to scream, but before the sound could escape his lips, Anderson drilled him through the head.

Wehring rolled off the back of his saddle and fell into a chokecherry bush. The horse gave a frightened whinny and galloped away.

The Indians laughed. Sammy Spoon gave a whoop.

The two women and young girl wept. The half-breed girl stared at the dead men, expressionless, hands tied behind her back.

Anderson shook his head and holstered his pistol. "Goddamn grangers been chafin' my ass long enough."

He turned his horse up the trail and put it into a trot.

A mile behind Anderson's group, Cuno had heard the gunshot and reined his horse to a halt. He listened, staring ahead.

The second shot sounded like a distant branch snapping.

"Jesus Christ," one of the mounted men around Cuno exclaimed. "You s'pose they're killin' the women?"

"It hard to say what they're doin'," Cuno said, heeling Renegade into a gallop. The seven others followed suit—a motley crew of unshaven men more at home on wagon seats than saddles. Their determined, angry expressions belied their reticence. They were not expert trackers or shooters, and most of them had their doubts they would be able to do the women any good.

For God's sake, that was Rolf Anderson and Sammy Spoon up there. Armed with at least eight war-painted Sioux.

Fifteen minutes later, Cuno reined his horse to a halt

and gestured for the others to do likewise. He stared ahead. The trail wound through towering pines, and in the shade of the pines, a man bent beside his horse, checking the horse's left front hoof.

The man was an Indian—straight, black hair, a bow and hide quiver fixed to his back.

Cuno turned to the men behind him, waving them back around the bend in the trail, out of the Indian's sight. Cuno followed them. Dismounting, he threw one of the men his reins.

"Looks like one has a lame mount. I'm gonna take him down. When I'm done, follow me and bring my horse."

"You be careful, young man!" Mendel Jefferson whispered.

Walking quietly, Cuno stepped into the trail, bending at the waist to see around the curve. The Indian was still studying his horse's hock.

Cuno walked ahead. Dodging behind trees, he approached the Indian. Just as the warrior was straightening and preparing to mount his paint, Cuno unsheathed his bowie knife and gave a whistle.

The Indian jerked around, facing him.

Crouching, Cuno stared at the brown chest, and tossed the knife. End over end it arced, winking in the dappled sunlight and making a soft crunch as it plunged hilt-deep in the warrior's chest. The horse whinnied and lit up the trail.

Cuno was pulling his blade out of the Indian's body when he heard hoofs thudding on the trail ahead. Looking up, he saw two shadows slide along the ground. He was about to bolt to his left, but froze. The Indians, no doubt riding back for the man Cuno had just killed, had spotted him.

Both men yelled exclamations and reached for arrows. Clawing his pistol from his holster, Cuno leapt into the trail, raised the gun, and fired. The Indian to his right tumbled off his horse, dropping his bow. The other man calmly nocked and loosed an arrow.

Cuno dove left, narrowly dodging the feathered wand. Springing back to a knee, he fired twice. The Indian's screaming horse ran into the trees while its rider rolled painfully on the trail behind it. Cuno shot the man again, silencing the warrior for good.

Hooves clopped behind him, and the other men jogged up with Mendel Jefferson in the lead. "Hey, that wasn't bad, kid," the black man said.

"Let's just hope there's more where that came from, 'cause I have a feelin' the rest of Anderson's crew is dead ahead. They probably heard the shots and will be coming back to investigate."

One of the horsemen cursed and mopped his brow with a filthy bandanna.

Cuno took his horse's reins from Jefferson, turned Renegade around, shucked his Winchester, and slapped the horse back down the trail. As Renegade whinnied and ran, shaking his head, Cuno turned to the men gathered around him. "You men fan out in the trees, try to drygulch the crew when it returns. I'm going to climb this ridge here and take as many as I can with my long gun."

Jefferson nodded and turned to the others.

"Just be careful you don't hit the women," Cuno warned. "And try to leave Anderson for me."

The dismounting riders regarded him curiously as the broad-shouldered young man with what had become an unruly mop of dark-blond hair scampered up the opposite slope, disappearing behind trees and shrubs. "Come on, boys," Jefferson said. "Let's get rid of these horses. I think I hear 'em comin' already!"

On the ridge, Cuno moved quickly, crouching and staying at least fifteen feet from the crest, skirting shrubs and pines. From below rose the clatter of hooves on the hard-packed trail, which had no doubt been used for centuries by game and Indians.

Cuno paused behind a boulder, slid a look down at the valley floor. Beyond the slender tree trunks, riders moved. Dark-skinned riders armed with bows and arrows, some with lances, the stone tips catching the golden afternoon light filtering through the trees.

Cuno waited, brought his rifle to his shoulder. He'd just jacked a shell in the breech when a shot rang out from below.

"Damn," he whispered to himself. One of his riders had gotten impatient.

The Indians whooped and chortled and slid cleanly out of their saddles, bounding into the trees. Several flung arrows as the shooting started in earnest. The wagoners yelled above the pistol and rifle volleys, their voices tinged with panic. One man screamed.

Cuno lowered his rifle and bolted down the slope, weaving around the trees, hurdling shrubs. An Indian ran across the trail before him, threw a lance, and a man screamed. Cuno lifted his rifle and shot the the Indian through the shoulder, spinning the man around. Cuno jacked another shell and fired again, blowing the Indian against a rock, off which the Sioux rolled onto shrubs.

As Cuno ejected the spent shell casing, another Indian appeared, turning back from the trees, his face a brown, devilish scowl. Seeing Cuno, the man whooped and nocked an arrow, ran toward Cuno, and let the arrow fly. Cuno dodged, lost his footing on the slippery slope, and fell on his ass, losing his rifle.

In a second the Indian was on him, knife in hand, thrusting at Cuno's throat. Cuno held the man off with one leg and arm while he grabbed the Frontier Colt from its holster, hastily thumbed back the hammer. The Indian was amazingly strong, and the knife tip was poking into Cuno's throat when Cuno rammed the barrel into the savage's naked side and pulled the trigger.

The gun barked. Instantly, the man relaxed, wild eyes dimming. Cuno slapped the knife away, kicked the man off his body, and scrambled to his feet. Semiconsciously, he noted that the gunfire had ebbed to the point that only one wagoner seemed to be firing.

He was running down the slope to the trail when he saw another Indian stumble out of the trees, hands clutching his side. The man saw Cuno and dropped to his knees. Cuno lifted his revolver to kill the man, but stopped when he heard hooves pounding behind him.

Cuno whipped around to see a man barreling down on him, whooping like a demon, reins in his teeth, pistol in one hand, carbine in the other. The greased braids and high-crowned, black hat with hawk feather in its band bespoke Sammy Spoon. The half-breed crouched low in the saddle and bore down on Cuno, triggering the pistol and carbine.

Hearing lead stitch the air around him, Cuno flung himself back off the trail, landing in shrubs and shale. On his back, he lifted the pistol and emptied the cylinder as Spoon passed like some ghoul from a child's horror story.

Blue smoke hazed the trail. Through it, Cuno watched Spoon's horse slow a hundred feet down the trail. The dun turned broadside to Cuno, who opened his Colt's cylinder and jerked out the spent shells. He plucked fresh cartridges from his belt and thumbed them into the chambers. The kneeling warrior across the trail from him lifted his head and began clumsily nocking an arrow. Cuno coolly lifted the Colt toward the man and fired. The Indian grunted and crumpled.

Cuno climbed to his feet, extending his Colt at Spoon, who sat heavily in his saddle. He'd dropped the carbine in the trail. The half-breed was breathing heavily, whistling through his teeth. Blood dribbled down from the holes in his face when Cuno's bullet passed sideways through his mouth.

The man lifted his head and grimaced. *"Ay-eeee!"* he howled as he reined the horse toward Cuno, coming at a ground-eating gallop.

Cuno pushed himself to his feet, raised the Colt, and fired. Simultaneosly, Spoon triggered his own weapon. The bullet carved a furrow across Cuno's right temple, making him wince and grind his teeth. Cuno's own slug ripped through Spoon's right elbow, causing Spoon to drop his Remington and to tumble off the right side of his horse, rolling when he hit the ground.

"Eeee-ahhhhhh!" the half-breed raged, rolling in place as he clutched his arm.

The horse galloped away. Through its dust, Cuno regarded the cursing half-breed. Satisfied none of the other attackers was an immediate threat, Cuno walked over to Spoon. The half-breed gazed up at him, fiery recognition in his narrowed eyes.

"Leave me be, white boy!"

"The name's Massey," Cuno said tightly. "Cuno Massey. Remember?"

Spoon stared at him hard, his face and eyes bright with pain, blood running from the holes in his swelling face.

"Valoria, Nebraska. The Pasttime Saloon."

The half-breed's expression did not change.

Calmly, Cuno bent down, grabbed Spoon's right hand, and gave his arm a jerk, causing a thick eruption of blood from the elbow.

"AHHHH! *You sonuvabitch!*"

"You killed my pa. That's why you just died, savage."

Spoon tipped his head back with a howl. Cuno put the Frontier Colt to his forehead and silenced him with a slug through his brain plate. Spoon's head bounced off the ground, his arms and legs twitched, and he relaxed with a loud fart and a sigh.

Cuno didn't have time to admire his handiwork. He ran into the trees and found three Indians and all the wagoners dead.

Running back to the trail, he cast his gaze up the draw.

Anderson and the women . . .

29

TWENTY MINUTES EARLIER, Anderson and the girl were riding near the rear of the column when what the hider recognized as Sioux curses rose behind him. He turned.

One of the two Indians riding drag had stopped to inspect his horse's left front hoof. The other warrior—a short, stocky kid with a pudgy, painted face and bloodthirsty eyes—jerked an admonishing finger at him and read him the riot act. At least, that's what it sounded like to Anderson, who could make out only the Sioux words for "mother," "dog," "queer," "lazy," and "dimwit."

Apparently, the first warrior hadn't properly cared for an injury his mount had incurred sometime in the recent past. He was thoroughly dressed down for it at the moment, however, and fell back as Anderson and the other man continued, leaving him to doctor his mount solo.

They'd ridden maybe five minutes when again Anderson heard a Sioux curse behind him. Turning again, he saw the pudgy-faced warrior rein his mount around, shaking his head and gigging his Appaloosa into a canter, heading back the way they'd come through the narrow, ridge-shaded valley. Apparently, the pudgy-faced warrior didn't think the other kid—probably a brother or a cousin—could watch his own backside. Or maybe the second kid had promised some formidable old crone he'd watch out for her lazy grandson.

Whatever the reason, the two Indians were gone, and Anderson was riding drag, enjoying the caress of the blond girl's breasts against his back, when shots rang out from the canyon behind him.

"What the hell?" he grunted, reining his horse around and scowling.

The Indians had heard it, too. They came on the gallop, pausing around Anderson and scowling in the same direction the hider was, keeping their agitated mounts on tight reins.

"Where Little Weed and Running Fox?" the warrior asked Anderson.

"They had to fall back. Lame horse. That must be them slingin' lead, or gettin' lead slung at 'em."

The leader pinched his eyebrows down as he looked back at the cleft by which they'd just traversed the pine-clad mountain. "The wagon train? They come?" the lead warrior spat at Anderson, as though it were the hider's fault.

"Well, someone's back there, Sundog!" Anderson wailed. "Take after 'em—less'n you want 'em gettin' their greasy hands on your badly needed rifles, not to mention your women!"

Frustrated, the leader glared at Anderson, then shifted his gaze to the trail ahead. They were supposed to meet White Bull on the north bank of Pine Creek by the time the shadows grew long. Sundog wanted to continue, but two of his men had been attacked. And the best place to attack their pursuers was in that cleft, where there would be no escaping Sundog's braves.

"Haaah!" Sundog yelled, healing his bronc into a ground-eating gallop, extending his war lance high above his head. The other Indians cut after him in a fog of dust.

Anderson turned to see Spoon sitting his horse nearby, staring after the Indians, holding the lead rope of the mules carrying the rifles.

"Well, what you waitin' for, Samuel?" Anderson grouched. "Toss me that rope and get after those sumbitches. I'll stay here with the women."

The half-breed glanced at Anderson, hesitating, vaguely suspicious. "Don't worry—I ain't goin' anywhere, dammit!" the hider raged. *"Ride, bucko, ride!"*

Spoon glanced at the mules carrying the rifles, then at the women. Then he looked with alarm at the hider. "What're you gonna do?"

"I'm gonna wait right here, Samuel. Ride! Those savages might need help!"

Reluctantly, Spoon galloped off through the dust kicked up by the warriors. Behind him, Anderson smiled. He doubted their pursuers from the wagon train had any chance against Spoon and the Sioux warriors, but anything could happen. And if something happened to Spoon, all the rifle and women money would be Anderson's alone.

He'd be pure-dee, double-d, damn rich.

"It isn't gonna happen, mister."

He turned. The half-breed girl sat her horse to his right, mussed hair hanging down around her pretty, oval face with its suntanned skin and high cheekbones and blue eyes. Her mouth was grim but her eyes were insolent as she studied the hider.

"What ain't gonna happen?"

"You ain't gonna get away. The man leading those men from the wagon train—I've seen him fight. He's good. Besides that, he has a bone to pick with you. A big bone. He's your worst nightmare, Cuno Massey is." Her lips spread a hard smile.

July knew Cuno was on their trail. She could sense him, feel his strength way deep in her bones.

Anderson frowned and wrinkled his nose, thoughtful. Where had he heard that name before? "Massey?"

"You may not remember him now," July said, "but you will."

Annoyed, Anderson gave a grunt. "I have a lot of people with bones they think they can pick with me. None of 'em done it yet. Now, shut up girl—you're gettin' on my nerves."

With that he reined his horse around, the lead ropes in his hands, and heeled his buckskin up the trail, glancing around at the cleft, then at the horses and mules bearing the women and the rifles. Satisfied everyone was in line, he kneed the horse into a trot. He'd be at the rendezvous point with White Bull within a half hour . . .

As he rode, he heard more shooting—a fairly short burst, then a few more sporadic shots. He glanced over his shoulder but the cleft had disappeared down the grade in the distance. The half-breed girl was smiling dubiously. Cursing with annoyance, Anderson turned back to gaze over his horse's ears.

He could not deny a slight prickling of the hair along his collar. When he saw the chasm of Pine Creek open a hundred yards ahead, like a wide shadow in the rolling green highlands, he gigged his horse into a gallop and gave several savage jerks to the lead ropes in his hand.

Cuno was galloping Renegade full out when he saw movement ahead of him, on the grassy bench surrounded by medium-sized grass- and pine-carpeted buttes with here-and-there talus slides and water troughs filling with afternoon shadows.

Not wanting Anderson to see him, Cuno dropped into a swale, took the swale to the south, dipping into a deeper cut, and rode west, paralleling Anderson's path above him, ahead and to Cuno's left. He galloped hard for about a hundred yards, and when Anderson and the women and pack horses came into clearer view, Cuno swung even with them and climbed a rise on Anderson's right side.

Cuno reigned Renegade to a halt, shucked his Winchester, planted the butt on his thigh, barrel up, and sat there, regarding the hider with challenge. Anderson had spotted him a few seconds ago. Now the hider reined his own horse to a halt, the horses behind him stopping as well.

Anderson and the women were about a hundred yards from Cuno, who gigged Renegade ahead now slowly, giving Anderson the first move. He noted that all the women but Daphne were tied to their mounts, and without having to give it much thought, Cuno knew why. It would be just like her to make promises to Anderson in exchange for his not selling her to White Bull.

Anderson dropped the lead lines and gigged his mount ahead, toward Cuno. Both men reined their horses down about thirty feet apart.

Anderson was smiling. "You're the last of the wagon train grangers, I take it?"

Cuno didn't say anything for a few moments. His heart was heaving and skipping beats, but you couldn't tell it by his expression—flat, hard, cold as late winter snow.

"That's right. And you're the last of your sons o' bitches."

His smile fast, Anderson shook his head. "No, hombre. I'm just the beginning."

He jerked his head to indicate the high plains continuing on the other side of the gorge yawning on Cuno's right. About a mile distant, a dark line stretched from north to south. Warriors, riding abreast, moving this way.

"Reckon I best kill you quick," Cuno said. "And here I wanted to take my time."

Anderson sneered and shook his head with disgust. He moved his arm in a blur. Cuno followed suit, brought his Colt up, and fired.

Daphne screamed. Recoiling with fear, she lost her hold on the hider and tumbled sideways off the horse, landing in a pile of skirts and hair and puff-sleeved blouse on the ground.

Anderson stiffened. Wide-eyed with exasperation, he glanced at the pistol half out of its holster. He looked at his left shoulder. A ragged hole shone through his buckskin tunic. In the hole, blood was beginning to gleam.

His glassy, acrimonious gaze returned to Cuno, who still held his smoking Frontier Colt chest-high. His face was as expressionless as before.

Slowly, a thin smile formed itself in the hider's red beard. His malicious eyes twinkled. He chuckled. Then, suddenly, he flung himself out of his saddle, on top of the fearfully grunting and trembling Daphne. As his horse galloped off, obscuring Cuno's view for the split second he might have been able to shoot Anderson again, the hider grabbed the girl, flung her before him as he stood and crouched behind her.

His hat was off, and his eyes were wild, his expression crazy.

"Oh, god, no . . . please!" she wailed.

"Shut up, bitch!"

Anderson tugged savagely on her hair. Suddenly, there was a knife at her throat, the curved point conjuring a bright bead of blood. She tipped her head back, away from the blade, but there was nowhere to go. Anderson's broad shoulder flanked her. His enormous, gloved left paw had her throat in a death grip. She couldn't move a muscle.

"What are you gonna do now, pistol boy?" Anderson raged at Cuno, who sat his saddle almost casually, pistol still drawn but held low, without immediate menace. Despite his aversion to Daphne, he didn't want to see her killed.

Glancing quickly across the canyon, Anderson said,

"Best drop that hogleg and ride out fast. Them Injuns'll use your scalp to sweep out their tipis tonight!"

Cuno's nose wrinkled. "Look at yourself, you pathetic, murdering bastard. Hidin' behind a girl. I'm gonna do you a favor."

Keeping his Colt low, Cuno thumbed back the hammer. The gun jumped in his hand. The corner of Anderson's face poking out behind Daphne's head turned red. The hider gave a grunt and staggered backward, throwing his arms out for a balance he never attained.

Daphne screamed.

Dropping the knife, Anderson fell in a heap.

Daphne dropped straight down to her knees, face in her hands.

"Shit," Cuno muttered.

It had been too easy. But there had been no time. The Indians were drawing near the canyon. In a few minutes, they'd follow the game trail down the opposite ridge, heading for this side—all twenty or thirty of them. They'd beat it up this side a few minutes later, and Cuno and the women would be dead.

And the Indians would have the rifles.

Glancing at the bouncing, jerking line of riders moving quickly this way, Cuno dismounted, jerked Daphne to her feet, and set her on the rear of July's horse. He cut July free of her tethers, then ran back and did the same to the other three females. To July he said, "Lead them all back the way you came—through that canyon behind us. Ride as fast as you can and keep riding."

"What are you gonna do?" July asked, massaging the feeling back into her hands while regarding Cuno doubtfully.

"I'm gettin' rid of these rifles. Go, July. There's no time to argue!"

She snarled at him, grabbing her bridle reins. "I wasn't

gonna argue. You wanna get yourself butchered by Injuns, it's no skin off my nose."

She reined the horse around and, grabbing the reins of the other mule on which the two older women and the child sat, appearing catatonic from the hair-raising experience, gigged her mule into a lope, heading south and west. The other mule followed July, the women and child hanging on for dear life.

Wasting no time, Cuno ran to the lead pack mule, led the animal to the edge of the ravine. He looked across the chasm, which was about seventy or so yards across. The creek ran at the bottom of the rocky defile, which was as deep as it was wide, with occasional brush snags. A game trail angled down the opposite ridge, crossed the creek at a rocky ford, then angled up this side, meandering around boulders.

It appeared to be the only way down. And the only way back up.

Cuno cut the straps of the makeshift panniers on the first mule, and the rifles clattered to the ground. One and sometimes two at a time, he whipped the long guns into the chasm, bouncing them off the boulders, breaking their stocks and bending their barrels. Several hit the water with silent splashes.

By the time he'd disposed of a third of the rifles and was leading the second mule up to the canyon's lip, Cuno heard hooves pounding in the distance. He looked north as he cut the straps of another pannier, the rifles dropping with a loud clatter. About twenty-five warriors sat their mounts on the canyon's opposite lip, watching him. The man in the group's center wore a full headdress and wielded a feathered lance.

He waved his arms angrily, his lips moving, shouting orders Cuno could barely hear. Several riders began descending the trail, tracing a forty-five degree angle down the opposite slope.

Cuno ran to Renegade, shucked his Winchester, and jacked a shell as he stepped toward the canyon. He dropped to a knee, aimed carefully, and when the riders were halfway down the slope, he fired. The lead rider tumbled off his horse.

Cuno jacked a shell and fired again, and the second man in line was flung from his mount. By the time he'd hit the ground, the three other warriors had leapt from their horses, which followed the first two into the ravine. The warriors stood whipping their heads around, looking for cover. There was very little—only a boulder about twenty yards straight down, across shale.

One made a run for it. Cuno fired at him. The slug pinged off the shale near the man's right ankle. Cuno fired again, and the man dropped, clutching a knee, his mouth a knife slash of grievous pain and venomous anger. Cuno silenced him with a bullet through his chest, knocking him flat, arms akimbo.

When Cuno had levered another shell into the Winchester's breech, he paused to watch the other two warriors scramble up the opposite slope as the mounted braves reined their horses back from the canyon. Several flung arrows from atop their agitated mounts, but all arced high and thudded low into the slope below Cuno.

The men afoot made the ridge crest and ran toward the others gathered in a milling, angry cluster about fifty feet back from the canyon. They knew they were within rifle range, but the crazy, lone White Eyes tossing their rifles into the canyon was beyond the reach of their arrows and lances.

All they could do was watch as Cuno continued tossing away the rifles.

He cut the straps of the last pannier and was sending the rifles into the canyon when, out of the corner of his vision, he saw a shadow move on the gold-washed grass to his right. He spun around on his heel.

Rolf Anderson—face bloody from the gaping hole in his cheek—held his broad-bladed bowie high over his head, point down, a savage grimace drawing the hider's lips back from his teeth.

As the knife began its downward thrust toward Cuno's face, Cuno reached up, grabbed Anderson's wrist, and slowed the plunge until he had the knife stopped two inches from the third button down from the collar of Cuno's shirt. Grasping the knife's handle with both hands wrapped around Anderson's right, Cuno worked the blade around, until the point pricked at the hider's tunic.

The hider's face became a mask of red hate and vexation and fear. He stooped toward Cuno, his wide shoulders slumped forward, grimacing and wheezing, blood from his head dripping onto Cuno's shirt. His face was only six inches from Cuno's.

"You raped and murdered my step-ma, you son of a bitch!" Cuno told him, staring savagely into the hider's savage eyes. "Then you killed my pa . . . in the saloon. Remember?"

Cuno paused, licked his lips, pressing the knife's razor point through Anderson's tunic. The hider's eyes widened with horror as the point cut through the skin and began inching through flesh.

"No! It-it wasn't me!"

"You remember that, you cowardly sack of shit?" Cuno asked him, his voice a snarl of barely controlled rage. "I've dogged you a long ways, and now I have you, and that's why this knife is goin' into your ribs—*like that!*"

"Uhhh!"

"Bet you wish you'd never come back to Valoria."

"Uhh-ahhh!"

"And now I'm gonna ram it right through your heart!"

Spinning the hider around, the man's back to the canyon, Cuno shoved the knife through his belly, angling it up toward his sternum.

The hider crouched over it, both hands wrapped around the hilt, beneath Cuno's. Hot blood washed over both men's hands like steaming water poured from a pail. Sweat and blood streaming down the hider's face, he stiffened and rasped like a dying animal.

"When you see Spoon in hell," Cuno said in his ear, "tell him hi for me."

Then with one more savage thrust, he heaved the knife home.

He released it and stood there as, eyes dimming, the slouching hider shuffled backward over the side of the canyon, his body slanting out and plunging in a slow, backward arc through the open air, hands slowly releasing the knife as his arms spread like some awkward bird futilely working to achieve flight.

He plunged into a boulder at the bottom of the canyon with a woodlike snap, painting the stone red as he rolled off into the creek, where he lay face up on the rocky bottom. The clear, brown water tumbled over him, tugging at his arms and legs, washing the blood from his face, the sun glinting off his hair.

Cuno stared at him, transfixed. Then he finished tossing the rest of the rifles into the canyon around Anderson while the Indians watched, helpless to stop him.

When the job was done, Cuno mounted up and turned another gaze at the Indians. He was reluctant to ride away. The red men would no doubt follow him, hunt him down—twenty against one. And he did not want to lead them to the women. He would remain here until dark if he had to, making sure they did not traverse the canyon, giving the women ample time to get away.

But then White Bull kneed his white stallion to the edge of the canyon. The warrior looked solemnly down at Anderson, whom the dying light revealed now only as a vague smudge in the creek. White Bull looked around at the broken rifles.

Lifting his gaze to Cuno, he sat stiffly for several seconds. He raised a stiff arm and fist high above his feathered head.

Cuno hesitated, curious, then raised his own hand to his hat brim and watched as White Bull reined his stallion around and rode back the way he had come, the other warriors falling in behind him, heading north and east, swallowed by the rolling prairie and thickening shadows.

Cuno glanced at the creek again, at the shape of Anderson lolling there amid the rifles. Then he reined Renegade around and gigged the horse into a lope.

When he'd threaded a route through the cleft where the wagoners, Spoon, and the Indians lay dead, he reined his horse to a halt, frowning into the darkening distance, where a lone rider sat on a rise brushed with the last salmon light of the fast-falling sun. July's hair whipped around her in the wind.

Cuno's chest heaved of its own accord—from the enormity of all he'd been through.

And then seeing her there, waiting for him . . .

With a raspy choke, eyes burning, he kneed Renegade into a gallop.

ABOUT THE AUTHOR

Peter Brandvold was born and raised in North Dakota. He's lived in Arizona, Montana, and Minnesota, and currently resides in the Rocky Mountains near Fort Collins, Colorado. Since his first book, *Once a Marshal*, was published in 1998, he's become popular with both readers and critics alike. His writing is known for its realistic characters, authentic historical details, and lightning-fast pace. Visit his website at www.peterbrandvold.com. Send him an email at pgbrandvold@msn.com.

"MAKE ROOM ON YOUR SHELF OF FAVORITES FOR PETER BRANVOLD."
—FRANK RODERUS

THE DEVIL GETS HIS DUE

A LOU PROPHET NOVEL BY

PETER BRANVOLD

On the trail with Louisa Bonaventure, "The Vengeance Queen," bounty hunter Lou Prophet is caught in a bloody crossfire of hatred between an outlaw who would shoot a man dead for fun and Louisa, who has sworn to kill him—even if she dies trying.

"THE NEXT LOUIS L'AMOUR."
—ROSEANNE BITTNER

0-425-19454-X

AVAILABLE WHEREVER BOOKS ARE SOLD OR TO ORDER CALL 1-800-788-6262

B248